Spectral Living

UNIVERSITY OF CALGARY
Press

Spectral Living

a novel

Andrea King

Brave & Brilliant Series
ISSN 2371-7238 (Print) ISSN 2371-7246 (Online)

University of Calgary Press
2500 University Drive NW
Calgary, Alberta
Canada T2N 1N4
press.ucalgary.ca

This is a work of fiction. Names, characters, businesses, places, events, and incidents are either the products of the author's imagination or used in a fictitious manner. Any resemblance to actual persons, living or dead, or actual events is purely coincidental.

LIBRARY AND ARCHIVES CANADA CATALOGUING IN PUBLICATION

Title: Spectral living : a novel / Andrea King.
Names: King, Andrea, 1980- author.
Series: Brave & brilliant series.
Description: Series statement: Brave & brilliant series, ISSN 2371-7238 (print), ISSN 2371-7246 (ebook)
Identifiers: Canadiana (print) 20210195673 | Canadiana (ebook) 20210195851 | ISBN 9781773851471 (softcover) | ISBN 9781773851488 (PDF) | ISBN 9781773851495 (EPUB) | ISBN 9781773851501 (Kindle)
Classification: LCC PS8621.I555585 S64 2021 | DDC C813/.6—dc23

The University of Calgary Press acknowledges the support of the Government of Alberta through the Alberta Media Fund for our publications. We acknowledge the financial support of the Government of Canada. We acknowledge the financial support of the Canada Council for the Arts for our publishing program.

Editing by Aritha van Herk
Copyediting by Naomi K. Lewis
Cover images: Colourbox 8876843 and 1431775
Cover design, page design, and typesetting by Melina Cusano

Chapter One

May 2011

Just look at Rémy up there, ignoring the podium, pacing
confidently to the rhythm of his French arguments,
occasionally glancing down his nose at his conference paper,
but otherwise letting his gaze float from face to face, affecting
an air of professorial gravitas. He's the very picture of scholarly
achievement. It doesn't even matter that he's short.

In her cartoon, Marian gives him Biblical robes and a stone
tablet. Caption: "Scholar on the Mount."

Did he just say that *the whole of literature is a palimpsest
of the original Word, which is man's greatest achievement and
greatest paradox?*

Of course he did.

She should start over. Self-portrait.

She levitates, rising above the heads of the other conference
attendees, who watch in awe, bedazzled by her arguments.
Before they can stump her during the Q&A period—ask her to
transform vast non-questions into questions in her head and
respond with an equally vast non-answer (in French!)—she
wings out of the room. Zip! Applause.

The applause is for Rémy. He nods and creases his forehead,
a trick of his that conveys modesty. His Q&A begins; eager
hands rise. Marian gazes beyond a few of them and out the
window. A low, verdant mountain appears grey and hazy

behind sunscreen blinds. "Nestled in the Laurentians at kilometre 67 of Le P'tit Train Du Nord trail," the inn's website would have her know. "Luxurious by nature." She wishes she were steeping in the outdoor hot tub or admiring the gentle froth of the waterfall. The Canadian Association for French and Francophone Literatures doesn't usually succumb to indulgence, but this year is its thirtieth anniversary. Even CAFFL lets loose every three decades. Marian torques her upper body, stretches her lumbar muscles. She and Juliette should play hooky from the afternoon's presentations, borrow a couple of the inn's retro bikes, and peddle the trail. When did she last take a vacation? Last year, around this time, after she defended her dissertation proposal at Waterton University and three days before her twenty-sixth birthday. She and David stayed overnight at a B&B in Gananoque.

She's lucky to be here now on a bursary. Living large.

"Montre-le-moi," Rémy says when he sits down next to her.

"Hm?"

"I could see you from up there."

Marian reluctantly shows him "Scholar on the Mount" and wills herself not to blush. She takes care to hide the cartoon of herself etched on the flip side of the page.

He smirks. "Can I keep it?"

She snaps her notebook shut. "I'll make you another someday."

The current presenter, an eco-critic from l'Université de Moncton, goes over her time by ten minutes, oblivious to the moderator's signals. Marian taps her heel—she's up next and feels like a trapped animal about to chew off her own leg in order to escape. Juliette slips into the room and waves encouragingly. She sits down a couple rows in front of Marian and Rémy.

A sprinkle of applause signals Marian's turn.

"You nervous?" Rémy asks.

She holds out her shaking hand.

"Merde," he says, and firmly clasps her wrist.

Rémy feels a mix of empathy and pleasure as Marian blushes at the podium, eyes downcast, both hands clamped onto her paper as though to secure it against a gust of nerves. He wants her to struggle. There must be obstacles, or the whole exercise is pointless. He yawns and wishes for coffee. She's presenting a distilled version of the first chapter of her dissertation, which examines female ghosts in the Québec novel, linking them to various feminist social issues that have never interested him. He tolerates feminism in her work because he believes that one must leave room for all scholarly approaches. Diversity of thought, et cetera. Overall, he finds her dissertation project satisfactory. She will not change the face of scholarship, but she will shine a light onto obscure literary spectres, keep the shadowy train of academe chugging forward. Not everyone can be Roland Barthes.

To be fair, he may never be Barthes, either, and for this reason, he identifies with Marian and her weird little ghosts, thinks they are not so different from his own former interest in metaphors of desire in the work of Hubert Aquin. Narrow, but thorough. He tries hard to concentrate on her ghosts when she comes to his office for meetings. He finds these meetings unsettling because Marian belongs to the second and most distracting of his student categories, of which there are three: 1) men, 2) attractive women, 3) unattractive women.

(He can admit this classification to himself. Not to admit it is to eschew self-knowledge.)

She continues to blush appealingly as she reads the final section of her paper. She is, objectively speaking, independent of his own gaze, attractive. It is not his fault that he notices this. She arrived this way; he observed. (Short, delightfully curvy. Pouty. Crowned by curly brown hair.)

Marian clears her throat twice during the inevitable dead time that follows her presentation. For twenty long seconds, the audience members decide whether they should bother to gather their thoughts and arrange them into speech. Rémy knows what she is experiencing. First, she is wondering if there will be any questions at all. This uncertainty will never go away, no matter how many papers she gives. Second—because she is inexperienced—she's wondering if the lack of questions might be a good sign. It's a terrible sign, in fact. In a room of French-speaking academics, dead air means that nobody liked what you had to say.

If the silence continues, he will have to step in. It is his duty.

Finally, a goateed professor Rémy doesn't know stands and strokes his peach-coloured tie. "Merci pour cette belle communication," he says. "I'm unfamiliar with the author you're working on. But your interpretation of the apparition as the prosopopoeia of a single psychic wound doesn't account for the potential heterogeneity of lack. It therefore seems more appropriate to speak not of wounds, but of *traces*. How do you intend to account for this as you rework the paper for publication?"

Rémy digs in his pocket for some breath mints as Marian spends too long jotting notes on the back of her paper. Even he is wondering if an appropriate response to this question is possible. The man with the peach tie follows a logic evident only to him, like a dog sniffing for a spot to crap.

"I hadn't thought of that," she says finally. As she awkwardly recaps what she said in her introduction, Rémy is reminded of everything that's right and wrong with academia. Assembled here are people whose sole purpose in life is to read books and talk about them, and reread them and talk about them all over again. What's not to love about such a life? But there's also the showboating and Molotov questions lobbed every which way.

Regardless, such is the game, and she must learn how to play it.

Marian thanks the peach-tie man for his question, gathers her papers, and sits down next to Juliette Delvaux, who, according to Rémy's system of classification, is also a Category Two, but is tall and therefore less distracting, less unsettling.

Marian waits well into their dinner on the patio before Rémy affirms that he liked her paper.

"Well received," he says, and she feels her chest relax. "Don't worry about that heterogeneity question. Purely performative." He takes a bite of lamb. "Fantastic. Bold yet tender. What is that? Rosemary?"

Good paper, better lamb. While he and Juliette chat with the eco-critic from Moncton, Marian enjoys the susurrant rush of the waterfall and shifts her chair out of the way of a server who is straining to light a tiki torch. Conversations from the other tables thrum in the background as Rémy describes a conference he attended at a plush Provençal resort last year. His voice is resonant and coupled with a low, confident laugh.

Until two months ago, Marian and Rémy only exchanged the occasional nod in the corridor. It wasn't until Professor Cloutier, her old dissertation supervisor, accepted a position in Montreal that Rémy took over her project. Cloutier called her at home to break the news that he was offered a Tier One Research Chair position in Québec Studies at McGill. He said that because she was at the beginning of her dissertation project, it would make the most sense for her to switch advisors. She didn't argue. Cloutier was fatherly and kind but obsessed with dead male philosophers. He often invited her into his office, poured her a cup of bad coffee from an old brown Thermos, and asked her to integrate into her work Hume and Hegel and Benjamin. "Our Hegel," he would begin, as though the philosopher were something he and Marian had in common. She would nod and take out her pen. "Pears, brown rice, toilet paper, ketchup," she wrote once. "Light bulbs, dog food, cheese."

When she dropped by Rémy's office the day after Cloutier's phone call, he was hunched near the window with his back to the door, fussing over a large potted plant.

She knocked on the doorframe. "Can I speak to you?" she said in French.

"I keep rotating her, and she's still fuller on this side," he muttered as he straightened up and turned to face her. "Yes, of course, come in."

"I was wondering if you could supervise my dissertation."

"Ah, so it's serious," he said, and she wasn't sure if this was his idea of a joke.

Awkward, she'd thought then.

Now, on this balmy spring evening, birch and poplar leaves tickling the breeze, the waterfall pouring in white ribbons behind him, he's transformed. She hardly even notices the speck of rosemary stuck between his teeth.

In the lounge after dinner, Rémy orders a glass of port for each of them, inwardly thanking Juliette for flirting with the bartender, who has given an extra generous pour. Marian complains that her feet are swollen. They carry their drinks over to a grouping of club chairs and chat boozily.

"We came all this way, and we've hardly done anything interesting," Juliette says, having made quick work of her port. "I didn't even have time to use the outdoor spa." She mashes her black hair into a bun as if to punish it for this injustice and secures it with a clip she draws from her purse. "Looks like we'll just have to go now."

Rémy sips detachedly. Marian unbuckles her shoe and massages the arch of her foot. She has unusually pretty toes.

"The spa closed at nine," Marian says.

"So we hop the fence."

"And I don't have a bathing suit."

"But you have nice underwear. I'll help you choose the best set for a swim."

"I should really make a phone call."

Juliette pats at her upswept hair. "At a resort like this, isn't the point to ditch the technology?"

Marian refastens her shoe and looks to Rémy as though to say, can you believe this?

He smiles and rolls the stem of his port glass between his fingers, creating tiny waves up the side of the glass. He's enjoying this little theatre.

"What are you grinning about?" Juliette says. "You're coming."

The sea in Rémy's hand grows quiet. "You can't be serious."

"Oh, but I am. Come on, now. Don't be a drag."

Thoughts of the university's labyrinthine policies on professional conduct slog through the various drinks he's imbibed and soon lose their way. Never mind. It's spring, darkness has fallen, his paper on palimpsest and Christly imagery was a success, and two pretty women are inviting him to enjoy the outdoors.

Marian says, "I guess no one will recognize us in the dark."

He downs what remains of his port. "It would be a shame not to make the most of the facilities."

On her way down to the outdoor spa with Juliette, bundled in a terry bathrobe with the inn's monogram embroidered at the chest, Marian wonders if she's serving as a front for a crush Juliette might be nursing on Rémy. But Juliette was flirting so obviously with the bartender that this hardly seems likely. She's probably just tottered to the far side of her work hard/play hard binary. Marian has witnessed this before. It usually results in her throwing a ridiculous theme party or dragging Marian to FastLane for what she calls 'ironic bowling.'

"He won't come," Marian says.

"Twenty dollars says he will."

Juliette tests the wooden gate and finds it unlocked. As they make their way up the walk, a motion sensor light clicks on and Marian sees she's lost the bet. Rémy dangles his calves in the swirling water, three towels stacked beside him. He's hairier than she imagined, but not unattractive. A primal version of the Rémy she knows from school.

They leave their robes next to a potted hibiscus. Marian glances down at her black bra, no longer confident it won't become see-through when wet. She doesn't like padding. "How's the water?"

Rémy tightens the cord on his black swimming trunks and lowers himself into the hot tub. He rests his head against the deck. "Perfect. Come on in."

The hot tub huffs alluring breaths of steam. Marian plunges in with a little cry and places her back against one of the jets, careful to keep her chest underwater. Juliette pauses waist-deep on the hot tub stairs before immersing herself up to her shoulders. They discuss today's keynote address on the history of literary publishing in Montreal, then move on to department gossip: a feud between the medievalist and the Provost; which professors haven't had their research grants renewed; rumours of further cuts to the operating budget. They could be chatting anywhere—in the hallways of the Modern Languages building, or at The Pint, the university pub, but they are here, warmly growing drowsy under the moon.

After a while, Juliette stretches, leans against the hot tub banister, and taps the imaginary watch on her wrist. "Enough rebellion for me. But don't let me break up the party."

Marian can't tell if this comment is meant to be suggestive. She decides against it, since Jules is David's friend, too.

Juliette retrieves her robe and pads up the walk. The motion sensor light clicks on and off.

"No use trying to talk her out of it," Marian says, and Rémy grunts in agreement.

Marian draws water in one cupped hand, holds it in her palm, and lets it trickle down her arm in a slender stream.

Rémy shifts as though to watch her. "It's been a real pleasure spending time with you these past couple of days."

Languidly, Marian reclines and floats her feet on the water's surface. The wine, the close air, and the gentle force of the jets slow her thoughts. A pleasure, a real pleasure spending time with her. The words become buoyant, errant, bumping against one another on the jet-whirled water. She can't tell where they'll go next, or even where she wants them to go, but she feels lulled by their warmth, even though a distant part of her whispers, Why am I attracted to this professor, this man who isn't David?

A hinge creaks.

In French, a man's voice: "What are you doing? Can't you see the spa is closed?"

Marian squints against the light. The corpulent night manager is hurrying towards them.

Rémy pulls himself onto the deck, dripping. "Oh, we thought that at a place like this, the spa would be open twenty-four hours."

The manager drags the cover from where Rémy rested it against a lounge chair. "Madame, out of the Jacuzzi. Please."

Marian flees the water like a panicked duck and crosses her arms over her chest.

Rémy tosses her a towel. She winds it around herself and darts up the walk to the inn.

Chapter Two

For the past three months, the most distinctive feature of
Rémy's walk to campus has been a giant hole.

A ten-foot chain-link fence stretches between him and the
abyss. Affixed to it is a sunny sign that reads:

Danger

Construction

Even on this last day of August, inside the fence workmen
holler and a dump truck growls. An excavator perches on
the edge of the hole. It coughs and stretches its neck before
swooping and clawing the earth. Hardhats bob out of its way.
These hats must be one-size-fits-all, or at least big enough to
fit the head of the university president, Philip Hodgins, who
smugly sported a white one on the cover of last spring's issue
of *Alumni Advancement.* "Breaking New Ground," read the
caption, an inexcusably lazy metaphor, even for propaganda,
and further cheapened by Hodgins' grip on a shovel that
shone like it had never met dirt. The magazine article glossed
over the twenty-five million dollars required to build the new
Student Activities Building—already dubbed the SAB—and
the widespread faculty opposition to the project. It highlighted
instead the SAB's state-of-the-art fitness centre, computer
labs, study pods, food market (*not* a cafeteria) and Centre for
Excellence in Teaching and Learning. Education 2.0.

SAB. President Hodgins, S.O.B., Rémy thinks, tickled he
can serve up this little slice of English slang, however dated.
He covers his ears against the excavator's racket. Hodgins'

innovation, Hodgins' edifice. Twenty-five million dollars
and counting, thirty-two million if you count corporate
sponsorship: an American hotel corporation will sear its logo
into the face of the building. Hotel SAB. Enjoy your stay. Would
it not have been more logical for the capitalists to claim the new
and also state-of-the-art student residence on Murphy Street?
Private baths and double beds in the single occupancy rooms;
leather couches and big screen TVs in the common areas.
There is only one such building on campus—ninety percent of
first-years live in less luxurious quarters—but the university
tour guides make sure to lead all potential recruits through the
super-dorm.

Oh, Rémy doesn't blame the students. He can't. Who would
opt to share a room with an imperfect stranger, who would
want to crap publicly in those metal stalls? But everywhere he
looks there is newly poured cement and newly forged steel. It's
an arms race. The Cold War of higher education. Universities
competing for prestige. Who will dominate this year's rankings
in *Maclean's*? Who can boast the best quality of 'student life'? A
state-funded educational system can't afford opulence. Rémy's
classes have tripled in size in only five years, not because
enrolments in French are rising—alas, the opposite is true—but
because the department has reduced course offerings to offset
budget cuts, new tenure-track lines aren't being opened when
professors retire, and the students have no choice but to cram
themselves into the classes that remain.

The construction site behind him, Rémy turns onto
Waterton Drive, the main road through campus, widened last
year to make room for budding grandeur without purpose:
silver saplings adorn a grassy median. Elm trees, or maybe
oak. Someone has painted a few of the trunks blue and white,
Waterton U colours. There goes a few thousand dollars more,
lost to spirited vandalism.

In the face of all this change, the Modern Languages
building remains unaltered. Reliably shabby, old enough to be

named only for itself. Its tangled ivy defies any who might wish
to give the limestone façade a good scrubbing. Rémy climbs
its eroded steps, heaves open the wooden door. Inside, waxed
flooring the colour of mushrooms clashes with the chipped
turquoise paint of the running boards and banisters. The stench
of bleach cuts through the subtle must of the lavatories. He
ducks into the men's room and holds up his arms in front of
the mirror, evaluating the half-moons of sweat that darken the
white cotton of his shirt. His kingdom for an air conditioner.
He snatches some paper towel, carries it up to his office, shuts
himself inside, and pins the paper towel under his arms for
a few seconds. He tosses it once it has soaked up less than he
would have hoped, half-unbuttons his shirt and pries open the
window, to little effect (no breeze). Two bikini-topped students
are lounging on a plaid blanket on the lawn. Propriety stripped
away—this is what heat does to people. No, inexact. Students
have no propriety to begin with. A half-naked Marian flits
across his mind's eye. It startles him that this is a memory and
not an idle fantasy. He has gone hot tubbing with a student in
her undies. What came over him that night three months ago?
Nostalgia for his grad student days, no doubt. Wine, flirtation,
freedom. The usual suspects. A twinge of desire, no more.
No more? Did he not go out of his way to avoid talking about
Delphine that weekend? Marian, who has a husband—David?—
mentioned him only minimally. An unspoken code. Lies of
omission.

If only she could see him now, damp and stinking, a clutch
of chest hair escaping the confines of his shirt. He is brambly,
perspiring, ridiculous. If indeed she finds him sexy in some
forbidden, professorial way, she should question her judgment
and get back to work. Everyone must get back to work. "You,
too, bikini girls," he mutters aloud in the direction of the open
window, feeling a pleasurable mix of voyeurism and paternal
outrage. He thinks: For heaven's sake, put some clothes on.

He picks through his email account, ignores the electronic version of today's meeting's agenda, and wonders idly what sort of meeting this one will be. There are only two kinds: those where nothing happens because no one can agree, and those where nothing happens because the issue has already been decided well in advance, behind closed doors. He consults his watch: ten minutes. He plans to hide in his office for another nine, at which time he and at least one other colleague will emerge into the hallway simultaneously and rush down the stairs to Room 113. The trick is to appear too busy to waste even a single moment of productivity, and also to avoid small talk around the seminar table.

You would think that in a department of seven, collegiality would flourish. But the linguists, Aurélie Thériault and Philomène Mulumba, consider themselves too quantitative for this milieu and prefer to fraternize with professors in psychology and mathematics; the nineteenth-century specialist, Babette Queneau, is quietly awaiting retirement; the Renaissance scholar and feminist, Flo Adam, has been trying for the past three years to defect to Women's Studies; Adèle Faucher, postcolonialist and chair of the department, rarely leaves her office; Yves Perrin, eminent medievalist, author of six monographs, laureate of the Otto Gründler Book Prize, Distinguished Chair of Comparative Literature, is too temperamental to befriend. Rémy misses and resents Jean-Louis Allard, who was hired a year after Rémy, drank beer with him on Thursdays, won three consecutive SSHRC grants, went up for tenure early, and left the department last year to become Dean of Arts.

Rémy fumbles to lock his office door as Normand Latour across the hall does the same. Normand is a Visiting Assistant Professor in Acadian literature. 'Visiting' is a euphemism for transient, underpaid, and generally put-upon, and this is why Rémy doesn't include Normand in his collegial count. Rémy likes him well enough and feels badly that his situation at the department isn't more permanent. He makes a mental note to invite him to lunch. *Salut, salut,* they greet each other, and exchange stiff pleasantries as they hurry down the stairs. Rémy opens the door to the second floor, and Marian, in the flesh, moves briskly past him, holding her cell to one ear and cupping her hand to the other as though to block out any noise she might encounter.

"Oh my God," she says as she descends the stairwell. "Just— oh God. Twenty minutes."

"I wonder what that's about?" Rémy thinks aloud, and Normand furrows his sparse brows and says he hasn't a clue, as if the question hadn't simply landed on him by accident.

"Bon," Adèle says once they are seated. "On peut commencer."

Lucie, the department secretary, poises her fingers over her laptop, ready to take minutes.

The first item on the agenda is the selection of representatives for committees. The usual avoidance tactics are deployed: downcast eyes, doodling, the consultation of electronic calendars on smartphones. Finally, a reluctant hand creeps up and Lucie takes down a name. Repeat, repeat. In response to the call for a representative on the Library Committee, which meets only once a year, three eager hands make a bid, including Rémy's, except he doesn't raise his as high as the others, because he's worried about his underarm sweat moons. Sold to Babette. Rémy gets stuck with the Curriculum Committee instead, which meets bimonthly. Adèle moves on to the next agenda item, the elimination of the minor in French Canadian Literatures of the West. The department's specialist in that area retired three years ago and his courses will disappear from the books this year. It is a pipe dream to believe that these courses will ever be offered again. Motion to strike the module made by Adèle, seconded by Flo. All in favour? Carried.

"Agenda item number three," Adèle says. "The budget."

Yves Perrin grunts. Flo stops texting.

"The dean's office has acknowledged receipt of our letter underscoring the detrimental impact of last year's three percent budget cuts on our program offerings. I have the response here for you to read."

The letter circulates. *Due to severe financial constraints we are unable to grant your request . . .*

"As you can see," Adèle continues, "The Administration won't budge. When I called the Dean to badger him further, he told me that another five percent cut is imminent."

Yves Perrin, medievalist extraordinaire, folds the letter in four, makes a tent out of it on the seminar table, crushes it. "I propose a motion. No, let's divide the motion, just for fun. Firstly, might I move that we call the neoliberals by their names. 'The dean,' as you say, 'the Administration'—capital 'A'—is a seconded member of our own department, and I refuse to call him by any other name than Jean-Louis, which is the name his mother gave him when he was a mewling, puking brat."

Adèle's eyes grow large, Babette trembles, Flo smirks, Normand and the linguists remain impassive, and Rémy admires Yves' childishness, pomposity, and gravitas.

"Secondly," Yves says as he rises and gathers his notebook and agenda, leaving the mangled letter where it is, "Might I move that if the smooth functioning of departments is deemed *unnecessary* to the university's advancement, that we all pack up our books, turn out the lights and go home."

He slams the door on his way out.

"Another five percent?" Babette says after a respectable period of silence.

"Lucie and I have been over the numbers," Adèle says too quickly. "There are things we can do without. No more coffee in the lounge. All events, including book launches, can be potluck. We can suspend the faculty computer budget. We've traditionally given four hundred dollars for the A.S.

Charbonneau Prize for the best student essay, but an inscribed book will do. We'll eliminate the visiting scholar position . . ."

All eyes, including Rémy's, latch themselves onto Normand, who visibly shrinks. Rémy, feeling sorry for Normand and ashamed by his own stare, mutters, "Well, surely there are other cuts we can implement first."

Adèle stiffens, realizing her gaff. She continues hurriedly and too loudly, like a woman pretending not to have farted audibly. "If we get rid of the faculty phone lines, we'll save nine thousand four hundred and fifty-nine dollars—"

Rémy laughs, then claps his hand over his mouth when he realizes she's serious.

"Everyone has a cell phone these days," Adèle says, defensive.

"*I* don't have a cell phone," Rémy says.

Flo hangs her mouth open. "You don't have a cell phone?"

Adèle makes a note. "Rémy, you can share a phone line with Normand."

Babette timidly raises her hand. "I don't have one, either."

"You can share a line with Rémy and Normand," Adèle says, apparently not embarrassed by her proposal. "Next item: the sofa in the lounge . . ."

Chapter Three

Kong, a nine-pound terrier cross, leaps and paws the air and snuffles around Marian's legs. She steps over the dog to hug David, slips her arms around his billowy white shirt and tucks her head under his chin. "Poor sweet Edna," she says. "Poor woman."

"She was just lying there on the master bed in her costume. Bonnet and all. She even put the velvet rope back across the doorway before lying down." David pulls away and runs the back of his hand under his chin, the way he does when he's nervous or distraught. "Sometimes she got quiet, I guess, but mostly she seemed happy and really upbeat. I guess she had to, though. Because of the visitors."

"What did you do when you—when it became clear—"

"I locked the door behind me and waited outside for the ambulance. What else could I do?"

The Acorn House, a two-storey frame house overlooking the Saint Lawrence River, erected in 1805 by Loyalist bachelor and entrepreneur Jeremiah Acorn—owner of the local grist mill and general store—now a minor tourist attraction: not the spot Marian would have chosen to end her days, but to each her own. David is curator and interpreter of the site, which means he polishes silverware, and arranges pamphlets, and rubs smudges off glass display cases, or sometimes calls over to the Upper Saint Lawrence Historical Society to report a bat in the attic or cracked paint on a frieze or lintel. All this he does wearing breeches, a waist coat, and a silk kerchief, for the benefit of nostalgic visitors who come to experience a day in the life of an insignificant historical figure in the year 1812.

As for Edna, she plays—*played*, past tense—Jeremiah's housekeeper and cook, and had adopted this role long before David's arrival on the scene in May. This is the latest in a long string of jobs that David has held since Marian started her graduate work four years ago. Telemarketer, assistant florist, line cook. After they finished undergrad and got married, and while Marian was saving up for grad school, they both did a year-long stint as phone operators for a roadside assistance company. At least the Acorn House job has to do with history, which was David's major in university.

"Sounds like a drag," Marian said when he first told her about spending his days with seventy-year-old Edna, waiting for tourists to trickle through.

David shrugged. "I guess she's not so bad. She sure likes backgammon." He later described to her how Edna sang along to Wilco on her iPod each morning before the tourists arrived, told ribald jokes about historical whores, and got pissed off when tourists assumed that her character remained unmarried because she couldn't get a man. These were the tidbits that trailed after him when he came home after yet another shift of repeating the same day in 1812.

Marian met Edna when she toured the Acorn House in July. In character or out of it, she always went by her given name. No need to change it for something more historical. 'Edna' matched her chintz dresses and cotton petticoats just fine.

She described to Marian the finer points of the slate-lined fireplace, turned balusters, and acorn newel posts, and taught her to stuff a lump of sugar in her cheek before sipping her tea.

"Lots of folks who come through here ask about ghosts," she said, when Marian mentioned her research. "What do you make of that?"

Marian explained that unfortunately she had no wisdom
to offer regarding the ghosts who say 'Boo!' and the people
who conjure them. Her understanding of ghosts, spectres, and
doubles was limited to the literary and the theoretical. Psychic
boundaries being violated, feminine erasure from the literary
tradition, misogyny, unacknowledged desires . . .

"Uh huh," Edna said. "What's it all mean?"

"It doesn't mean just one thing, exactly," Marian said,
stalling as she struggled to come up with an answer, and feeling
the rising mercury of self-doubt: was her work worthy of being
talked about with someone like Edna? Did it actually have
meaning outside of academia, and more importantly, outside of
her own head?

"The 'so-what' factor," Edna continued when Marian didn't
answer. "There must be one."

The so-what factor. Indeed. "I've mostly discovered that the
popular understanding or definition of the ghost doesn't really
apply all that well to literature," Marian said. "The ghosts who
appear in movies or campfire stories or folklore want to avenge
some wrong, or act out their innate evil tendencies, or express
what was left unsaid in life. They have their own desires, their
own agenda. But the ghosts of literature are most often pure
projection: they convey the needs of the characters or authors
or societies that they haunt. They point to a lack or a desire,
but never their own. Basically, they reveal the questions and
anxieties of others. Anyway, sorry to bore you," Marian trailed
off, embarrassed, although Edna was following her description
attentively. "I'm not used to talking about this stuff with
non-academics."

Edna puckered and nodded as she sucked her sugar. "People
who come to the Acorn House want to know if I hear noises or
voices, and if objects get moved around from room to room."

"What do you tell them?"

"What they want to hear. What else is there?"

"I picture her getting ready in the morning," David says as he changes out of his costume and into a T-shirt and jeans. "Tying her apron, pinning her hair up, like any other day, except this time she stuffs her purse full of sleeping pills."

"It's so sad. So incredibly tragic." These words sound inadequate to Marian's ears, like she's channelling ready-made platitudes about death. But if there are better words out there, she can't seem to access them.

David tosses his wool trousers on the dresser. They slide to the floor and he doesn't intervene when the dog settles down to gnaw on them. "I suppose the funeral will be on Friday."

Marian pictures Edna in her dusty-rose dress, couched in the polyester satin of the casket, hands folded, face painted in the hues of life. Death on display; death concealed. Made up and yet profoundly real. Nothing like the dead women that Marian studies in books.

"Would you like me to come with you? Dr. Perrin is giving a talk, but I can skip it."

"It's up to you," David says, and she's relieved. Mourning makes her deeply uncomfortable. The questioning, the groping sadness. The grip it has on the living. Maybe this is why she studies death in literature: because it's never real and is seldom final. The ghost is present even when the person is absent.

"I mean, if you wanted to come, that would be fine," David adds, and looks away as though he feels vulnerable.

Deep in Marian's stomach, her flight instinct flutters. "Is that what you want? Because if you need me, I'll come. But otherwise, there's the Perrin talk."

For a moment he doesn't reply.

"I guess I didn't know her that well," he says.

On Friday, he comes back from the funeral stiff jawed and red around the eyes. "A dozen people there. No family, except some second cousin from Buffalo. A forty-minute memorial. That's what a life can amount to."

Marian wonders if he's thinking of his own parents,
who divorced right after she and David met, and now are so
wrapped up in their own lives they seldom bother to call him.
Jan and Tom's mutual discontent transformed over the years
into distrust and then loathing, and by the time they decided
to separate, they had grown eight arms that they used to
wrestle over finances and more nebulous emotional spoils, like
subcategories of blame. Tentacular divorce. Now Jan lives with
a fisherman in Newfoundland, and Tom has moved to Italy and
is dating a glass blower. They placed an oceanic buffer between
them in order to survive, and somewhere along the way, they
left their son stranded.

Did David tell Edna all this? Maybe she was a confidante, a
psychological refuge.

His confidences buried with her.

David places the funeral program face down on the kitchen
table, drinks a beer, and lies down for a nap. Marian drifts to
the living room window, watches dusk settle around the other
buildings of the stout apartment complex, which borders a
respectable, bungalow-laden neighbourhood a half-hour from
campus, appropriate for dog walking if not child-rearing. No
parks, no fancy schools—mostly retirees trimming hedges and
growing clematis. Lots of mature trees for the dog to mark.

Marian takes Kong out and waits while he lifts his leg on
an elm. Back inside, she measures out his food and watches
him dine with his usual commitment to ritual and precision.
He selects two bits of kibble, drops one on the floor, chews the
other contemplatively, and picks up the second. Repeat. When
he finally lies down, he makes his body round, his head flat, and
peers at her with the half-closed eyes of a crocodile. Eating is a
serious business. It levels him.

David emerges from the bedroom. He blinks heavily,
as though shoving away sadness. "The day before she killed
herself, she cleaned the baseboards of the parlour. Like she
wanted to do a little extra to make up for the inconvenience.

Then she brewed tea and talked about lingonberries. Said her maternal grandmother was a Swede." He rubs his knuckle to his chin. "She had to know I would be the one to find her. What does that mean?"

"That someone had to find her."

"Did she think about that beforehand? She must have."

Marian tries not to imagine the thoughts that would have gone through Edna's head in the days and weeks before she killed herself. "I know you want it to mean something. To make sense. But it doesn't. It's just shitty, that's all. Really shitty."

"You interpret the hell out of everything. Except this."

Marian crosses her arms, and David follows suit.

"I guess I don't see the point." Marian feels her voice rise and is helpless to stop it. "I mean, we can never know, right?"

"You could have come."

"You told me I didn't have to!"

"You should have wanted to."

"I can't read minds." She knows she's being partially disingenuous, but her instinct tells her it's dangerous to capitulate—if she does, she'll have to explain herself. The truth is ripe for misinterpretation and will make her sound callous. In her mind, Edna's death is an event that can't be explained, or can only be explained via circular logic: Edna killed herself because she wanted to die. Or, more precisely: Edna killed herself because she didn't want to live. If there's a more complete explanation, they will never arrive at it. So why circle the question?

But even though she's holding fast to deniability, she feels remorse. Because she doesn't want to leave David alone with Edna's death.

"I can make us some pasta," she says.

"Awesome. That will solve everything." David disappears into the bedroom, and she calls after him that she's sorry, but he closes the door and protects himself with sleep.

Marian eats half a box of crackers and lies down on the sofa. Her eyes skate over the text of Derrida's *Specters of Marx* until the book grows heavy and the words drift away.

A bonneted corpse in a dusty-rose dress pokes her with a stockinged foot.

"Good evening, dear," Edna says.

Marian yawns without covering her mouth, observes the corpse reclined at the other end of the sofa. "Good evening, Edna."

They share the silence of the dead.

"I'm really sorry you didn't like life," Marian says after a while, because she doesn't know what else to say to a suicidal ghost.

"Don't be." Edna stretches her toes farther into Marian's zone of the sofa. "I'd looked at this world long enough."

"Are things better now?"

"I don't exist anymore. That's something."

"You should tell David that."

"Nah. He's busy grieving." Edna smiles sweetly, revealing gleaming dentures that Marian doesn't remember her having in real life.

"Nice of him to come to the funeral," Edna says.

Marian looks away in shame. "I'm sorry I wasn't there."

"Pssh! It wasn't exactly the party of the year. A little ironic you were afraid to go, though, eh?"

"It seemed like a reasonable option at the time."

"Can't say I blame you. Funerals creep me out something awful."

"Can we talk about something else?"

"As you like." Edna cracks a gnarled knuckle and folds her hands over her dress. "How about you tell me what you were doing in that hot tub?"

Marian digs under the sofa for her Derrida book. "I need to get back to work now."

"Liar," Edna says.

Chapter Four

The bell in the clock tower sings as Marian eases into a vinyl
armchair in Mackintosh Library's fireside room. The room
overlooks Waterton Drive, bustling now between class periods.
Outside, the tops of maples blaze, flickering orange and red
while inside, the faux logs in the fireplace lie sleepy and grey.
She came to the library to feel the back-to-school hum, still
palpable two weeks into the semester, when the undergrads
are not yet buried in assignments. She thinks the undergrads
a nuisance—the long lines they form at the pita place, the
keg parties on the lawn, the crowded city buses, the fact that
she practically had to swat one away in order to claim this
armchair—but their return to campus is necessary. It marks
the passage of time. Another ring in the tree trunk. They must
leave campus in the spring and return a few months later like
migrating birds. Their arrival allows her to forget the summer
semester, its cycles of procrastination and subsequent guilt.
Again this year, her best intentions blew away like beach
sand. By the time she was done putting in hours at her crappy
summer job shelf reading at the law library, she had no desire to
work on the second chapter of her dissertation, even though it's
on La Corriveau, who is fast becoming her favourite ghost.

An old existential anxiety creeps into Marian's chest. Is she
cut out for academia? Yes. No. She checks her cellphone. The
checking doesn't bury the anxiety, just reminds her that her
attention span—the attention span of students everywhere—is
being sacrificed to a pocket-sized god. She reads an email from

her mother; feels a mix of tenderness and further unease. Her little chickadee of a mother, tap-tapping at the keyboard two fingers at a time, brow furrowed before the monitor. She's sent Marian an article on meditation for stress reduction. She believes her daughter to be high strung and obsessive, and isn't wrong. It's stressful being the daughter of recovering hippies. All that happiness to pursue. As for obsession, well. If Barbara were here now, she would no doubt tell Marian to go find herself a banana or some trail mix. Only once blood sugar has been regulated will Barbara admit the possibility of less than optimal moods. She believes in snacks and mind-over-matter.

Marian leaves her jacket on her chair and wanders down to the library snack counter to buy cranberry juice and a raisin cookie. When she returns, she sheds crumbs as she chews, loses a raisin down the crack of her armchair, and pulls out her notebook. La Corriveau's story is pure excess and melodrama. Maybe it just doesn't like being squished into academic prose.

On one side of the page, she writes. On the other, she draws. The result is more of a commonplace book than a chapter or story. Prose and illustrations and newspaper clippings transcribed in their old-fashioned font. Comics of only a few frames: scenes of murder and betrayal. Hatchet, gallows, gibbet. Molten lead; bottle of poison. Birds, beasts. Cabinet of curios.

Glass tomb.

'GREAT HISTORICAL CURIOSITY'

Hard to say where you first saw La Corriveau. She's always been there, on beer cans or bus shelters. The subject of live theatre or lame TV specials. Your little cousin's costume last Halloween— black wig in disarray, ghoulish face, tattered dress and, of course, the cage.

She is born Marie-Josephte Corriveau, in 1733 in Saint-Vallier, Québec, to Joseph Corriveau and Françoise Bolduc. The only child of nine not to succumb to the various perils of the era— stillbirth, smallpox, typhus—she is destined nonetheless to meet an unfortunate end thirty years later as Québec's most infamous murderess, convicted under British martial law of killing her second husband and hanged in chains near the Plains of Abraham in 1763.

At sixteen, she marries Charles Bouchard. They raise three children and work their parcel of land until Charles dies of putrid fever. A little over a year later, in July 1761, Marie-Josephte marries her neighbour, Louis Dodier.

Dodier quarrels regularly with his in-laws, who own the house in which the couple lives. Scuffles erupt between him and Joseph Corriveau over unpaid rent or access to their co-owned horse. During a disagreement over use of the family bread oven, Corriveau launches himself at his son-in-law wielding first an axe, then a hoe. And who can blame him? By all appearances, Dodier beats Marie-Josephte.

She flees Dodier, takes refuge at her uncle's house, and appeals to the local authority of the time, one Major James Abercrombie, who convinces her to return home where she belongs. A few weeks later, early in the morning on January 27, 1763, Dodier is found dead in the barn, bloody wounds to the head marking his demise. A dung fork lies nearby.

Witnesses gather: the parish priest, a British captain of militia, eight or nine villagers. Suspicion falls on the father-in-law. But Joseph Corriveau is an upright member of the parish and shares a surname with a large number of its inhabitants. The honour of the community is at stake. It is in the best interest of all to declare the death an accident. Taking on the role of coroner, the parish priest in his report to the authorities writes that Louis Dodier was kicked in the head by a horse. The body is expeditiously buried—no time for a wake. Later, during the trial, one villager will complain that Dodier was buried without so much as a clean shirt.

In the village, rumours crackle. The brother of the deceased files a petition with Abercrombie and demands justice. Abercrombie orders that the corpse be exhumed. The surgeon

who examines the body details the nature of the head wounds:
a fractured jaw and four deep punctures, perfectly spaced three
inches apart. He concludes that no horse hoof could inflict
such injuries. Joseph Corriveau is charged with murder and his
daughter Marie-Josepthe charged as his accomplice.

The French have recently lost to the English at the Battle of
the Plains of Abraham. The Conquest is complete. All cases are
tried in military courts, as British civilian courts do not yet exist.
The makeshift court martial is held in Québec City's couvent des
ursulines. The trial unfolds in English, and it is unclear how much
Marie-Josephte and her father understand of the proceedings.
Unclear, too, whether or not the British military men who
comprise the jury understand the various French testimonies.
Twenty-four witnesses take the stand: neighbours of Dodier,
other villagers, the parish priest, the captain of militia, Major
Abercrombie himself. Hearsay proliferates: the father is violent
and quarrelsome, the daughter a slut and a drunkard who has
been seen throwing up in her children's bonnets. The defense
lawyer, a French Canadian, is unfamiliar with British martial law
and is unable to build a solid case. Impossible to poke holes in the
witnesses' dubious testimonies—there is no cross-examination in
courts-martial. Joseph Corriveau is found guilty of murder and
sentenced to death by hanging. Marie-Josephte is sentenced to
*Receive Sixty Lashes with a Cat and Nine Tales upon her bare back,
at three different places viz under Gallows, upon the Market place of
Québec, and in the Parish of St Vallier, twenty Lashes at each place,
and Branded in the Left hand with the Letter M.*

M for Murderer.

This beating and branding will never take place. The day
before Joseph Corriveau is scheduled to be hanged, a priest is
summoned. Joseph confesses that he did not kill his son-in-law—
he was merely his daughter's accomplice after the fact. The priest
tells him that by remaining silent, he is committing murder against
himself, thus endangering his immortal soul. The words resonate.
Joseph accepts a pardon in exchange for his statement: "The Night

of the 26th of January about ten O'Clock, this Declarant being
then in his Bed, his Daughter knocked at the Window, and said in
a low voice, Father come."

He let her into the house.

"Dodier is dead. I killed him."

Joseph in his statement says that upon hearing this, he called
his daughter a "Vile Wretch" and sent her away, but later helped
her drag the body from the conjugal bed to the stable. He says,
"It was Marie Josephte Corriveau who killed her Husband in his
Bed, with a Blunted Hatchet." Afterwards, she burned the bloody
sheets.

On Friday, April 15, 1763, Marie-Josephte is tried a second
time under martial law. She confesses to killing her husband in
his sleep because he abused her. She is sentenced to be hanged in
chains, and she must pay for the iron gibbet herself.

The trial lasts no more than half an hour.

'Hanged in chains' means hanged twice for good measure. The
first hanging is unexceptional by eighteenth-century standards: a
scaffold erected at the city's highest point, a noose, a crowd hungry
for grisly entertainment. It's not personal: all this Marie-Josephte's
father, too, would have suffered, had he not hoisted his daughter
onto the gallows at the last moment, thus saving himself from the
charge of murder.

But Marie-Josephte is a woman who has killed her husband.
She is not only murderous, but insubordinate. A traitor. The
sanctity of the patriarchy has been violated. She must be made an
example of. For this reason, the second hanging is anything but
routine. Once the life is wrung out of her, Marie-Josephte is taken
down and encased in a tight-fitting, iron exoskeleton and hauled
to a well-travelled crossroads in Pointe-Lévy, where she is put on
display. For five weeks she publicly decays in her cage, dangling
from a hook like a macabre Christmas tree ornament, after which
time Governor James Murray allows the body to be taken down
and buried. (It is best not to offend the sensibilities of Britain's

newest subjects. The display of power over the French Canadians has been made. No need to rub it in.)

No wonder the French Canadians' memory of Marie-Josephte Corriveau is long and fantastical. As far as infamy and humiliation are concerned, they will never see her equal. Gibbetting is unknown to them. Even the British usually reserve this gruesome punishment for the most heinous and traitorous male criminals. Her demise is the stuff of legend.

Years pass, and the story transforms, filtered through legend and literature. It pickles in its own piquancy. It wasn't one husband that La Corriveau killed, but two husbands or five or seven. She slipped arsenic into food, butchered spousal flesh with her axe. She hanged one husband, poisoned another with herbs, poked yet another in the navel with an awl. Occasionally she is hilariously inept—when she fails to strangle one of the husbands in his sleep, she goes at the job again with a hammer, then a pitchfork. Over the years she metamorphoses into a witch courted by werewolves, a ghost who rattles her cage and haunts unsuspecting male travellers on the high road at night. Villainous, sterile, decrepit, drunk, she needs the help of these travellers in traversing the blessed water of the *fleuve*. She wants to dance with demons on the other shore.

The first husband's putrid fever is of course entirely forgotten. La Corriveau killed him, too, by pouring molten lead into his sleeping ears.

In 1851, eighty-six years after her death, Marie-Josepthe Corriveau goes on the road.

Her cage, one bone still rattling inside, is accidentally exhumed, then stolen, from a Pointe-Lévy cemetery. In August 1851, the cage is displayed first near the Bonsecours market in Montreal, then in a cabinet of curios in Québec City. For only twenty-five cents, you can view the gibbet that contained French Canada's most notorious murderess! Better get there fast—she won't stick around long. An American agent already has his eye on her.

By the end of the month, La Corriveau—both legend and
cage—has crossed the border and debarked in New York City.

If you are browsing the *New York Daily Tribune* on August 26,
1851, you may find yourself tempted by *Silks! Silks! Various
Importations*; or a cake of *JONES'S Chemical Soap*; or *a new
romance, THE CORSAIR—A Venetian Tale, by George Sand,
author of Consuelo, Indiana, &c., &c.*; or a *NEW MAP of the
VILLAGE of YONKERS*. Or perhaps you are interested in hiring
one of the women who offer their services as chambermaid, nurse,
housekeeper, ladies' maid, washer, seamstress. Or you're more in
the mind to hire a capable young man as a clerk, foreman, book-
keeper, or salesman. It's possible that you just want to make sure
that your own want ad has been printed correctly: your notice that
you have a *good country physician's practice for sale*, or that you are
seeking to hire a *middle-aged respectable widow as Cook, with a child
of 12 or 14 to assist in light work.*

But perhaps you're just a New Yorker looking to enjoy the
best the city has to offer that week. In that case, you'll skim over
the above and feel a sizzle of interest when you see what's new at
P.T. Barnum's American Museum at the corner of Broadway and
Ann Street. You've already seen the dwarfs, giants, giantesses, fire-
eaters, and Swiss Bearded Lady; you've marvelled at the World's
Fattest Man/Woman/Baby/Twins; you've popped in twice to
see the elephants, gorillas, and camelopard; you've familiarized
yourself with the particulars of shoes, snails, crystals, mummies,
and optical instruments from around the globe; you've grown so
worldly that curious ladder feats no longer amaze you; and as to
the cosmoramas, they've become downright routine. You have been
meaning to see:

The every-where-talked-about-and-admired **HAPPY FAMILY**,
a large collection of Birds, Beasts, &c., by nature hostile to each
other, but taught by a **Mysterious Process** to dwell together in the
utmost harmony and affection. Cats, Rats, Dogs, Pigeons, Owls,

Mice, &c., &c., all **Educated to Peace**, may be here witnessed
in a state of **Christian Communism**, having laid aside all their
destructive instincts to assume those of **Social Tranquillity**.

And you have your excuse! Because now, for your 25¢, not only can
you view miraculous beastly harmony, but also the latest:

GREAT HISTORICAL CURIOSITY—IRON GIBBET OF
OLDEN TIMES, and thrown aside by the progress of civilization
during the last century; one of these public death instruments
found in Point Levy, Canada East, in the course of May last, had
been used under the Government of Sir G. Murray, first Governor
of Canada, after its capitulation, in the year 1763, for the execution
of a female who had murdered three successive husbands. It will be
exhibited during a few days, at No. 252 Broadway, 2nd floor, room
No. 11, from 8 A.M. To 9 P.M., where historical details of her
criminal life may be procured.

You gather your wife and kids and don your hat, because where
else in the city can you find such wholesome family entertainment
for only twenty-five cents a head?

What did Barnum and his visitors see in this little Québécois
ghost? Which part of her story piqued international interest, made
her cage worthy of a prominent display in the throbbing heart of
New York City? Female violence and revenge, safely contained,
patriarchy restored? Or was it the human and therefore uncanny
form of the iron artifact that fascinated so? Perhaps it was the
allusion to serial killing? Or the evocation of foreign (Canadian!)
barbarism? Whatever the reason, P.T. Barnum—America's most
famous humbug-naturalist-Orientalist-opportunist—thought
Marie-Josephte Corriveau marketable enough to trumpet the
arrival of her cage among his 'million curiosities.'

    A long and illustrious career. La Corriveau is still newsworthy
one hundred and eighty years later, in 1931, when the *New York*

Sun profiles her cage, acquired now by a museum in Salem, Massachusetts. Just down the street from the sorcery museum in the witch capital of the USA, the gibbet hangs "in fitting comradeship with a guillotine blade which was in service during the French Revolution."

Fine company indeed.

It is more than two hundred years after her death when feminist writers such as Anne Hébert claim her. In Hébert's *La Cage*, first staged in 1989, Marie-Josephte is a prisoner of her sex, of male violence. She is born with her cage.

One morning, having eaten your multigrain toast with butter and Bonne Maman jam, but not yet finished your bowl of cottage cheese, you read that the Musée de la civilisation has repatriated the cage. She's finally come home! She'll be on display for only five days.

You take the number 21 bus to the museum's Maison Chevalier. Six bucks to descend into the vaulted cellar—a temporary, rubble stone crypt. There she is under the stone arches: a supine skeleton of rusted, pitted hoops, your iron beauty asleep inside a glass cage.

Linger over her display; get some selfies with the cage. She's destined for storage.

And when she's gone, don't fret. She will live a thousand more lives. Another story will be born, and another and another.

You can always count on a ghost to refuse to stay dead.

Chapter Five

Marian returns to the library several days in a row to immerse herself in the legend of La Corriveau. As she descends the stairwell on her way out one day, she spots Rémy below, returning books. Their interactions since the conference in May have been few. She saw him at a dissertation defense in July, after which he greeted her exuberantly but professionally, and asked if she'd been out of town. He said they really needed to go for coffee sometime, though nothing came of it. She assumed, with a twinge of disappointment, then guilt, that his memory of the evening they had spent in the hot tub had evaporated.

Rémy is trying to shove too many books at a time into the return slot. He doesn't notice her until she's a few feet away. "Ah te voilà," he says, as though he has been searching for her and expecting her to appear any moment. "The slot to book ratio needs to be reexamined."

"A question for the physics department."

"Engineering, I was thinking."

With both hands he holds out a book on the American short story, and Marian clasps the other end of the book, not knowing why, and feeling silly.

"Procrastination," he says.

"From what?"

"The most onerous of tasks."

She lets go of the book and his arms drop. "Laundry? Grading?" she says.

"My tenure file."

"Oh, I'm sorry," she says, as though offering him heartfelt condolences.

"They make me justify my existence here," he says, doleful. "That is the way of things."

"Let me know if there's something I can do."

"If only you were serious."

"Why wouldn't I be?"

"I wouldn't want to impose . . ."

"*Is* there something?"

"It's just—it's in English, this damn tenure file."

"I can look at it," she says quickly.

"I couldn't possibly—"

"No really. It's not a problem."

"I would be grateful. Are you busy now?"

She hesitates. "Not really . . ."

"You can see my new office. Though Cloutier didn't make it easy for me on his way out. Damn pack rat." He slides the last book into the return slot and shepherds her through the library's theft detectors.

Outside, a few students have set up a folding table on which they've laid a couple of clipboards and some pamphlets. One of the students calls out to them as they round the corner. "Are you guys worried about the funding cuts?" The student sounds more earnest than aggressive. He has a hipster beard and wears a faded T-shirt condemning the construction of the Keystone pipeline out West; the wrappings of a former cause. "Five percent cuts across campus! I'm in the political science department. The chair has already laid off members of the non-unionized administrative staff."

"I've heard there are cuts in our department, too." Marian glances at Rémy, who is hanging back.

"There's zero budget transparency," the student continues. "New buildings are going up around campus, yet there's never any money for departments. The president just does whatever he pleases. There's no consultation."

"You're right," Marian says. "It's not okay. And it's not just staff, either—I've heard there might be less bursary money next semester."

"So you'll sign our petition?" The hipster gestures to a clipboard on the table.

"Of course." Marian scribbles her name and holds the pen out to Rémy.

Rémy waves the pen away. "The faculty are organizing their own petition."

The student nods, noncommittal. "We all have to do what we're comfortable with."

"That's great there's another petition going," Marian says to Rémy as they continue their walk to his office.

He rubs at his head, sheepish. "This is embarrassing, but there isn't one. I don't know why I said that. It just came out."

"Oh. You felt you couldn't sign because you're a faculty member?"

"Well, it's probably best not to sign as an *untenured* faculty member."

"Ah." It had never occurred to Marian that her professors— that Rémy—could feel vulnerable. "It's a shame you have to be afraid," she says.

"'Afraid' isn't quite the right word. Prudent, let's say. Anyway, you were right to sign. These cuts aren't okay. Sometimes I feel like the business of learning is the last item on the administration's agenda."

As they climb the steps to the Modern Languages building, Rémy touches her arm and asks about her summer. She rattles off details of a few sunny events and avoids talk of her dissertation.

The building is mostly quiet. Inside one of the classrooms an evening Chinese class is taking place.

Rémy unlocks the door to his office and turns on the light. "Do you like it?" He makes a sweeping gesture around the room, keys and jacket in hand, like a magician ready to amaze.

When it was Cloutier's, the office had been inviting and warm, swaddled in wall textiles and area rugs. The once-amber walls are now institutionally white. With the exception of a lush potted plant, the room slaps with the white hand of minimalism. The fluorescent lights buzz unpleasantly.

"It's different, anyway."

"Carl was nice enough to have it painted for me."

"Carl?"

"The building manager," Rémy says. "I'm a socialist." He raises his eyebrows self-mockingly. "Man of the people."

"Just no petitions," Marian says.

Rémy laughs. "Touché." He gestures to a black rampart in the centre of the room. "The best is that now I have room for a decent table."

The table is three times the size of the desk where she and Cloutier used to have meetings. On it there is no cozy old Thermos, no set of matching mugs. A pitcher of filtered water and one glass are its only accoutrements.

Rémy sits in the leather task chair on the south side of the table. Marian perches on a plastic chair on the opposite side of the barricade. Everything interesting lies on his side of the room: the bookshelves, the desk, the window with its view of the St. Lawrence, the plant. She feels tiny on the other side amid the empty space.

He gathers some papers from his printer tray, slips them into a brown interdepartmental envelope, and wheels his chair over to her side as though sensing her discomfort and wanting to bridge the gap between them. "Normally I wouldn't ask a student to do this. But it's you, and—" he hesitates. "It takes a certain amount of trust, you understand?"

"I won't tell anyone what's in the file," she says.

He exhales, relieved. "Maybe you won't find my English so bad." He says this haltingly in English, his accent strong.

"I doubt that," she says in French with a little smile.

"Smart girl."

Chapter Six

"Doggy bomb!" Marian releases Kong onto David's curled
body. The dog nuzzles his snout into David's neck, and David
groans and locks him into an affectionate half nelson. It's eight
forty-five in the evening. Light from the hallway angles across
the bedroom floor.

Marian squeezes herself onto the sliver of bed beside David
and lies with her butt hanging off the side like an oversized
spoon. "We're going on a date," she says.

"Actually, we're not. We're sleeping."

"You've been sleeping too much lately," Marian says,
keeping her tone light. "It's unhealthy. You should at least add
some beer to the mix."

"Mm," David says, his eyes still closed.

Marian leaps up, flicks on the light, tosses him a shirt.

They end up at Molly O'Neil's, the type of Irish pub that
serves Blarney Chip Nachos and Pot 'O Gold Potato Skins.
David orders them each a pint and Marian tries to ignore
her reflection in the shamrock mirror while they stand in
the corner waiting for a table to become free. They talk about
Kong's new habit of turning around and backing himself up
like a little truck when he wants a lift up onto the couch, and
the theft of David's runners from his gym locker—who would
want to wear a stranger's grimy shoes?

David transfers his pint from one hand to the other and
wipes condensation onto his jeans. "The board is hiring

Edna's replacement next week. They asked me to sit in on the interviews."

"That's decent of them." Marian sips foam from the top of her beer, nervous to engage in the subject of Edna, and already faintly nostalgic for the few minutes where they were able to talk about normal, unfraught things.

"I told them I wasn't interested," David says. "What's the point?"

"You *will* be spending all day with this person."

"So I spend all day with her."

Marian sighs, then hums along to the folk music to keep her tongue busy. In the end, she succumbs. "You only worked with her for four months. Don't you think your reaction is a bit . . . intense? Disproportionate, maybe?"

He doesn't meet her gaze. Glances around the bar.

"Never mind," Marian says. "I just thought it was worth mentioning. Since you brought it up."

He shifts his body away from her. "Thank you for that," he says.

For a few minutes they stand there, pinning down each end of the silence between them, watching other people in the bar have fun.

Marian finishes her pint and makes a trip to the bathroom. While she performs acrobatics in order not to touch the dubious surfaces of the toilet and stall, she thinks, Why is the person closest to you always the touchiest, the most likely to feel aggrieved? As though proximity rubbed away all the usual buffers. She just wants David to feel better, to be his old self. She just wants them both to be happy.

David has found them a spot at the bar, and as she joins him, a gaggle of women descends. They order beer and shots, squawking in the emphatic tones of the already inebriated, and several of them flaunt white sashes like Miss America's: BRIDE, BRIDESMAID. A bridesmaid scoots onto the bar stool on the other side of David. "My cousin's getting married," she says to him over the music, more loudly than necessary.

"That sounds like fun," David says, his tone diplomatic.

"I guess."

Marian shifts to observe the woman. She appears to be about their age, or a little older. Under her sash she wears a sleeveless green dress that shows off her form: slim and taut like an elastic. Her bare crossed legs shimmer with some special beauty product.

"He's in med school," the bridesmaid says. "The groom, I mean. My cousin says she likes his personality." She leans in and says something that Marian can't hear, and nudges David with her shoulder. David stiffens and reaches for his beer.

"This is my wife, Marian," he says, gesturing with his pint, but one of the other women is already half-shouting in the bridesmaid's ear, asking if she'd like another shot.

Once the bridesmaid has chased the shot with a swig of beer, she makes a face and turns back to David. "This is a lot of work."

"I can imagine."

"What do you do for a living?"

"I'm a historical interpreter."

The bridesmaid doesn't follow up on this ambiguous job title at first, just holds her pint up to her mouth with both hands and drinks.

"You mean at a tourist site or something?"

"The Acorn House."

"Hey, I know that place! It's just down the road from my aunt's house. She took me there a couple times when I was a kid." The bridesmaid leans in and Marian can hardly hear her when she says, "There was a suicide there not too long ago, wasn't there? My aunt told me about it."

"That was—it was my colleague, in fact." David blinks and looks away, as though he, like Marian, is surprised by the

emotion that has leaked from his voice and is spilling towards
this stranger.

"Oh, I'm sorry." The bridesmaid lowers her head and casts
her eyes down. "That's awful. It must be so hard for you."

David nods, downs the last of his pint. "I think she might
have been bipolar," he says.

Marian leans back to stare openly, letting go of any
pretence of not eavesdropping. David has never mentioned
this theory of Edna's mental health to her, and yet here he is,
revealing it to a shiny-legged stranger.

Is he punishing her? Or confiding in her through this tipsy
medium?

The bridesmaid remains oblivious to Marian's scrutiny.
David, however, bristles; his jaw tightens in recognition of her
stare.

"Anyway," he says. "You look like you're in for an
interesting night."

The bridesmaid uncrosses her legs and pushes her chest
out as she adjusts her sash. "We're doing a scavenger hunt. My
friend needs the signature of a guy named Steve. Is your name
Steve?"

"Nope."

"What is it?'

"David."

"Too bad."

Marian reaches behind David and taps the bridesmaid on
the arm. "He's just messing with you," she says. She can tell
by the way the bridesmaid swivels and stares that she's seeing
Marian for the first time. "His name's Steve. Check his ID."

The bridesmaid blinks confusedly. Next to her the bride
winces and adjusts the jewelled strap of her shoe, supporting
herself on the edge of the bar. She loses her balance and bumps
into the bridesmaid. Beer sloshes onto the bar. The bridesmaid
puts down her glass and flicks beer off her hand. She floats a
cocktail napkin over the puddle. Marian tries to catch David's

eye but he's reaching over to help mop up some of the spill with his own napkin.

"Why would you tell me your name is Dave?" the bridesmaid says. "That's not very nice. What if I asked for your number? Would you write Dave-555-whatever and let me text some old lady and feel stupid? Are you one of those guys?" She's on the verge of tears. Her eyes are slightly too close together and she wears her eyeliner cat-eye style as though to compensate. Marian hopes her eye makeup won't run. She wants her to stay pretty and intact.

"I'm sorry," David says. "It's just that my name isn't Steve."

"Of course not."

"No, really—"

"Whatever. It's fine." The bridesmaid ignores what remains of her beer while two of her cohort square up with the bartender and leave an ungenerous tip.

"What else is on your scavenger list?" David asks.

"No clue. It wasn't my idea."

The other women are now tucking their sashes into jackets. The bridesmaid stands and smooths her dress down over her shiny thighs, ready to go outside as is.

"We have to bar hop now. Wanna come?" she says, apparently having forgiven him and surrendered to drunken optimism. "We're gonna end up at Electrix. You can bring your friend if you like." She casts a diplomatic glance at Marian.

"I think we're okay here," David says.

"I guess we'll have to find another Steve."

"Good luck," Marian says, trying to sound kind.

The bridesmaid pretends not to hear her and unsteadily leads the way out of the bar.

David shrugs on his jacket.

"You that tired?" Marian says.

"You shouldn't have sold me out that way."

"Sorry?"

"You want me to end up signing some bachelorette's boob with a Sharpie?"

"It was a joke!"

"Doesn't bother you at all, eh, to watch some other girl hit on me."

Marian buttons up her own jacket and takes refuge in its hood. How can she be bothered when she knows the outcome of the evening, that they will go home together as always? But wasn't she also picking a fight, and wondering, just for a moment, what would happen if David got up and followed some stranger out the door?

"What's this bipolar business?" she says as they make their way to the exit.

"Never mind. It's just a theory."

"You can tell Miss America about it, but not me?"

"Drop it," David says. He pivots away from her as he holds the door open for a forty-something couple who, as they move past, share a glance—that of one couple observing another's dispute. Marian thinks she knows what they are feeling: discomfort at witnessing a private but familiar discord, and gratitude that it has nothing to do with them.

Chapter Seven

The next morning, Marian calls Juliette to tell her about the debacle at the Irish pub.

"The worst fight I ever had was over cats and dogs," Juliette says after Marian has finished venting. "Literally."

Marian laughs. "That's quite the meta-fight."

"It was when I was at Paris III. I was seeing this guy from Toulouse. He had an English bulldog, and at the time I had a Siamese that I had left behind at my parents' house. I said something about missing Lili, and he tried to convince me that cats were a lesser species, blah blah, and that I should spend more time with his bulldog. It was completely absurd. I have no idea how we got there, but it practically ended in blows. As you can see, we broke up. *S'entendre comme chien et chat.*"

When Marian hangs up, she's grateful to her friend for helping her make light of the weird encounter with David and the bridesmaid. She herself made sure to frame the story as one long sitcom misunderstanding. Deep confidences would just bog everyone down.

She plugs her cell phone in to charge and half trips over Kong, who is curled in the shape of a kidney bean in the hallway. Unalarmed, he rolls onto his back and lets her rub his downy belly. Oh, to sleep soundly and dream only of chicken. Last night she and David were deep sea diving, submerged in a great indigo ocean, and he was talking to her from within his spacey helmet. His mouth moved like that of a fish and indecipherable sounds came out. Benign and even funny in the

light of day, like so many nightmares. In the past she would
have told him about it; they would have laughed it off over
peanut butter and banana toast. This morning she kept her
unconscious to herself, sensing he wasn't in the mood for levity.
David, too, has been having nightmares these past couple of
weeks. He's always been a vocal sleeper, and lately has been
spitting out gibberish in the night. He makes no mention in the
morning of what kind of night he has endured. When she asks,
he says, "It's nothing," and waves his hand as though it were all
too trivial to discuss, or too complex to discuss with her. This
both worries and wounds her. But if he says it's nothing, she
should believe him, right? Which, okay, 'nothing' never means
nothing, but maybe he just wants to be left alone? Maybe he
knows that he's in a funk, and just wants to stay that way for
a while. She won't go so far as to use the word *depression* to
describe his state. Because clearly it's temporary. Just a funk,
that's all. But still, would it kill him to talk to her? To say . . .
anything. She would settle for "please pass the peanut butter
and banana toast," if the tone were right.

But *nothing* is fine too. If that's where they're at.

That afternoon, she concentrates on finishing the corrections
to Rémy's tenure file. She's spent three days going over the file,
fixing the unfortunate use of articles and prepositions (too few,
too many), rejigging verb tense sequences, and chopping down
typically French clause-on-clause sentences.

His curriculum vitae, if you don't count the wonky
capitalization, required very little work. At first the contents
seemed impressive to her. Umpteen conference presentations, a
handful of articles, a couple of smaller grants. But she couldn't
help but notice that he has not yet signed a contract with an
academic press for his monograph, *Palimpsestes: Le roman
québécois au vingtième siècle*, and that his only forthcoming
book is a collection of articles that he edited with a colleague at
Laval. Even she knows that the monograph is the key to tenure.

She attended Rémy's research presentation on palimpsest last fall—part of the department's "Regards sur le récit" series—and suspects that his book, should it come to fruition, will represent a substantial contribution to Québec Studies. According to his theory, the Québec novel continually recreates its Biblical origins, at once erasing and paying homage to a problematic Catholic history. Before there was a Québec literary tradition, there was scripture. Every man, woman, and child knew the word of God. The Church was omnipresent, and thus scripture formed the basis of the culture's literature. The novels of the Québec canon, he said, can be classified into two types: creation stories and the fall of man. Either authors create the world, or exile themselves and their characters from it.

Marian didn't agree with Rémy's categories then, nor does she now. She finds them too neat, too compelling. It's the kind of theory that academics latch onto for a brief period until they discover some newer, sexier part-truth. And yet she recognizes that this is precisely the type of research that moves ideas forward, gives other scholars something to get riled up about and push against. Imperfect theories such as Rémy's keep literature departments in business, and for this reason, she was surprised to learn that his palimpsest book is not under contract.

Even more surprising is the section of his CV titled "Fiction." Rémy, she has discovered, is a creative writer. Or *was* a creative writer: the last of his five stories was published in 2006, just before he was hired at Waterton. It appeared in a student literary journal that is now defunct, but Marian managed to order an electronic copy of it, along with the other stories, on interlibrary loan from l'Université de Montréal.

Taken as a whole, the stories form a strange and imperfect palimpsest. In each, a self-centred male character errs in some way, loses his girlfriend, and never quite arrives at an epiphany. The depictions of the female characters are thoughtful without being generous; the male protagonist—it seems to Marian that there is only one, despite superficial differences in age or social origin—is appealingly clever but comes off as rigid. Overall, she thinks the stories competent but lacking in emotional depth. But having read them, she feels moved and even protective of Rémy: here is a man who has faith in the power of narrative, and who struggles to raise his skill to the level of his vision. A man who believes the perfect story is but one keystroke away.

Chapter Eight

Rose-Anna Lacasse in Gabrielle Roy's *Bonheur d'occasion* has
just learned that her eldest daughter, Florentine, is pregnant
out of wedlock. Montreal, 1940. Florentine has fled the house
in shame, and Azarius, Rose-Anna's sweet but lazy husband,
has neither earned enough money to pay their back rent, nor
found them another house now that they are being evicted.
This is how Rose-Anna ends up whispering so as not to disturb
another woman's sleeping children, stepping around emptied
boxes and foreign furniture. The strangers are the new rightful
tenants. When they knocked on the door, what could she do
but let them in?

But now Azarius comes home and through a fog of
humiliation and worry, Rose-Anna hears him say that he's
found them another place—a place of their own . . .

Rémy looks up from his copy of the novel, whose margins
display a graffiti that is barely legible, even to him. He says,
"Who can tell me which of the three types of *focalisation* is
operating in this passage?"

A few students make a show of consulting their notes.

"Let's back up, then. What *are* the three types?"

The students hunker down into a deeper silence. All but
one avoid eye-contact. The boy in the front row whom Rémy
has come to think of, in English, as Sweater Kid stares at Rémy
fixedly but without malice. Sweater Kid attends every class, sits
in the front row, never speaks, and never takes notes. His only
occupation is ocular attentiveness. By all rights, Rémy should

dislike him—his weird intensity, his refusal to participate—
but it's the sweater that throws Rémy off. Grey with a black
moose blazoned on the front. Hand-knit, which suggests that
someone loves the kid enough to measure and sheathe his
lanky torso. That he has worn it to every class since the middle
of September, the collars of various polos poking out at the
neck, suggests that he is either sentimental or chilly or both,
and therefore vulnerable. No, despite all, Rémy almost *likes*
Sweater Kid. And yet he intrudes on Rémy's field of vision with
the force of his apathy, sapping a disproportionate amount of
his energy in any given class.

"*Focalisation interne, externe,* and *zéro,*" Rémy reminds the
class. "Which do we observe in this passage?"

The silence grinds on. Sweater Kid uncrosses his knitted
arms, revealing the moose, and sprawls in his chair as though
settling in to watch a movie he's already seen. Behind him
a friendly slacker named Alain munches on a breakfast
sandwich, whose greasy, eggy odour nauseates Rémy but also
triggers a craving for the day's third cup of coffee. Next to
Alain a girl named Fiona fidgets with her green bangs, her
book open to what is certainly the wrong page. By the window,
three blonde girls bloom like potted daisies; they pretend not
to eye the cell phones they've carefully positioned next to their
notebooks, whose screens light up like slot machines as text
messages roll in. That Rémy cannot reliably identify the three
blondes has been a paradoxical source of relief for him this
semester—it's not *only* the two Chinese students in the second
row—Rose-Ling, Ling-Rose—that he has trouble telling apart.
But why should he bother telling anyone apart *when nobody
puts up their hand*?

"Let's review," he says, more indifferent than frustrated,
and also a little bored. Narratology is taught at the CÉGEP level
in Québec. Still, these are concepts the students must learn. "*La
focalisation interne* is when the narrator zooms in on one of

the character's thoughts and actions and limits himself to that character's point of view."

Pens wag as though this definition were new, and not pulled wholesale from today's theoretical readings, an excerpt from Gérard Genette's *Figures III*.

"*La focalisation externe* is when the point of view is external to the character: we only know what we can see from the outside. We have no access to the character's thoughts or feelings. It's like the narrator is a cameraman filming the story."

"*La focalisation zéro* is your omniscient narrator," Rémy continues. "He knows all and tells all. He has access to all the characters' thoughts at once."

He pauses to write the three terms on the board. The blonde closest to the window—whose name may or may not be Denise—raises her hand. "So why not just talk about *point de vue* and *omniscience*?" she asks. "Like, 'omniscient narrator' and 'third-person limited' or whatever. Why the extra terms?"

"Because this terminology is more precise," Rémy says quickly, acknowledging to himself that this is only true in some cases. Sometimes the terms are effectively useless—for instance, when authors use two or even three of the *focalisations* interchangeably in a single passage, such that you can't tell where one ends and another begins.

"In the passage we just read," Rémy says, shoving away his internal quibbles, "the *focalisation* is limited to Rose-Anna. We are privy to her view of the world: her shame in the face of her poverty and her daughter's pregnancy; her elation when she learns that her husband has found them a new home. We can therefore label this passage *focalisation interne*." With his nub of chalk he draws an asterisk next to the term. "Now, it is also important to position the narrator with regard to the *diégèse*. That is to say, where does he stand in relation to the world of the story? We can differentiate between five types of narration: *extradiégétique, intradiégétique, autodiégétique, hétérodiégétique* or *homodiégétique*." Having added these terms to the untidy list on the board, Rémy pauses to wipe the chalk from his hands onto his pants and survey the class. A gap opens up between what he sees and what he understands, like when he stubs his toe and a split second passes before he feels the pain. Sweater Kid has opened his notebook and uncapped his pen. The pen is bright orange, like a dog's Frisbee or a pylon. A beacon of apathy. Until now.

Rémy blinks hard as though to clear his mind's eye of what he has just seen. "Of course," he says distractedly, "what we observe in *Bonheur d'occasion* is the type of narrator that we call *extradiégétique*. The *narrateur extradiégétique* is external to the *diégèse*."

Sweater Kid, who turns out to be left-handed, shoves up his sleeve to reveal a slender wrist. He touches his pen to the first page of the virgin notebook.

"The *narrateur extradiégétique* guides us without ever becoming an agent in the story," Rémy mumbles, still distracted by Sweater Kid, who is scribbling industriously, his gaze shuttling between the contents of the blackboard and his notebook. Having lost his train of thought, Rémy, too, fixates on the narratological terms on the board. They appear foreign to him, as though written in someone else's hand. He tries to decipher the role of these words in Sweater Kid's awakening, but can't fathom what the kid sees in their esoteric arrogance. Even as he attempts to understand, he feels himself inching away from the board and towards the window, putting distance between himself and these scraps of Gérard Genette's *Figures III*, unwittingly, as though propelled by an outward force.

He reaches the opposite side of the room, *Bonheur d'occasion* still open in his raised hand. Stands there like a statue of a poet or a prophet, outwardly frozen, inwardly screaming, *Put the pen down!* The blonde girls' cell phones flash, green-haired Fiona yawns, the Chinese students whisper to each other, and Sweater Kid completes his copying of the words from the board and resumes his silent stare, gripping his pen.

Rémy momentarily forgets that he is a body in this room.

Outside in a treetop a squirrel fight breaks out.

He thinks, If the last library on Earth were on fire, I would save this book. And that has nothing to do with narratology.

Rémy observes the frantic flight of the squirrels from the treetop and after a moment speaks. "We can pick this novel apart and dissect its pieces. We can give these pieces names and use the names to make arguments. But I fear that it is not the point."

He pauses, not knowing what he's going to say next. A few students lean forward. Some look intrigued, others distrustful.

"The point is that I'm not sure I have words that do justice to what Gabrielle Roy is doing here. She's invited us into the world of a poor family from the quartier Saint-Henri, a family suffering from a uniquely human illness: hope. Azarius has just come home and announced to his wife that he has found them a house. *Chez nous*, Rose-Anna thinks over and over, hearing the news. Home. Her desire for the security of home is so great that she wakes her sleeping children and tells them that the family will pack up and move this very instant. The midnight move energizes and enchants: suddenly the world is rich with possibility. What will the new house look like? Which child will have his or her own room? Each year the family migrates to a smaller, more ramshackle house. This year, it will be different. The house will be bigger, it will have a veranda, a yard; Rose-Anna will plant a vegetable garden. The children, under the spell of their mother's excitement, help to place the family's meagre belongings in the cardboard boxes that she never throws away, boxes that she breaks down and keeps in the storeroom all year in anticipation of the next eviction."

Rémy leans against the window ledge and asks Fiona to read aloud the passage where the Lacasse family squeezes into the cab of the truck that Azarius has rented for the night, a

jumble of boxes and mattresses in the back—the passage where
Rose-Anna cradles her youngest daughter on her lap and
inwardly scolds herself for questioning the goodness of God.

Fiona reads hesitantly, mispronouncing the French words
here and there and looking up to Rémy for verification. He
gently corrects her, all the while thinking of his old apartment
in Montreal, Côte-des-Neiges, his commute to campus on the
métro, his endless walks through the Plateau or the Quartier
Latin. He remembers how he used to stop on a random street
corner to love the city in stillness while the city, beautiful and
indifferent to his love, rushed on. How in these moments,
anything seemed possible.

When Fiona has finished—when Rose-Anna has touched
her husband's arm and said, "Eh bien, partons!"—Rémy
caresses the cover of the book and says, "The Lacasse family
hopes. And we hope with them. They arrive at the new house
in the dark, they lay out their mattresses, and the night is rich
with possibility. And when the first freight train thunders past,
shaking the floors, rattling the windows, and we understand
that the house is only a few feet from the tracks, the loss we
feel is physical—it digs deep into the pit of our stomach. When
Rose-Anna thinks how she will never sleep through the night
in this house, when she bargains with herself, saying, "Il doit y
avoir des avantages avec les désavantages," the sadness in our
gut spreads. Because it hurts to watch her grope in the dark for
a second-hand happiness."

Rémy gazes out at the empty treetop. The sincerity of
Gabrielle Roy's prose grips his chest. Bare pathos and empathy.
Not a hint of irony. Does sincerity belong to a bygone era?
Would it be possible to write this novel today?

He turns back to the class. With the exception of Sweater
Kid, who maintains his motionless stare, the students are
fidgeting, shifting in their seats, uncomfortable with his
contemplative silence. It is his job to fill the airtime. But what
is there left to say? Shall they read the next passage, look up at

each other and say, "This is beautiful, profound"? And the next passage, and the next, saying over and over, this is beautiful, this is genius? Is their role here simply to dwell together in awe?

Five novels on the syllabus. Each tells the story of what it means to be human. Thirteen weeks and thirty-nine instructional hours in a semester. Too many hours to fill with the same story. One must settle for dissection, for theory. For arguments as neat as filing cabinets, and the labels to slap on them.

Rémy's limbs feel heavy, as though filled with sand.

He says, "That's all for now." After a moment, adds, "Next class: *le modèle sémio-pragmatique.*"

Chapter Nine

Marian chews at a piece of chapped skin on her lip and tastes
blood.

"I really don't want to be the dissertation police," Rémy
says. "But I do have a responsibility here. Your second chapter
is two months late. Is there something I can do to help move it
along?"

Marian thinks of her weird piece on La Corriveau. Many
times she's considered showing it to Rémy, but if he doesn't like
it or thinks it a waste of time, she will feel even worse than she
does now.

"I did start working on the chapter, but I just couldn't get
the tone right. I wrote this long section that didn't fit. I don't
even know what it is."

"It's easy to get off track. But you need to keep to a schedule
and focus on program completion."

Marian hesitates. "*You* didn't," she says finally.

"Sorry?"

"You wrote stories."

His brow twitches. He looks away.

"I read them," she says, softened by his discomfort, and
relieved that she's managed to shift the focus away from herself.

"What did you think?"

"They're really similar to each other," she says, and
immediately wishes she hadn't. "Not in a bad way," she rushes
to add. "I liked them. Really."

"I was just trying to get something right." He shakes his head in self-disdain.

She wants to ask what that something was, but decides this would be going too far. "Why did you stop?" she asks instead.

"Because the result was never as good as I hoped."

"So you gave up?"

He exhales bitterly. "That's not what this job is about. No tenure committee is going to care about that stuff. To them it's just fluff."

Marian nods sympathetically and lets the silence stretch out between them. "Is it weird that I'm feeling sad for you?" she says.

"No. At least I hope not. I appreciate it, actually."

"I want to believe that you'll find your way back there again."

"That's kind of you."

"You mean naive."

"Not only. Stay the way you are. The alternative is to be jaded."

They smile shyly at each other. Student laughter bursts from the hallway, and Rémy shakes his head as though coming out of a daydream. "Anyway. Sometimes when you're stuck, it's best to move on and come back to that part later. Why don't you start writing chapter three? You can get a fresh start and build up some momentum. I've got something for you that might be relevant." He rises and searches his bookshelf, which is double-shelved. He pulls books down by the handful in order to dig behind them, and a few minutes later hands her a copy of Lacan's *Four Fundamental Concepts of Psychoanalysis*.

He pats her arm, and she can't tell if he's flirting or being paternal. "Onward," he says. "Your dissertation won't write itself."

Over the next couple of weeks, she makes a habit of dropping by Rémy's office, and he in turn makes a habit of keeping her there as long as possible. Each time, the supposed topic of their meetings is her dissertation. Instead they talk about his teaching frustrations, and the joy of slipping one's foot into a new pair of socks, and his childhood growing up in Sherbrooke, and hers growing up in Thunder Bay. The perfection of Anne Hébert's clipped sentences or the clever humour of *Astérix*.

Today he asks her: "Why Québec?"

"You're referring to my research?"

"Mm. Your family is French, right? You're some sort of heritage speaker?"

"My grandparents spoke Norwegian and German. Which is okay," she adds quickly, registering his surprise, "because my parents learned a few words of French on their honeymoon."

He ignores her feeble joke. "You have no ties?" He looks confused, or vaguely troubled.

"Do I need them?"

"Of course not," he says quickly. "We're talking about an object of study. Scholarship is indifferent to kinship."

She nods not because she agrees, or thinks him sincere, but because she wants to defend her motivations against further inquiry and speculation. She could tell him about her longtime fascination for the tensions between Québec and English Canada, the way they rumble beneath the surface and occasionally peak, or about her affection for the Québécois accent, whose sounds smoosh together like socks in a drawer, or even about her embarrassing affinity for Acadian singing sensation Roch Voisine. Little badges of sincerity or authenticity. But the truth is that in Thunder Bay, Ontario, she did not grow up watching *Passe partout* or *Babar*, never learned to mythologize the Plaines d'Abraham, never completed a school project on Jeanne Mance, Maurice Richard, or Marguerite Bourgeoys. In short, she is not *Québécoise*, and so she lets the topic of conversation die, feeling that her moral claim is tenuous at best, and knowing, too, that Rémy will not want to hear that what she likes, above all, is studying ghosts. That ghosts are abundant in Québec literature suits her just fine.

Chapter Ten

Marian pulls skirts out of her closet, evaluates her butt in each, and chooses a leopard-print number that her mother sewed for her last Christmas. She sets it on the bed and tries not to feel bad about using it for impure purposes. Not impure. Ambiguous. And since when was there any law against looking attractive? She roots through a stack of sweaters, extracts an ivory V-neck, and sets it next to the skirt. Together, they are plush and sleek—a great cat sprawled beneath a baobab, lazily surveying the savannah through half-closed golden eyes. She would like to channel the spirit of the creature but is having trouble getting into her black tights. Has she gained back those pesky five pounds? She must have put the tights in the dryer, or else there's a cosmic force of feminist resistance operating against her, preventing her from dressing in a sexualized way for a man.

Shut up, cosmic force! Have you not heard of the third wave? The sexy feminist hasn't been a subject of serious debate since the nineties.

Suit yourself, the cosmic force replies. They're your buttocks.

The tights are on—the elastic has found her hips, and the crotch no longer hangs low. She dons the skirt and V-neck. While she searches the apartment for her peep-toed pumps— last worn to her master's convocation—the tights twist her panties into a rope between her butt cheeks. From a box in the storage closet she unearths the shoes, which are sprinkled with a fine layer of dust.

Before long, her left Achilles tendon begins to cry like a girl.

"I've just gendered my Achilles tendon," she says aloud to herself as she hobbles to the bus stop.

"Écoute," Rémy says, leaning back in his task chair and clasping his hands behind his head like he's relaxing on the beach. "I understand your resistance to spending too much time with a male psychoanalyst from a previous century. But this is French Studies. Psychoanalysis hasn't gone out of style."

"*Desire is the desire of the Other,*" Marian says. "I've heard it a hundred times. But I can't help wondering: whose desire? What are the different ways we can interpret the word 'Other,' ways that Lacan didn't intend? Women are erased from the discourse of desire even as they're made the focus of it. Anyway, you're not giving me enough credit. I read the Lacan you leant me."

"And?"

"Correct me if I'm wrong, but for him, the basic premise of seduction is that pleasure can only be derived from circling *around* the object of desire." With her finger she draws a circle on the surface of the table, wondering if she's being too obvious, but also noting how Rémy leans towards her as she does so.

"That's more or less it, yes." His eyes follow her hand until it settles again on her lap.

"You're saying that there is no pleasure to be had in possessing the object."

"Well, no, in the strictest terms, the object cannot be *possessed,* that's true . . . or at least, not precisely . . . because the desire is the desire of the Other, so . . ."

"See, that part I understand. But how can I know what the Other wants?"

"Well, you can't, because the Other doesn't exist as such . . . it only exists insofar as you believe this to be the case."

"So I believe that the Other desires. And my belief in the Other's desire makes me desire in turn."

"Correct."

"But I cannot *possess* what the Other desires." She affects a yawn. "That seems simple enough."

"I'm glad you think so. Many would disagree."

"Oh no, it *is* simple. Like most esoteric arguments, that is."

"Here we go," he says, grinning.

"The trouble with Lacan—no, the trouble with *most* theorists—is that they take something real and poof! make it vanish into words."

"Go on," he says, still amused.

She rises and feigns interest in his potted plant, rotating it so that its back leaves can now enjoy the sun. "Because no normal person would ever argue that desire isn't real. That it can't be felt in the flesh. Or that *possessing* the object of desire is impossible."

"You're taking it all too literally," he says, the vein at his temple visibly throbbing.

"But that's just it," she insists, "at some point, one has to be *concrete*." She pivots, and after a few moments of irrational deliberation—thoughts of her roped panties, and David, and the French feminists of the second wave—she plunks her skirted butt down on the corner of Rémy's desk.

He wheels his chair closer. If he moved a fraction of an inch, his knee would brush against her calf. He stays perfectly still. "You present a fine philosophical argument."

Later that week, he asks her to name his plant. She's tickled by this invitation and saunters over to the window to appraise it. A cluster of fuzzy leaves greets the morning sun, and a few stragglers round themselves over the edge of the pot, lolling downwards.

She bends low and lifts one inviting leaf in her palm.

"Colette, after the writer," she says finally. "This is an intimate plant. Soft leaves cozying together like a bundle of mittens. But a boundary pusher as well. Refusing to stay contained in that little pot. Moving towards the floor as though she wants to dance."

Rémy nods solemnly. "An excellent choice." He grabs the pitcher of filtered water that always stands at the ready on his table. "Colette," he says as he waters the plant, "I baptize you in the name of intimacy and audacity."

"And style."

"Of course." He smiles down at the plant's silvery patina, its ample leaves. "Je trouve qu'elle est en forme aujourd'hui."

"She really is, isn't she?"

Marian is watering Colette a few days later when a figure appears in the doorway, a slender, taut-postured woman. She has a straight blond bob and the delicate features of a pixie. Marian rests the pitcher on the table and looks to Rémy, curious. He shoots a desperate look at the clock on the wall. His gaze flits back and forth between Marian and the woman in the doorway.

"Delphine, this is Marian. Marian, Delphine—my fiancée."

Delphine takes a few steps into the office. "Ahh, la Petite," she says. "Enchantée."

"Enchantée," Marian murmurs, still processing the word "fiancée," and feeling her neck sting red. La Petite? Is this what Rémy calls her?

"Rémy speaks very highly of your work," Delphine says. Her tone is so sweet that it sounds like a question rather than a compliment.

"You're very kind." Marian continues to blush and covers the base of her neck with her hand.

Delphine looks Marian over, from her speckled neck right down to the toes that peek out of each glossy shoe. Finally, her eyes fix themselves instead on Rémy. "Es-tu prêt, mon amour?"

"Oui, un instant." Rémy grabs his jacket and keys. He passes Marian her book bag and ushers both women towards the door.

Marian powers downtown to meet Juliette at the novelty store. It turns out that six blocks is not far enough to digest Delphine, her existence, her sticky voice, and most of all her sly knowledge of Marian, her words implying that she has been a perfectly banal topic of conversation around the dinner table, that she is so small as not to be a threat.

Has she seen Delphine before? She must have attended some department event or another, yet Marian can't place her. But it's not her responsibility to place Delphine. It's Rémy's. What kind of man spends months—months!—editing out a person as essential as a fiancée? Rémy. Rémy does, and she doesn't know what to think of this, but thinking isn't the point, is it? Feeling is the point. What she feels is angry and embarrassed. Does he really call her *la Petite*? Little one? Like someone's daughter. *His* daughter.

Her conscience is mumbling things she prefers not to hear.

Yeah, so? So what? She's not as bad as Rémy. At least she *mentions* David to Rémy from time to time. Maybe not as much as she could, sure, and maybe she *occasionally* leaves David-sized holes in their conversations. But she would never belittle Rémy to David, make him seem insignificant. If anything, she has to stop herself from talking about him a little too much.

Little hypocrite, she thinks as she turns onto Main Street, enjoying her bitterness and self-pity, and perspiring from her exertion. *Little fool. You're nobody to him.*

Chapter Eleven

"Why the fixation on pirates?" Marian asks a few minutes later, straining not to sound grumpy as she and Juliette cruise the aisles of the novelty store. She's feeling misanthropic and is dreading that evening's costume party, which Jules is holding at their friend Patrick's house because her own place is too small.

"It's Halloween," Juliette says.

"True enough."

"Call it Bacchanalian. Necessary release. Something like that." When Marian still looks skeptical, Juliette continues: "You've got to humour me. We don't have such parties in France."

"Why not?"

"The French take themselves too seriously."

"Not even if you're a student?"

"Don't get me started on the grad students I met at Paris III before I transferred to Waterton. They only want to talk about seminars and literary theory and how little they slept the night before because they were up reading Deleuze. Then they go and rip out the pages of library books so that their classmates can't prep for their exams."

"Ouch," Marian says. "Maybe you got a bad cohort."

"*Bof.*" Juliette puffs out her cheeks in a French show of disdain. "I'm glad I'm here now. The department wasn't a good fit anyway. I was having trouble finding a supervisor for my dissertation. There are hardly any feminist scholars in the literature departments over there. And then what of my topic on twentieth-century feminist productions of Molière's plays? Hm?"

"What about the French Feminists?" Marian says. "You know, with a big 'F,' the ones everyone talks about. Where have they disappeared to?"

"Simone de Beauvoir taught high school."

When Marian makes a face of disbelief, Juliette says, "So did Jean-Paul Sartre," as though this evened out the score. "Oh—great skull! Check it out—we're definitely buying this." She holds up a neon skull on a string.

"That *is* cool," Marian says, letting her unpleasant encounter in Rémy's office fade into the background.

"I think I saw pet costumes over in the next aisle," Juliette says. "We could dress up Kong. Wouldn't that be cute?"

Marian grabs her arm. "I want to be a parrot," she says, the desire coming over her even as she speaks the words.

Juliette hoots with delight. "That's the spirit."

This is how they end up back at Marian and David's place, tacking blue and yellow boas to a white shift dress that Marian has bought second-hand. When they're done, Marian lets Juliette sweep her hair up into a chignon. Juliette plucks a few feathers from the dress, nests them in Marian's hair, and helps her examine the back of her head in the bathroom mirror with the aid of a mirrored compact.

"It's like a bird that got caught in an updraft," Marian says.

Juliette stabs at some scraggly bits with a comb and achieves a more subtle 'bird-riffling-in-the-wind' look.

Marian glances down at the boas. "You're sure I don't look like a stripper?"

"Nah. Strippers have those clear plastic stilettos."

David comes homes from work and asks if they've bought him a cutlass and tricorn hat.

Juliette unsheathes the pieces of his costume from a plastic shopping bag. David takes the hat from her, visibly pleased, and snugs it onto his head.

"You don't mind dressing up when you already do it every day?" Juliette asks.

David raises his hand to the brim of his hat. "It's not work, right? And honestly, I'm looking forward to the party. It'll be nice to put on something else for a change. Get away from that place." He removes the hat, severs its price tag with his teeth, and turns to Marian. "Where's your beak?"

"No beak," Marian says.

"It's not a parrot costume without a beak."

Patrick's house is full of pirates, save for a couple of wenches, one parrot, and a treasure map, embodied by Juliette—she's wearing leggings and a t-shirt, both beige and painted over with dotted black lines, compass points, a blob that may represent a fish or a whale, and a rudimentary palm tree. A large red X marks her forehead. "To put it anywhere else would have been gratuitous," she says as Marian passes her a bag of chips that she and David bought at the convenience store on the way over. Juliette coos in French at Kong, who's dressed in the crocodile costume that they bought for him that afternoon. He's supposed to be the character in *Peter Pan*.

The living room is darkly radiant—Juliette has replaced the lamp bulbs with black lights. Patrick saunters over, gives David a friendly slap on the shoulder, and hands Marian a hot-pink drink with a tiny umbrella wedged between some ice chips. "You're looking plucky this evening, Lady Marian," he says. He winks his right eye, the one not hidden behind an eye patch.

"Patrick, charming as always."

"Piracy suits me."

"You look great," Marian says. "The lighting, too."

"He had nothing to do with it," Juliette interrupts before he can answer. She holds up the serving bowl that contains the chips. "Should we put these in the living room or next to the rest of the food?"

"I leave such subtleties up to you," he says.

Patrick's battered kitchen table has been transformed into a tropical fruit plantation. Kiwi and pineapple rounds rub up against lengths of papaya and melon. A motley pirate peels himself a paper plate and harvests mango balls from the tray in the centre with a skewer.

Marian scans the room to see where Kong has ended up. Always hungry, he huffs in hopeful circles at the base of the table and rubs the top of his head against its legs, trying to remove the hood of his crocodile costume. Patrick calls him over. The dog casts one last yearning gaze in the direction of the spread before trotting over to lick Patrick's black boot. Patrick smiles down at him and turns to David. "Should I get you a drink? But you're at home here."

"I'd almost be offended if you did," David says, and wanders off into the kitchen. He lingers by the fridge, beer in hand, chatting with a couple of people he knows from the gym.

Patrick leans down to give the dog a few thumps on the back. He scoops him up and holds him with his green crocodile belly exposed. "And you, my god-dog. I have nothing to offer you, but that has more to do with your lovely owner than with me."

"No feeding him party food," Marian says. "He'll puke."

Patrick winks and makes his way to the front door with Kong in his arms. "This is my god-dog, Kong," she hears him say to a couple of guests who have just arrived. "Named after the monster." He saunters back and deposits the dog on the carpet. Marian asks him how his research is going, and he feigns distress. "You dare ask me this at a party?" He sighs. "My audio samples are corrupted. I fear I may be doomed."

The night stretches long, shot through with spirited talk and laughter. Bits of costume lie abandoned here and there: tricorn hats, moustaches, pistols and cutlasses, a single knee breech. Marian's legs grow tired, and she sinks into a ratty armchair. Across the room by the stereo, for the amusement of some guests from the political science department, David is telling the story of their third date, during which they were attacked by an aggressive goose on a walk near Pine Lake. He gestures comically, alternately playing the role of the couple and the enraged bird. No melancholy tonight—just sweet, silly David. *Good for you*, Marian thinks, not entirely oblivious to her own poutiness. *Glad you're having fun for once.* She looks down and with her thumb probes at a few gaps in the feathers of her costume. Well, shit. Under the black light she doesn't look anything like a parrot, but rather like a speckled hen, or that nasty goose, mottled and maybe even fat, the white of her dress oozing from a mess of plumped feathers. She didn't think ahead, did she? The feathers, the light bulbs, the sugary pink cocktails—how many has she had?—someone else has been mixing them. Maybe if she eats more chips. *La Petite, la Petite*, she thinks, noting the immaturity of her get-up and surroundings, then resisting this judgment. What does Rémy know about her, anyway?

She hears a gurgling noise and looks down to see that she's run out of cocktail. Sneaky, those fruity drinks. Posing as juice, pouring down easy like in a Floridian citrus commercial. But she's smart, she knows they leave their mark, they sugar it into you. An extra-pink tongue, for starters. A few hours later, an extra fuzzy head. Not a warm fuzzy wool toque head, either, but a weird flossy pink fungus head. She decides to hold off on having another cocktail and gazes around, eyes liquid. The two wenches are chatting on the couch opposite her, their flounced skirts tucked up beneath their crossed legs. Something glows before them in the black light.

It's the soft white curve of the chip bowl.

She wants to walk over and claim the bowl—certainly the wenches won't mind, they've already been holding the chips hostage for a while. She tries to hoist herself up, but oops! collapses into the chair. Her legs won't cooperate, weighed down by feathers and pink rum. She chuckles and kicks her feet, checking to see they still work. One-two, one-two. All systems go. She gathers her legs beneath her and heaves with her hands. Up!

That wasn't so bad, she thinks as she stumbles in the general direction of the wenches. "Do you mind?" she asks, pointing to the chips.

"Not at all," the first wench replies.

"Go for it," the second urges. She hands Marian the bowl.

Marian moves obliquely back to her armchair. Once seated, she lays one protective hand over the bowl while the other gropes for chips.

"Smile, or I swear I'll get up and dance."

David is leaning over her. She's crushing chip crumbs against the side of the bowl with her thumb, forcing her leaden eyelids to stay open.

"I'm drunk," Marian says, sounding whinier than she intends.

"I mean it," David warns. "I'll make you do it one way or another."

She shrugs. This many drinks in, it's her God-given right to stay glued to this chair.

"Don't say I didn't warn you," David says.

On the stereo a Tragically Hip song ends, and a nineties rock anthem pipes in. David leaves his tricorn hat on the floor next to Marian. He draws himself up and shoves the coffee table out of the way.

"You really don't have to do this," Marian says.

He closes his eyes as though in concentration. "Oh, but I do."

It begins with a subtle head bob. Then his knee and heel jerk in unison; it's as though he's working a pump with his foot. He performs a spin, elbows crooked and hands flapping at his sides like fins. Resembling a disoriented fish, he shimmies to the left and back to the right, leading with the thrust of an ear. When he comes back to Marian, he raises his arms over his head in fists, somehow remaining bent at the neck and shoulders. He looks like a hunchbacked gymnast at the end of a routine, or a superhero with a bad back. From this posture he bounces to the music: boom, boom, la, la, laaa. Now he throws his head back, arms still high, and grins at Marian—a big shit-eating grin. He knows he's ludicrous and is loving it.

The wenches, who have been watching from the threshold to the kitchen, sashay closer and engage in their own strange aquatic dance.

"You're a fucking goof," Marian yells at David over the music.

"La la laaaaa," David croons, and wriggles his finger at Marian, inviting her to dance.

"Ah fuck," she says. He offers her his hand, and she takes it, leaving the empty chip bowl on the floor. She bops next to him like a spastic bird, the feathers of her boa sticking to her sweaty armpits.

David catches her by the waist. "Hottest woman I've ever met," he says, and holds her against him, swaying and humming contentedly.

When they get home, he lifts her by the butt and she wraps her legs around his waist and clings there, a joyful, lustful, booze-soaked barnacle. He kisses her drunkenly but not clumsily, still sober enough to flick her tongue with his own. His breath smells of the bourbon he was drinking near the end of the night—spice-licked vanilla—which reminds her of cake mixes and waffle cones and more elaborate confectionaries, like marzipan or profiteroles or a whimsical wedding cake, complete with bride and groom and trees and mushrooms and even bunnies: bunnies who are under-the-influence, over-the-top, over-the-moon . . . hilariously dirty *let's-fuck-like*-bunnies . . . and now she's carried, giggling, into the bedroom, and David lays her diagonally on the bed and hovers over her. She kisses his nipple and presses her face to where his chest and underarms merge and smells the pleasantly pungent scent of his underarm, pheromones that have long reminded her of

cumin or animal pelts or leather couches. Combined now with
the spicier edge of the bourbon, the cuminy armpit dispels her
thoughts of conjugal bunny cakes, and evokes instead a cigar-
clouded men's club, an antiquated haven . . .

David reaches over to the bedside table, and into this
smoky haven introduces the shocking yellow modernity of
her vibrator. He comically brandishes it, and she giggles some
more and admires the vibe's sunny-smooth, scoop-tipped
oval ergonomics. He presses the magic button and tucks the
vibe between their pelvic bones and slips inside her with a
happy grunt, and they wiggle and grind, and ride and ride the
drunken euphoric silicone waves.

Chapter Twelve

By the time she starts in on him, they are already on their second lap of the path, because as usual, once isn't enough for her. Delphine zips along, unfazed by the late autumn chill, her arms and hips working in quick sequence. And as though her words are also part of some sequence, as though she's responding to a question he has just asked, she says, "We could get married in the spring, outside with the trees and the bugs."

Rémy is suddenly very sorry he consented to be alone with her here, in the woods, on the Arrow Point conservation trail.

"Sure," he says. "And we'll hand out fly repellent as wedding favours." It sounds like a bad joke told a few seconds too late. It *is* a bad joke told a few seconds too late, but it's the best he can do, feeling ambushed here in the woods.

"A more civilized venue, then. The Jardin botanique. A small reception at Sofitel, like Luc and Isabelle."

"We don't want to be like Luc and Isabelle. They drive a minivan and have a goldendoodle."

"It's an SUV, isn't it? And Guimauve is such a nice dog."

"She seems to walk and crap obediently enough."

"You're cranky this morning."

"Just tired."

"I'm sorry. We'll slow down. I get geared up and forget that you like to take it all in."

He doesn't like to take it all in—he's indifferent to nature, and she should know that by now, so he chooses not to reply. Nor does he reply when she points to a stump and says, "Look

at the hole . . . I wonder who lives there?" But when she asks
how his grading is going, he does tell her, somewhat sorely, that
it feels particularly heavy this year, and that he wishes he didn't
bust his tail just to be confronted with concrete evidence of
what his students haven't learned.

He unzips his jacket. Complaining about the least of his
problems opens the valve on the worst of them. He's glad she
posed this banal question about grading, because it means she
understands what needs to be said and what doesn't, what can
be accomplished and what can't. It means he can keep puffing
away, quads aching, his presence here enough.

She says, "What about the inn you stayed at last spring? It
sounds romantic. We could hold the reception inside, stay a
couple of extra days to relax at the spa."

"It wasn't all that romantic."

"Waterfalls, Jacuzzis, nature trails . . . Didn't you say the
food was excellent?"

"I don't recall."

"I do. I remember you saying the lamb was perfect."

"The soup was bland. That much I remember."

"You don't even like soup."

"Other people do. Anyway, that area is probably nicest in
the fall, and you know how busy I am during the school year."

"Yes, I suppose I do know," she says, her tone light yet
forced. "So many people to see to. So terribly involved."

He glances at her and she stares straight ahead, breathes
in through her nose, out through her mouth. She couldn't
possibly mean another woman. If she did, she wouldn't circle
the issue. There would have to be a scene—shouting, crying, the
pounding of fists on his chest. She must mean work generally.

He waves vaguely at the air. "Being a professor isn't a job.
It's a way of life. I have no choice but to take my work home
with me. I've sometimes wished for a nine-to-five job like yours.
It simply wasn't my calling. You've always said you understood
that."

Delphine stops, and her eyes search his face. There aren't enough trees in the woods to hide him. She says, "If you don't want to marry me, why did you ask me?"

For a moment he's silent, torn. Should he soften or harden?

"Don't make this about me," he says. "We both agreed we'd take it slow, so that we don't become one of those couples."

"Which couples? The ones who go through with it?"

"The couples who dive headfirst into their own fairytale garbage. You want to figure out that you like the idea more than the person after the wedding guests have gone home? Is that what you want? Of course not." He lowers his voice and makes it sound wounded. "We agreed we'd take it easy. I'm surprised you would even think about going back on your word." He caresses her cheek through his glove.

Voices reach them. An older couple with hiking sticks approaches. Rémy and Delphine separate as though caught in some illicit embrace. Let the couple move past.

"We will get married," he says. "I just need time."

She laughs softly, as though sincerely. "Mon cœur. Of course it will happen. I know you well enough for that."

Chapter Thirteen

A bitter November wind blows off the river. The streets and sidewalks are dirty with sand and salt—a five o'clock shadow on the grim limestone face of the university. An ache settles into Marian's toes as she hurries from the library to the International Centre to meet Patrick for lunch, a welcome break from staring at the pages of a book on dead female muses and repressing thoughts of David. After their jolly fuck the night of the Halloween party, he retreated back into moodiness, this time swapping talk about Edna for nondescript silence. He doesn't even bother to complain about Edna's replacement—the wife of one of the board members, wanting to keep herself busy with a job now that her youngest kid has gone off to university.

To Marian, David's stony mood seems like a wall designed to keep her out. And when she cracks dumb jokes and he doesn't laugh, or drags him out to a movie to distract him, she's just trying to help. But there's no cajoling him out of his funk. He sometimes replies, "You just don't get it." Which is true. She doesn't get why he would invite her to burrow her nose into his cuminy pheromones and then push her away again. Didn't he like being his old self?

The International Centre is located in a brick Victorian house on Waterton Drive, between the Alumni House and Health Services. Marian stops in front and waves to Patrick coming towards her on the opposite sidewalk. He wears his toque low and his scarf high. Only his eyes are visible. Dangling from his gloved hand is a plastic bag that must contain rice and the sauce he makes out of cassava leaves, her favourite of his Sierra Leonean dishes.

"Long time, Lady Marian," he says once he crosses the street. "You've been working on your diss, I bet."

"Slowly and very badly."

"No such thing," he says.

On the porch of the International Centre a young woman speaks Arabic into a cell phone while her friend pats her gloves together and motions for her to hurry up. Marian and Patrick move past them and through the front door, which is bordered by two stained glass windows. One bears the motto *Incipit Vita Nova,* and the other consists of an abstract mosaic in primary colours.

They wipe their boots and hang their coats on a hook by the door. Straight ahead are mismatched couches and armchairs and a kitchenette area. Upstairs are what must be offices. Marian can make out a couple of doorways decorated with colourful posters.

A man powers down the stairs; he is massive like an old-growth tree and yet wastes no time. He raises the binder that he carries in one hand. "Big Pat!" he booms. Emphasis on both words, a one-two punch of a greeting. "Real good to see you again, man." Large red sneakers jut out from his wide-legged jeans.

"Three times a week you tell me this," Patrick says. "But I like hearing it, so I come back. Marian, this is Boone." Boone is a PhD student, too, Patrick tells her—a critical cartographer in the Art History department. He works part-time at the International Centre as the events coordinator.

"I'm not familiar with critical cartography," Marian says.

"Boone studies the relationship between maps and art," Patrick says. "He creates these cool maps using all kinds of materials you wouldn't expect. There's one on display here, in fact." In the next room, above a paisley couch, hangs a large piece of artwork with a concave black hole in the middle.

Marian steps closer. A sky-blue linen cloth stretches across a jagged frame. Three stripes of paint—a wider black one shored up by two white—extend downward from the right corner and seem to disappear into the hole at the centre. The fabric is frayed at the borders where the blue merges into other bright colours. The black and white stripes extend throughout the frayed edges. "Which country does this represent?" she asks.

"Botswana," Boone replies. "I made it for World AIDS Day last year. The motif is borrowed from the national flag—the black and white on the flag are said to represent racial harmony. The textile I brought back with me after my last trip home."

"Are those the colours of the surrounding countries at the edges?"

"AIDS affects their industry and culture, too. And to a disease, borders are inconsequential."

"This map made Boone into a professional," Patrick says. "The director of the Centre saw it on display at the Sweeney Gallery last December and asked if he could purchase it."

Boone grins. "My first patron."

Patrick holds up the plastic bag that contains their lunch. "Are you in a hurry? You should eat with us. Marian is an artist as well—she only moonlights as a French student. Last year on my birthday she drew a cartoon of me as a UN delegate and framed it. The caption read: *The Future of West Africa and Eastern Ontario*. A very flattering representation."

"That was a gag gift. We also bought him a selection of import beers."

Boone shifts the binder under his arm and grins. There's a slight space between his front teeth. "I was just at a lunch meeting and would like to get outside for a few moments. But I'll sit with you a bit. I want to get to know this moonlighting Marian." When he says her name, the last syllable stands strong: "Mary-Anne."

Boone leads them over to what he considers the best spot at the Centre, the purple corduroy chairs in the corner whose springs aren't broken. They sit and he unsnaps a piece of blank paper from his binder and passes it to Marian. He digs in the pocket of his jeans and extracts a fountain pen and a stubby pencil, and holds one in each palm, as if assessing their utility. He hesitates before offering Marian the pen. "Under the circumstances, I think it would be best for you to draw me."

Marian looks to Patrick.

"Let her settle in!" Patrick grabs the pen out of Marian's hand.

"Precisely." Boone smooths his palms over his jeans and lays an elbow on the armrest. "What better way to 'settle in', as you say. We'll introduce ourselves via the most appropriate medium." He snatches the pen from Patrick and offers it again to Marian. "No need to worry: what I am proposing is a trade. I will offer you a map in return for your sketch." He waggles his pencil and taps at the open binder: a question, or a challenge.

Marian notices that the pencil has no eraser. It's a defect that levels the playing field a little. She takes the pen from Boone. "A sketch for a map. But I want the binder to draw on."

Boone rips out a blank page for himself and hands the binder over. He spreads the paper over his sizeable knee.

"Hold on," Patrick says. "We came here to eat."

"Soon," Marian says.

"Five minutes, Pat," Boone says. "You can be the timekeeper."

Patrick rubs at his forehead and Boone's face fills with concern. "Oh, I didn't mean to leave you out," he says. "You can play too. But wait, we'll have to go looking for another pencil."

Patrick pushes up his shirtsleeve to reveal his watch. "That won't be necessary. On the count of three..."

Marian pops the cap off the pen.

"Two... one... go."

Boone hunches over the paper and points the pencil to the centre as though getting his bearings. Marian studies his face, and before long, a figure begins to form under her pen.

It's Boone, posing in front of Mackintosh library. She gives him a globe to hold under his arm and tries to exaggerate the folds above his eyes. These details make him look scholarly, she hopes, and slightly concerned, like he understands the world he's got tucked at his elbow. After a few moments of indecision—she doesn't want him to look clownish—she draws a pair of prominent feet.

Somewhere in the background a woman answers the telephone and a microwave beeps.

"That's time." Patrick tugs his sleeve back over his watch.

"You first," Marian says.

Boone grips the paper on each side. He looks like a large fourth grader giving his first class speech. "I'm not quite done. I wanted to try some sort of juxtaposition. . ." He passes the sheet to Marian. Patrick leans over to examine it as well. The map represents the intersection of Waterton and Murphy, near the hospital, but inside-out: the sidewalks and roads tower above the buildings. It's as if the buildings have passed through a giant sieve and now lie dormant beneath. A few forms evoking cars and humans zip along the prominent roads and sidewalks.

The right corner of the map is blank.

"You didn't even finish it?" Patrick says. "This was your idea!"

"I will indeed finish it. I promised Mary-Anne from French a map."

"It's okay. You can finish it later." Marian passes Boone her own drawing.

Boone considers it gravely then smiles wide. "Outstanding! Observe this Cartoon Boone. What an expression of resolve and intelligence."

"I was going for concern, but I'll take resolve."

"The feet are certainly true to life." Patrick removes a pink Tupperware container from the plastic bag next to his chair. "I assume you no longer need a chronograph." He heads to the kitchenette and waits his turn to use the microwave.

Boone crosses one sturdy leg over the other. "So, you're a writer and an artist. A kindred spirit."

"Oh no. I doodle. And I'm a researcher, not a writer. I take things apart and shove the pieces around a little."

"From the pieces, do you not make something new?" Boone sniffs the tip of the pencil and slips it back in his pocket.

"I make something different. A composite. It's masonry, not art."

"You have no imagination whatsoever."

"None."

"Do you dream, Mary-Anne?"

"Yes. But so does my dog."

"Never mind your dog. Do funny things and people wander through your head when you're not looking?" Boone walks two large fingers through his cornrows and flips them up into bunny ears.

"Yes," she says, not sure where this line of questioning is going.

"Ah. What did you dream last night? If this is not too impertinent a question."

Marian looks past Boone to Patrick, who is placing his Tupperware in the microwave. He won't make it back to intervene, but anyway the honest answer is safe enough: she did not dream of sex with Rémy on the back of a giant tortoise (that was the night before last), nor of David slipping out the door with all of her underwear and the toaster. (That was Sunday night.) She didn't even dream of Edna, her funny little bonnet and probing toes.

"I dreamed that my dissertation defense was postponed because one of the committee members showed up naked."

Boone gives a satisfied nod. "An improbable scenario in the Canadian climate. The fruits of an active imagination."

"Come on. Everyone dreams."

"Precisely."

"You're suggesting that everyone has an artist's imagination."

"I am."

"Then we just need to learn how to access it, do we? Find the portal to the unconscious, where we'll discover a massive bank of stories and images?" Marian leans forward. "Ever heard the French expression 'Mon œil'?"

"No. Teach me. I like French lessons."

"It means 'Yeah, right.' And there's a gesture that goes along with it." She tugs on her bottom eyelid with her index finger and exposes its ugly red underside.

"Ha! The ironic eye. Like you're saying, 'I see all too well.'"

"Exactly. And you don't even need the words. You can say it with one veiny eyeball."

Boone uncrosses his leg and reaches down to tighten the laces of his sneakers. "Did I say we were all Van Gogh? No. But we sometimes start thinking with the wrong part of our brain. We should start with the dream-stuff and arrange it neatly afterwards. You must be someone who's good at arranging things. Most grad students are."

"Sure."

"Then you're halfway there. Now your brain must move backwards. Here, I'll lend you something you'll like." He rises and disappears upstairs. A minute later he emerges wearing his coat and holding a graphic novel. The title reads *Don't take this the wrong way, but.* On the cover is a punk adolescent girl. The book is translated from the French and published by Drawn & Quarterly.

"I think you'll enjoy this violation of the text-image barrier," he says. "You can give it back to Big Pat when you're done."

Marian takes the book from Boone's outstretched hand. "This is a library book."

"True. A wonderful place, the library. They let me walk away with their possessions without expecting much in return. Unless you count my numerous fines."

Patrick returns with the sauce and rice, now divided between the Tupperware and an extra plate.

"Catch you tomorrow," Boone says. "I'm going walking now. I must figure out how to finish Mary-Anne's map." He shakes Patrick's hand and wishes Marian *bon lecture*. She reminds him that the word 'lecture' is feminine.

He nods slowly, processing this grammar lesson. "Bonne lecture!" he cries out, visibly pleased with himself.

Once he's ducked out the door, Marian turns to Patrick. "Huh. That was . . ."

"That was Boone. Once he's gone, one is never quite sure what took place while he was there."

"His French needs work."

Patrick agrees and eyes the book Marian is holding. "Picture book?"

"For grown-ups."

Patrick hands Marian the plate. "We all need a distraction."

Chapter Fourteen

When Marian stumbles into the bathroom hunting for some melatonin to help her sleep, Edna is hunched over, her long pink nightgown hiked up, one foot resting on the side of the tub. She's clipping her toenails. "Little buggers just won't stop growing," she says. "All this clipping is hard on the back."

"Here, I'll help you." Marian directs her to sit on the closed lid of the toilet seat, and she herself perches on the side of the tub. She takes Edna's foot onto her pyjama-clad lap, noting what must be a rather painful bunion. Bluish veins and prominent tendons stretch like roots beneath the skin.

"Not too close, now." Edna passes Marian the clippers. "I'm prone to ingrown toenails."

"Noted," Marian says as she gets to work on the big toe. "I wasn't expecting to see you again. Given that we didn't really know each other."

"Surprise!" Edna throws her hands in the air like a Jack-in-the-box, then smirks and folds them in her lap.

"You have a very special sense of humour."

"Indeed. You know, you could always try talking to David about his depression. Seeing as how it's bothering you."

Marian gathers the first few toenail clippings that have fallen onto her lap and drops them in the garbage bin. "I never know what to say to him anymore."

"Saying *something* is usually better than saying nothing."

"You don't think that maybe he'll just come out of it? Because the other day, I googled grief and mourning. People need at least six months before they start to recover—"

"Suit yourself," Edna interrupts, and leans over to examine Marian's work. "But just for the record: your method is flawed."

"David, wake up."

"Mhm? What?" David pops up on his elbow and peers over Marian's shoulder at the glowing digits of the alarm clock.

"Tell me what's wrong."

"What's wrong with what? Did something happen?"

"No, not exactly."

"Then can we go back to sleep? It's two in the morning."

"I can't sleep. You're depressed."

He grunts. "I'm tired, is what I am."

"But not only."

"For Christ's sake, Mare. Can't this wait?"

"No."

He sighs into the darkness, wearily draws out his words. "Do you not find it self-centred on your part to wake me up in the night to talk about *you* being distraught because I'm depressed?"

She doesn't reply at first. Watches 2:05 become 2:06.

"I guess you're right. I'm sorry I woke you."

"It's okay." He adjusts his pillow and flips over. "Don't worry about me. It'll pass."

A hint of light flits across the ceiling, cast by a passing car. David's breathing grows regular and his arm twitches.

"It's just that before, you wanted to talk to me," she says, her voice jerking him awake again. "You wanted to tell me what was going on. And now you don't."

"In the morning," he mumbles.

But in the morning he's busy getting ready for work and doesn't bring up their conversation, and she feels silly for having disturbed his sleep—for letting worry amplify itself

in the dark—and the banal rhythms of daylight (coffee, dog
walking, hygiene) make her think that everybody is probably
going to be fine.

The Modern Languages building smells different to her, as
though she were no longer a part of it. It's ten after eight,
and she hopes to slip into the department office to check her
mailbox and slip out again, unnoticed, but as the janitor holds
the door open for her, Rémy saunters past. He's carrying a small
brown bottle and seems as surprised to see her as she is him.

"Tu vas être contente de moi," he says. "I've fed Colette a
good breakfast. I borrowed this from Lucie."

Marian sleepily peers at the bottle; it contains plant
fertilizer. It takes her a moment to remember who Colette is,
and another to switch on the French part of her brain.

"Bonne idée," she says. "Lucie's aloe plant always looks
really healthy."

"I moved her over a couple of feet as well. Lucie told me that
the electromagnetic field from the computer can interfere with
her growth."

"She sounds well cared for." Marian moves past him into
the department office. A wasted trip—she has no mail.

"The collection I edited with Thomas Leclerc over at Laval
comes out in the spring," Rémy says when she drifts back into
the hallway. His words sound like an apology rather than an
announcement.

You should be writing your monograph, she thinks
unkindly. She says, "Good for you," and the words sound bitter,
even to her ears.

"No, I mean, I wasn't looking for praise. But I was hoping
you could translate the jacket blurb for the online catalogues. I
could ask another student, but—"

"I'm the best translator." Marian grips the handle to the
stairwell door.

"Yes. That's not all, though." He touches her elbow and looks at her imploringly.

She lets her arm fall.

They are alone in the hallway except for the janitor, who pushes the floor polish machine in a slow march. Marian fidgets with the fleece lining of her mittens. She finds this silence awkward and uncomfortable, even though she is its author. The machine grinds and whirs, and the janitor keeps his eyes on the floor as he moves past.

"I haven't seen you in three weeks." Rémy holds his hands up as though to say, I don't know what to do. "Just—come," he says.

Marian is sweating in her winter coat and scarf. She tugs at the scarf and loosens it. Beside them the janitor fiddles with a setting on the machine. She wills him to go polish another floor.

"Okay. Fine." She follows Rémy to his office, feeling absurd. Even the university cleaning staff can see what she's caught in. A willing victim.

Rémy shuts the door behind them. She's caught by surprise when he pulls out a chair for her, uncharacteristically gallant. A print-out of the passage he wishes her to translate lies ready in front of her. How many days has he been waiting for her to come by?

He leans in behind her. "It's not very long—only a hundred words. And the publisher doesn't need it for a couple of weeks. Maybe when you're done, I could take you out for a drink at The Pint. To thank you."

His hand warms her shoulder and a new pressure system forms in her body. Light-headedness lifts the grogginess, as though she's already had that drink. "I'm pretty busy right now." She turns, stares at the base of Rémy's neck. Her breath comes shallow. He smells like the cedar wood of an old-fashioned sauna. She wants to move in close to his throat as she speaks; instead she presses her back against the chair. Her words collide, part English, part French.

"Quel bordel," she says. "Le pire des clichés. I have a husband et un chien." She laughs bitterly. "At least I don't have a mortgage."

As soon as she lets loose this drivel she wishes she could take it back. She leans forward and buries her head in her arms. She will disappear into her elbow. Whenever she resurfaces, her words will be gone.

Over her forearm she sees Rémy move to his side of the table. He sinks into his computer chair. "I don't have a mortgage either," he says in English under his breath. He slowly oscillates, eyes downcast.

The silence lasts a full minute. She sits up and wonders if she should leave.

Rémy clears his throat. "Nothing but transference," he says. The vein at his temple pulsates. "A necessary part of the student-teacher relationship. The professor is a screen onto which the fantasies of the student are projected. He or she, like a good analyst, will field these fantasies without participating in them."

Marian inhales and presses her hand to her forehead. Rémy's words are more half-cocked than her own. "Hold on. You know you were part of this."

He swivels and sits erect like a man surveying his own territory. "Well, I definitely had my head in the sand. And then of course you are what you are, which complicated things."

She doesn't know whether to laugh or spit. What sand? And what exactly is it that he thinks she is? An intelligent, attractive woman? A graduate student succubus?

"What kind of professor goes hot tubbing at midnight with his half-naked student?"

He sniffs. "That encounter was perfectly chaste."

Chaste. She pictures lace stays and picnic lunches.

"Who cares if it was chaste? I know the colour of your chest hair! And that you have a mole next to your left nipple!"

Rémy brings a protective hand to his chest. For a moment he seems stunned speechless. "Under the circumstances," he says loudly, "I think it would be best for us to spend some time apart. Your dissertation is of the utmost importance, and I cannot encourage you to jeopardize it. Here's what we'll do. We'll continue this separation. If you need my professional advice you can write me an email or leave a note in my mailbox."

"An epistolary advisor." Marian rises and goes to the door.

"Marian."

When she turns around, he's holding out the document he prepared for her.

She glares.

His face softens with apology. "You don't have to do it. If you're busy, I mean."

"Like most grad students, I have absolutely nothing to do. As you have so kindly pointed out."

"I didn't mean—" he breaks off. He sounds hurt, sad. His Adam's apple slides up and down.

"I know," she says after a moment, softened by his neediness. By him needing her. "Give it here."

Marian finishes Rémy's translation the next day, but decides to make him wait. Let him ask for it. She plunges down a research rabbit hole—spends the rest of the week picking through the evidence and testimonies in the *Copy of the Proceedings of a General Court Martial Held at Quebec the 15th day of April 1763, By Virtue of a Warrant from His Excellency Governor Murray, dated the 14th day of the same Month*. Marie-Josephte Corriveau's trial. Having studied the proceedings, she still doesn't know whether Marie-Josephte really did kill her husband, but in her mind's eye, the gaps in the historical record thrash to life.

Late summer, 1762. The tabletop cracks as a woman's skull pounds its surface. With his palm, Dodier grinds his wife's face into the grain of the wood. Three children freeze

in the background as though in tableau: two girls, six and
eight years old, and a boy just turned five. The middle child,
Marie-Angélique, flinches first: she drops her doll to the floor,
crouches slowly to pick it up, and holds it to her belly, eyes
trained on her mother. The eldest, Marie-Françoise, turns away,
stiff as a broom, and sets a pot of water to boil for washing.
Hand trembling, the girl drops a soap cake into an empty
bucket. Her little brother, Charles, stands motionless by the
washboard. He knits his brow and glares out the open window
at a crow perched on the fence, his hands balled into fists at his
sides.

Dodier releases his wife's head from his grip. He grabs a
heel of bread from the sideboard and tears at it with his teeth.
"Not much to say now, eh?"

Marie-Josephte straightens; palpates her screaming temple.
Notes that she can still see from both eyes. Traces the spot
where a bruise will bloom on her cheek.

The next day, around the far side of the barn, she happens
upon her son. She watches his actions without comprehending.
From a distance of several yards, he charges towards the fence
and throws his chest against the post. Collapses to the ground.
She shouts his name, but it's as though he doesn't hear. He picks
himself up and, in measured steps, walks backwards through
the grass. Plows forward and once again hurls himself at the
unrelenting wood of the fence. When he stumbles to his feet
a second time, Marie-Josephte runs to him, spins him round
and catches him in her arms. At first, his body is as rigid as the
fencepost, then he crumples and clutches her skirts. Heaves
ragged breaths against her dress. Leaves a trail of snot and tears.

As he staggers off and disappears into the barn, she
doesn't care if it's the devil who buzzes like a fly in the sun and
murmurs in her ear. She doesn't need the devil to tell her that
her husband must die.

Chapter Fifteen

Rémy resets the alarm for Delphine before heading into the bathtub, swiftly, as if in one smooth leap—a salmon jumping upstream. Or maybe it just feels that way because he's not yet caffeinated, and afterwards can't recall what was going through his head while the tub was filling with water.

When they first rented this apartment—the converted kitchen and pantry area of a nineteenth century manor—he worried that the lack of shower would disrupt his mornings, turn his day slow and tepid. Before this bathtub, this city, he would have read *Le Devoir* while chewing on a St-Viateur bagel, and taken a shower hot enough to turn his neck and shoulders scarlet. In the beginning, he had his Montreal newspaper delivered (this was possible, even in Waterton), but found it made him too mournful for the routine he had enjoyed on Côte-des-Neiges, and for the more spacious apartment where a giant cactus plant, abandoned by the previous tenant, pointed accusingly at the mangy tomcat who skulked across the balcony. Rémy never considered throwing out the plant or chasing the cat away. They looked tough, like they knew better than he did who belonged there.

"Mal du pays," his grandfather grunted when Rémy mentioned to him on the phone a while back that he had cancelled the newspaper subscription and adopted a new routine. Literally, sick for one's country. The old man is sharp—transitions don't make themselves, or else it's Rémy who makes them unnecessarily complicated. Is this what happened with

Marian yesterday? No, certainly not. He merely nudged her in the right direction at a critical moment. The situation was bound to be awkward, and he had no other choice, given all her talk about dogs and mortgages. He hadn't realized just how far things had gone—an innocent flirtation turned serious. His office that day had felt like a confessional, and it needed to be clear who was playing what role. Of the priest-confessor pairing, better to be the priest.

But did he not also wish for her to want him, just a little? He must be strict with himself, admit that rationalization will only take him so far. Indeed, the irrational is what carried him into that murky territory where he let Marian spend hours on end in his office, and he—be honest, now!—found himself eagerly anticipating each visit.

He reaches for the soap. He must cleanse himself of that awkwardness now. Down the drain, office infatuation! In its place: time and distance and the utmost professional conduct.

Maybe he's been selling himself short—maybe he really is good at transitions, has a knack for graceful change. Has he not hunkered down into this cast iron tub to read a few pages of *Ulysses* every morning for the past several months in order to improve his English? After five years, it's time that he got used to the *lingua franca*. He's discovered that the English words sound all right in his morning head, filtered through residual dream content. It's the reading ritual that has helped him grow used to this limestone town, the reading ritual and its sly unhurried way. After a few weeks—after Leopold Bloom had served his wife breakfast, read a letter from his daughter, and visited the privy—Rémy found he enjoyed his morning soak, this settling into wakefulness before eggs and coffee. (Impossible to get a decent bagel here.) Joyce himself would have sloughed off distractions in a clawfoot tub like this one, his imagination swimming, words rippling across the water before landing on the page.

Rémy turns off the faucet. The tub was the right choice on the part of the manor's former owner, a prominent local lawyer. He respects this man, who knew better than to install a banal shower while converting the manor into apartments in the sixties. He identifies with the need to ease from past to present and respect the essence of space. "Too good a space to leave it to someone less appreciative," Rémy once said to Delphine when she complained of the lack of light and storage.

"You're turning me into a troll," she replied.

"A stone princess." He loves the exterior walls; limestone creased like old flesh. Loves, too, the creaks and nicks and undulation of the apartment's wide floorboards. The place feels ancient, and thus sturdy, grounded. There is history here, even though it is not his own.

"We could be earning equity," Delphine said.

"We could be driving twenty-five minutes to work each day. You could do your running in a west-end suburb where all the garages jut out like snouts. Or even worse—we could be locked in, with no way back to Montreal." He still believes this, that it's possible to get a tenure-track position at l'UQAM or l'Université de Montréal if only he's ready to flee at any moment, can work up the nerve to apply and butt up against researchers with more pull, more grant funding. Until then, he tucks himself into this stone niche, hope periscoping. As does Delphine. She must know he has their best interest at heart. That's why she always drops the subject and tells him he's right and kisses the crinkles of his eyes, even though for a time afterwards she seems deflated.

He squirts dandruff shampoo into his palm and works it into his hair. His scalp isn't flaky, but he read somewhere that pyrithione zinc prevents a man from going bald. Grey isn't so bad, but bald is a crapshoot; you can't be sure you have a good skull until the hair is gone. He makes room to dunk his head by poking his knees out of the water, and when he resurfaces, he rubs at his scalp to make sure all the shampoo is gone. He picks up *Ulysses* and dimples its pages with his wet fingers. *Curious longing I. Water to water. Combine business with pleasure.*

The words swim, and Marian appears, shining wetly in the moonlight. Desire rustles through the trees.

He must keep his work high and dry. Protect it from complications.

He places the shampoo back in the plastic rack just above the tub, flip-top closed, label turned out, next to the soap in its black travel dish. There is a compartment for everything. (This is what Marian seems not to understand.)

Once out of the tub, he takes his time combing his hair. He doesn't have to go in to the office today, but needs to transition—there's that word again—from wet visions to reality, from the bathroom to the rest of the apartment, which seems to belong more to Delphine than to him. It's his own fault; he didn't want to be bothered with decorating. Still, she kept to what she knew he would like: stark walls, neutral-toned furniture, an out-of-sight place for everything unsightly. Kitsch touches are forbidden—no knickknacks or travel souvenirs or afghans. No pictures dangling from nails, and therefore no holes in the walls to patch later. While he likes this place, it's best not to inhabit it too deeply, leave a mark on it, as if carving his initials into a tree trunk.

In the bedroom, he switches on the lamp. Delphine stirs. She seems tiny, buried, a child snugged into a grown-up's bed. They don't speak—she needs a few minutes to warm up and grow into the day. After a quarter of an hour, she'll puff up and hustle and make him look lazy by comparison. For now, she presses a button on the alarm clock, sits up, kisses him on the cheek, and disappears into the bathroom. Rémy contemplates his side of the closet, the clothes arranged by colour and rank like so many soldiers, his dress shirts and pants hanging proudly in the centre. He grabs a pair of dark grey slacks and a blue shirt. He can't work unless he's properly dressed. No, that's not true. He can't work unless he is shod in good shoes, and he feels absurd sitting at the computer wearing nothing but boxers and loafers. The shoe dependency is a displacement of a childhood behaviour: up until the age of nine, he couldn't go to the bathroom without them. It exasperated his mother. "As if your bowels talked to your feet!" She stopped threatening to bring him to the psychologist when he started going to the bathroom in his sock feet and saved the shoes for his homework sessions.

It occurs to him that he would be embarrassed to tell Marian this. Delphine knows, but pretends she doesn't.

Of the ten pairs of shoes he owns, he chooses the tasselled loafers, juxtaposed at the bottom of the closet against a beat-up steel lunchbox. His grandmother wanted to throw out the lunchbox when his grandfather retired from the mines. Rémy rescued it. He pictures its contents: publication acceptance letters for each of his stories; one first-edition, signed copy of Hubert Aquin's *Prochain épisode*; a snapshot of him and Delphine in the outdoor Rodin sculpture garden in Paris, striking the pose of The Thinker.

He likes knowing that if the apartment were to catch fire, his personal history could be gripped in one hand and carried to safety.

Rémy drinks black coffee from a square mug, which is also black. Delphine takes quick sips of protein shake at the counter beside him. She's no longer sleepy, but edgy—not the precise energy of an athlete before a race, but the twitch and tremble of a rabbit. This is the pre-run Delphine: jacked up, alert, but still vulnerable, like she could at any moment drop dead from a loud noise.

"Research day today?"

"Mostly. I've got some grading to clean up as well."

"Nice not to have to go to campus, though."

"Definitely." Marian's high heels tap at his memory, and he wishes he had a reason to drop by the department. "How many kilometres?" he asks.

"Don't know. Haven't decided yet." Delphine finishes her protein shake and places the glass in the dishwasher, careful to line it up with those that are identical. She adjusts the headband that holds back her bangs. "I didn't get out these past couple of weeks, and I don't want to lose endurance."

"You had the flu."

"I'm better now, though. Almost a hundred per cent."

"You were coughing last night."

"I know. I'm sorry." She comes over and places a hand on his chest. An offering. "I know Thursday's your research day. I should have slept on the couch."

"Mon cœur, that's not what I meant."

"Oh, of course not. But I still should have thought of it." She pulls her jacket from the entryway closet and loads her pockets. Keys, iPod, Kleenex. She looks out the window, anxious, as though the road were already chasing her. "Unless you want me to make your eggs. I can make them before I go. Why don't I go ahead and do that?"

He tells her that's not necessary, but she's already taken off her jacket and is pulling ingredients out of the fridge. He feels guilty, but not enough to get up and do it himself, and part of him likes being served. She makes sunny side up on toast and leaves the pan to soak before shrugging her jacket back on and slipping out the door.

It's not quite daylight. He guesses that she'll be gone about an hour and a half. She'll come back wrung-out, docile, and pull on her scrubs with the cartoon molars printed on them, or the plain baby blue ones, which he doesn't mind as much, and leave for her eleven o'clock shift at Dr. Gauvin's office. When she gets home in the evening, she'll tell him how worn out she feels and fold herself into a hug, and he'll gently scold her and tell her he's going to have to make her take better care of herself.

At least she doesn't mind her job; he's grateful for this. She works for one of the two French-speaking dentists in town, although she preferred her former boss in Montreal, who allowed the hygienists to put in variable work hours and play local indie bands on the stereo rather than soft rock. That's where they first met—Rémy had come in for a routine cleaning and check-up. Reclined and bibbed, he stared up at the hazel-eyed hygienist whose gaze was fixed on the inside of his mouth, and who never scraped too hard.

"You're a student?" She pointed with a scaling device to his backpack.

Rémy let his jaw relax. "Just finishing up my PhD in literature."

"My brother did a master's in history. He teaches at CÉGEP now. Open up." She pressed at his back molar. "How's the dissertation going?"

"Your brother never taught you not to ask that question?" His words were slurred. Drool crawled down his chin.

"Oh, I didn't mean—I was just interested—" She wiped the scaling tool, dabbed at his chin, and set to work on a different tooth.

"Don't worry about it," he said, and she paused, waiting to get her hands back in his mouth. "It's not going too badly, in fact. I'm almost done." Every few teeth, he told her about his work on Hubert Aquin, how he was analyzing truncated desire in the author's novels from a psychoanalytic perspective. During the polish and before the fluoride (he requested mint, no childish flavours posing as fruit or candy), he told her how he'd already published two articles in *Études françaises* and had recently been invited to give a guest talk in a graduate-level seminar at McGill. Delphine peered thoughtfully into his mouth, and sometimes into his eyes.

"You must be very clever," she said as he swished the cup of fluoride that she passed him. "I admire people with such a high tolerance for school."

He spit the fluoride out in the sink. "It's not so bad."

She handed him a toothpaste sample. "We'll just wait for Dr. Ouellet, and then everyone gets to go home."

A twinge of disappointment—small but distinct—moved through him. He wanted to spend a few more minutes talking with the hazel-eyed hygienist. She made him feel small enough to pamper and big enough to be important. "I'm your last patient?"

She nodded.

"Would you like to grab some Indian food?"

She pushed the tray table away from her. "I would." She had an uncertain smile, her teeth small and rounded like wafers. "I mean, if that's what you want."

He was surprised when she took him back to her apartment after that first date. She had that same tense pre-run energy then, though he didn't recognize it as such at the time. An eagerness he hadn't anticipated. He remembers now that she spent a long time in the bathroom afterwards. He could hear water splashing. The next morning, she got up with the sun. From bed he watched her pull her spandex bra top over her breasts and stomach. In those days, his fingers would graze her soft belly until she nudged his hand away. Seven years later, the skin is stretched tight over her frame, though he can't see the precise outline of her ribs, thank God. He pushes out of his mind the skeletal version of her body that he would later come to know and would rather forget.

That first morning she'd returned after an hour and forty-five minutes, red-faced and breathing fast. He was sitting on the sofa rereading one of Aquin's novels. She poured herself a glass of water but left it on the counter and sat next to him on the sofa instead. "Maybe didn't eat enough." The words were garbled, as though she were talking in her sleep. Colour drained from her face. Her head wobbled; she lay down and rested it on his thigh. Rémy murmured and combed her damp hair with his fingers while her eyelids hovered and fell closed. She was motionless for a minute or so, gave a soft moan and buried her head in his lap. He asked if she had gone into a diabetic coma or something, and she murmured that it was just hypoglycemia from a little over-exertion.

"A little or a lot?" he said, and she didn't reply.

A month later she moved in with him.

There's no second bedroom in the apartment that could serve as an office. Rémy's desk is in the living room; it's a beat-up pine worktable, also inherited from his grandfather. He runs a finger over its pitted surface and is reminded that he, too, works with his hands. It's not all abstraction.

The desk doesn't go with the rest of the decor, which is for the most part smooth and white. Delphine would tell him it isn't white at all—it's eggshell or cloud or verbena. She keeps track of these distinctions. His computer is an old PC laptop that weighs close to nine pounds and taxes his shoulder when he totes it to work. He should buy a new one, but he can no longer put the expense through the department budget and he's cheap; he acknowledges this to himself, though he tries to hide it from his colleagues and students. (He's careful never to skip out on buying a round.) Unable to face his book manuscript, he opens a smaller, more manageable document named "Sainteté." The full title of the conference paper is "La sainteté contemporaine: *Hypatie ou la fin des dieux* de Jean Marcel et *L'immaculée conception* de Gaétan Soucy." Beside the computer lie his copies of the novels as well as an old electricity bill, on the back of which he has jotted: *transpositions et superpositions esthétiques, historiques, philosophiques. Sublimation masculine. Réappropriation artistique d'un passé catholique.*

Rémy doesn't work on Aquin anymore, hasn't written anything on this author in several years. There was a time when

his own political concerns were tightly knotted to the author's
ravelled prose—Aquin's textual violence, his sovereign rage,
used to exorcise a separatist demon in Rémy that now comes
out only rarely, when poked at: election time, national holidays
(he can't abide Canada Day and insists each year on being in
Montreal for Saint-Jean-Baptiste). Now he comes to Aquin's
novels feeling used up, indifferent, or embarrassed: has he
himself not defected to English Canada? Anger seems beside the
point. (Maybe that's what Aquin meant when he offed himself.)

Some days he wonders if he's become a fatalist. Others he
acknowledges that it's hypocritical to teach English-Canadian
students about Québec literature, accept a salary that is
partially funnelled from their tuition payments, and think of
them as Other, as 'Ontarians,' which Marian has pointed out
is a phantom identity. (According to her, Ontarians exist only
in Québec—just the sort of totalizing statement you'd expect
from someone who belongs to the cultural majority.) Maybe
his research interests have simply followed their due course and
are slipping away to natural causes. Like a death-bed atheist
crying out for his last rites—faithless but craving ritual, history,
meaning—he's become less interested in overtly political works,
and more so in authors whose work bears the mark of God's
retreat from Québec life. Scholarly salvation, a sacerdotal
march towards interpretive closure: when in doubt, he can
always relate his ideas back to the Catholic Church.

If he had ideas, that is. The trouble with writing a
monograph is that once you're halfway through, once that first
electric jolt of scholarly excitement has passed, you end up
bored stupid and spend your research day checking your email.

He also wonders why he's not the one making up new
narratives for scholars like him to analyze. There was a time
when he considered himself a writer. Maybe if he'd persevered,
draft after draft, he could have been an author to contend with.
And yet that's not what the university pays him for, and so
instead, he writes about palimpsest, writes about rewriting.

Or, rather, *pretends* to write about it. At this point he knows his book will not be finished in time for him to include it in his tenure file. He should be worried, but he recently watched a colleague in German get tenure without a monograph. When he asked his own chair what happened, Adèle said that the German department couldn't afford to lose the professor: given the recent cutbacks, the department would never get the budget line back—would not be able to bring in a new recruit—and their programs would be in danger. Rémy is crossing his fingers that his own tenure committee will find themselves in the same bind. In the meantime, he sits down at his desk every Thursday and goes through the motions—either works on the manuscript or actively ignores it—because what else can he do?

He stretches and massages his lumbar muscles. His chair at the office is more comfortable than this one, which is angular, modern to a fault. Maybe he should sit on tables like Marian. Does she go to the department on Thursdays? He can't recall. That translation he gave her should be finished by now. He imagines her playing with his words and making them a part of her, rolling them around in her own language. When she gives them back to him, they'll leave an imprint, like tracks in the snow.

Time passes.

The cursor blinks at Rémy.

Rémy blinks back.

Clearly he's not working well at home. He would be more productive at the office.

On campus, he stops at Roast to pick up his second coffee of the day and a chocolate-covered pretzel. It takes him a moment to realize that the wool-clad shoulders in front of him in line belong to Jean-Louis, his old comrade turned dean. He considers fleeing; realizes this is not possible without being spotted.

"Jean-Louis! Salut!"

Jean-Louis performs an elegant quarter-turn. "Eh, Rémy," he says, and smiles widely with his whole face, dimples creasing. "I haven't seen you in forever. How've you been?"

"Oh, you know," Rémy says, and trails off before he says something banal. *Keeping busy. Same old, same old.*

Jean-Louis nods like he really does know, like Rémy's words have content. He never makes Rémy feel irrelevant or inadequate. Rémy does that all on his own when he thinks about how successful Jean-Louis is.

They shuffle forward in line. Jean-Louis orders, turns back to Rémy, and places a friendly hand on his shoulder. "I've been meaning to talk to you about those budget decisions that came down the pipe." He shakes his head, blows air through pursed lips as though to say, what a doozy.

"Nothing personal, I suppose," Rémy says.

Jean-Louis nods his wise, slow nod, which Rémy considers a Jean-Louis classic, and one of the many reasons he climbed the ladder at the speed of a pre-pubescent acrobat. Who wouldn't want to promote that nod?

"That's the issue," Jean-Louis says. "I mean, with the university running a deficit, it's all about prioritization right now. *Everyone* is taking a hit."

You're not, Rémy thinks. "Tough times," he says.

"And how."

The barista passes Jean-Louis his Americano, warns him it's hot, for which he thanks her as though she were giving him unexpected and vital information.

"Rémy. We need to get together some time. I'll drop you a line."

And Rémy wants to believe him, because this is the man who used to play shuffleboard with him at The Pint after a pitcher of La Maudite, who used to argue with him about Foucault. But now that he thinks back, Jean-Louis never complained about other colleagues, or upper administration, or students; only nodded sympathetically when Rémy did, only smiled his dimpled smile and poured Rémy another drink.

"Isn't that the dean?" the barista says once Jean-Louis tips her handsomely and strides off.

A dean, Rémy thinks. One of many.

"In the flesh," he says.

"I saw him at my friend's convocation. I think it's cool he's so young, and he's the dean. He must be *really* smart."

Rémy messily eats his pretzel on the way to the department, burns his tongue on the coffee.

Lucie passes him a phone message from the registrar. Not urgent. Rémy checks his mail; in his box is an intradepartmental envelope. Addressed to him, but the box that usually bears the sender's name has been left blank.

There is no translation inside the envelope.

Instead, a cartoon featuring two characters, one female, one male. Him, Marian. *No*, he thinks, resisting. A man who looks like him, a woman who looks like Marian. Avatars.

The man carries a lush plant into an office, goes back into the hallway, invites a skirt-clad woman inside. The woman smiles at him and at the plant, perfect teeth, lips shiny. "Qu'elle est belle!" the woman says. "D'une beauté sans mesure," the man says. The plant appears to beam. The two characters whisper conspiratorially.

The man is now alone in his office. He is fertilizing the plant and looks at once self-satisfied and crafty. The plant gives off jagged bolts of light, as if juiced-up, electric. It rocks on its stand and continues to throw off a mysterious light-energy.

The plant is luminously transformed. It becomes a toothy, beefy Venus flytrap.

The man lures the woman into the office. The plant opens its ravening jaws and swallows the woman.

The man deposits the plant outside the office door. A janitor is sweeping the floor nearby.

The woman fights her way out of the jaws of the plant, wielding a pen like a scimitar. Behind her the man's office door is closed.

The woman walks away down the hallway. Her skirt is patchy and soiled, but the vanishing lines of the drawing make her appear defiant, triumphant. The janitor watches admiringly.

"Neat," Lucie says as she peers over Rémy's shoulder. "I didn't know you went in for alternative assignments. I had you figured for an essay kind of guy. Is that for French 236?"

He stuffs the cartoon back in the envelope. "I'm doing some creative response assignments these days."

"Your students must love you for it."

"Indeed." Rémy hurries away down the hall. He locks himself in his office, drops the envelope on his desk and throws himself into his chair, which rolls a few feet and bumps against the bookshelf. He was wrong about this chair: it isn't more comfortable than the one at home. It's a hot seat, a witness stand. He swivels. Colette the plant gleams in the sunlight, appears to accuse him. *Did you do this?* she seems to say. *Did you fertilize this attraction?*

The attraction was there, crouching, waiting! It came looking for him! It was cunning, insistent. Wore heels that tapped out a seductive rhythm on the tile. He tried to focus on his work, he really did, but that sound always snapped his mind back to where it wasn't supposed to be. Click-click, click-click, click-cl-click. In that little skip, resolve shimmied under the table and out the door, and in its place, the image of Marian's shoulders. Their bare contours that night in the hot tub. Interesting that she chose not to draw that encounter in her cartoon. It's the scene he would have chosen. Or else he would have ended the plant cartoon differently.

The man approaches, desirous and stealthy. The woman backs away, her chest thrust out: yes no yes no. They embrace and knock over the plant. Ceramic shatters and earth sprays. They grope and undress and moan into the dirt. The woman's hair tangles with the roots of the plant. The man's chest hair furls wildly. There is aching and thrusting and breath caught in the throat. A final shiver of release before the primal picking of dirt off each other's buttocks.

He is Tarzan. An atavistic avatar.

"Ostie!" he swears aloud as he grips his desk. This woman is sapping his wits. But if he's witless, so is she, because what kind of student puts an autobiographical cartoon in her professor's mailbox?

He pulls the cartoon from the envelope and examines it again. "Qu'elle est belle," the avatar says to the plant. Indeed. He recalls that blushy collarbone, the rise and fall of her accent. A mellifluous voice and the click-clack of a pair of heels. Is that all it takes to undo a man? No. So it must have been her pale form in the moonlight. And to be fair, who wouldn't wish that scene had ended differently? What man wouldn't want to kiss such an exquisite navel, rather than hurry to obscure it with a towel?

But the nerve to draw it all! It's as though he's been caught with an erection.

The cartoon stares up at him. You're responsible. You did this. You *participated*. But do you want this? Do you want *her*?

Yes, maybe. Maybe he wants her. But he doesn't want to be the guy in the drawing, the crafty, smirking, up-to-no-good opportunist. The guy who takes advantage of his student, becomes a professional disgrace. He's not that guy. Is he?

He sighs, feels once again the breathy mist around them, the thrum of possibility. But also, those long conversations: Lacan, the beauty of Anne Hébert's syntax, his own creative writing, the state of the publishing industry in Québec, the Montreal Canadiens (didn't he do most of the talking that time? she must be a good listener), teaching frustrations, the best brand of merino wool socks, the poetry of close textual analysis.

Maybe he is that guy. Is that guy so bad?

Better find out. He gets up, stumbles around in his storage closet, trips over the space-heater, fights aggressive dust bunnies and mounds of unsorted files and papers, and uncovers the university's Faculty Handbook. Flip, flip. Section 6.1.4: Faculty-Student Conduct. "Romantic relationships between faculty members and students are forbidden. If a faculty member should become romantically involved with a student, he or she must disclose the relationship to the head of his or her academic unit and arrange to transfer the student to another professor's class."

"Romantically involved." Well, that would be a bit of an overstatement in this instance, wouldn't it? *Nothing's happened*, he assures himself.

"Another professor's class." Another supervisor?

Indecision, confusion. After rereading the policy four more times, as though expecting it to hatch clarity, Rémy collapses into his swivel chair, calls home and leaves a message for Delphine on the answering machine. He's at work late taking care of an emergency, he explains after the beep.

He refuses to leave until he's figured out what to do.

jeudi 24 novembre 2011 19 h 42
Objet : [Aucun objet]
De : Rémy Leblanc <leblanc_remy@uwaterton.ca>
À : Marian Kristiansen <kristiansen_marian@uwaterton.ca>

Ma chère Marian,

How to respond to a fantastical cartoon? With an apology, followed by a request. I've dealt with this badly. Come and see me.

Rémy

Chapter Sixteen

Marian can't get comfortable, because Edna is perched on the bed and her butt has pinned down the quilt. She scoots up, places a pillow behind her back. David sleeps soundly against the wall.

"Shall I make tea?" Edna says.

"No. Thanks, though," Marian says, trying not to sound testy.

"I suppose you've thought about what you want."

"A little."

"Well?"

"If I had the answer, there would be no need to ask the question."

"You're a quick one. Ms. Doctor of Philosophy."

"Quick, or evasive?"

"I was just being polite. David is looking pretty pale compared to that Rémy guy just now, huh?"

"Shh. You're not supposed to say that out loud."

"And he wants to see you." Pause. "He's an interesting man. Charming in an awkward sort of way. Smart. Girls always melt for smart. I guess David is more of the nice-guy type. Nice guy, terrible at backgammon."

"Edna. I'm confused."

"Living will do that to you." Edna stabs at a silver curl that has sprung from her bonnet. "No tea for you, eh? What about brandy?"

"No brandy."

"Gonna be a long night," Edna says.

Tongue-tied, Marian sits primly at Rémy's table, on which she has placed the translation he wanted. Rémy called this meeting—he seemed decisive—but now he paces between the table and the window, talking about exam preparation and car maintenance and BLT sandwiches, and, yes, the weather. It's as though he were saying, Now that you're here, I don't know what to do with you.

To which she silently replies: I don't know what to do either. I drew a cartoon and sent it to you because you pissed me off, and now I'm feeling exposed and ridiculous. Too many words buzzing over my head. Maybe if I had a net, I could catch some of them and make my own sentence.

She discovered his email message this morning, after Kong refused to eliminate because a cacophonous garbage truck was making its way down the street, and David refused to get out of bed despite the fact that he needed to be at work in fifteen minutes. She tried to float above these domestic worries and imagine what to expect from Rémy. Anger and indignation? Plans for an afternoon rendezvous? Groping? She didn't expect this drawn-out monologue. She wants to crack a joke or even take off her sweater, anything to slow him down.

He stops pacing and his hands flutter in front of her. A man on the brink. Of what, she's not sure. The term 'mid-life crisis' occurs to her, though he's only in his thirties.

Abruptly, he bends down and kisses her, his lips soft and full, his hands gripping her shoulders. When he pulls away, his buzzing words are given the weight of stones. Months of desire, of wondering, press through her body and are released.

"That's better," she breathes.

He strokes her hair. "I need to step down as your supervisor."

She bats his hand away. His brain is broken. He's bending the rules of logic and probability. He's gone crazy. "Step down as my supervisor and step up as what?"

"This situation is compromising. I'm no longer an appropriate judge of your work."

"The only other Québec specialist in the department ditched us for McGill! Where do you expect me to go?"

Rémy sighs. "We'll find someone for the paperwork. We don't need another specialist. I'll still be here to guide you."

Marian snorts. "Oh, come on. Who's going to want to take me on with you breathing down their neck? Who will write my reference letters?"

"I'm ethically bound to protect you." He crouches down and caresses her face, absurdly gentle.

She shakes her head. His hands drop.

"You're protecting yourself," she says.

"I have to declare a conflict of interest. It's in the faculty contract."

"I can just see it—you walking into the chair's office and saying, 'I can no longer supervise Marian. She drew me a cartoon and I kissed her.'"

He retreats behind his desk. Oscillates in his task chair, gripping the armrests.

"Do you want the whole department knowing about this? Do you want your colleagues snickering behind your back?"

"I don't believe they would—"

"Forget what you believe. What if someone mentions it to Delphine? How do you plan to explain this at home?"

She thinks, *How will I explain this at home?*

"This sort of procedure is confidential," he says quietly, and she can tell he believes it. "We need to keep the personal and the professional separate."

"Nothing in this department is confidential! It's a reality show with jargon." She's almost shouting.

"Shh," he says, casting an anxious glance at the door. "I want to be ethical. I want to do my job." He sounds defeated, as though he's losing more than an argument.

"A bit late for that, isn't it?"

Either too late or too soon. Why would she let him step down as her supervisor when nothing definitive has happened? Just a kiss, no more. And if it were more? He wants her, that much is clear. But will he want her next week? Next month? If he changes his mind about her, she will be left with nothing. Her dissertation will dissolve, and therefore her whole degree.

"Just—don't say anything to anyone, okay? This is my life, too."

He sighs, disappointed or frustrated or both. "What would you have me do?"

She doesn't reply.

Affair, she thinks, startling herself, trying out the word for the first time. She forces herself to wear it, move around in it, but feels as though she's put on some older woman's clothes.

Fling, she thinks instead.

She makes her way to the door, feeling his gaze on her back. Sex with Rémy. Would it bring relief, certainty? Or further confusion? No way of knowing, though her path seems set, as though laid down by someone other than herself.

"Marian. What do you want from me?"

She pauses with her hand on the doorknob. "You could start by inviting me over," she says.

He nods deliberately, as though performing his own calculations. As though he, too, must come to terms with an inevitable series of events. He pushes back his chair and comes over to kiss her.

"Je t'écris," he says.

Chapter Seventeen

Later that afternoon, Marian distractedly helps Juliette with her skates. Each year, after the last of the apples and gourds have sold and Waterton has put on its long winter face, the city's market square transforms into a rink. She's never been before— she's wimpy about the cold—but Juliette rented two pairs of skates and talked about chai lattes and scones at Java House afterwards. The promise of spiced drinks and carbs probably wasn't necessary: the temperature still hovers above zero, just shy of Marian's freezing point.

That morning Juliette attended a workshop offered by the university's Research Support Centre: "How Not to Feel Like a Fraud."

"I didn't know you felt like a fraud." Marian tightens Juliette's laces one crisscross at a time, starting from the bottom, like her mother used to do when she was little.

"Everyone feels that way. Three-quarters of the participants were profs."

"Did you learn anything?"

"Only that I'm not alone."

They wobble onto the ice.

The air is balmy, and a few of the other skaters have removed their toques or gloves. They appear quaint, anachronistic. Marian thinks of glacier flow and global warming and music boxes that spin figurines. A feat of engineering beneath the ice keeps it frozen, but for now winter and its routines seem constant, an immovable continent on which she glides.

"Do you think skating would have the same health benefits as running?" Juliette asks.

"Hm? Oh, almost certainly." Marian herself should try jump-roping or marathon training—see that gravity demands its due at every step. But not yet. She's high on the exquisite euphoria of possibility, a vague deliciousness that her body can only grasp at, and her rational mind isn't equipped to apprehend. When she left Rémy's office a few hours ago, he promised he would write to her. She's checked her email on her cell phone dozens of times since. His invitation is imminent; its consequences seem far away.

"I would make an awesome Canadian," Juliette says as she zigzags, her arms held out for balance.

"You look very authentic on skates." Marian feels the urge to confide in her friend, to tell her everything. She even begins constructing the tale in her mind, editing it so that the relationship of cause and effect seems inevitable: the series of miscommunications with David, his withdrawal, the feeling of connection with Rémy, the desire to get closer and closer. But what if Juliette doesn't understand, what if she takes David's side or simply says something critical, rational, and breaks the spell? Marian isn't ready to be jarred from her euphoric float. Reality can wait.

Juliette pushes off and sprints around the rink; Marian drifts. A man in a puffy red coat skates backwards towards her, bent over and deliberate, surfing the ice. His friends, who spill onto the rink from the far end, clap in appreciation.

He turns and shears the ice with his massive hockey skates. "You are so serious, Mary-Anne. You must be admiring my moves." Boone grins and gestures broadly to his friends. "You see, I have coaches. We hold ARTus meetings at the rink."

Juliette glides over, and Marian introduces her to Boone.

"Julie-Mary from French," Boone says as he gamely kisses Juliette's hand. He tells her she looks like Juliette Binoche, and she doesn't seem to mind, even though she isn't usually susceptible to that brand of flattery. Marian looks past them to Boone's friends, who whoop and perform a sliding line dance. They sport vintage paisleys and corduroys, a faux-fur stole here, a neon scarf there, the kind of artsy group that Marian pictures her parents being part of when they were young.

The woman in the neon scarf, who is rounder and older than the others, breaks away now from the group, traces a slow figure eight, and winds herself into a single axel. Her purple hair fans and settles. She hovers and spins and collects admiring glances as she goes.

"You like Annick's moves better than mine. I'll try not to be offended. Her parents were figure skaters. I've seen videos on YouTube."

"For real?"

"You question the word according to Boone?" He chuckles. "Skating is not her only talent, you know. There are also the comics. You know this of course. You've read her."

There was no author photo on the jacket of the book Boone lent her. So this is its creator, a little chubbier than Marian expected, but just as vibrant. Marian recalls the story of a Montreal adolescent who joins a punk band; they set old country and western lyrics to their own music and play the city's underground scene. She loved how the cartoonist— how Annick—used abundant black gouache and stark white contrasting lines to create a sense of chaos and innovation.

"She skates as well as she cartoons," Marian says.

"She skates in our direction. Tell her you like her work. She will do a spin for you, maybe."

When Annick stops in front of them, smiling, Boone tells her that he has one admirer and two French speakers for her.

"Des louanges dans ma langue," Annick says in a strong Montreal accent. They chat for a few minutes and Marian learns that she is cross-appointed between Cultural Studies and Art History.

Boone tells Annick that Marian has been reading *Don't take this the wrong way, but* and that she once drew an excellent cartoon of him. "She saw deep into my thoughtful soul, which now hangs on the fridge."

Juliette nudges Marian's skate with her toe-pick. "Where's my portrait? I'll hang it above my carrel at the department. It'll create more demand for your work."

"You know I have plenty of work to do as it is."

Annick loosens her scarf. Beneath it she wears a bright pink feather on a silver chain. "My to-do list never respected my art. That's why I threw out the list."

"But you're an artist. That *is* your agenda."

Annick makes a French tut-tutting noise. "I'm a woman who gives herself permission."

"There's a skill," Juliette says. "They should have a seminar on that."

"Mary-Anne will learn," Boone says. "I can already see her brain churning. She is arted-up, I tell you."

"Boone, we've had this conversation. My brain churns scholarship. Mostly, anyway."

"Alors il faut tomber amoureuse," Annick says.

Marian blushes and looks away. This woman reads minds. Aloud.

"You must fall ass over ears in love." Annick motions to the appropriate body parts. "Create a character and love her and you will be able to justify anything on her behalf. What she wants, where she ends up. You'll give her places to go and you'll follow her as though she's all that matters in the world. And the people she meets along the way? You'll fall in love with them, too."

"Is that how you do it?"

"Every day."

Marian feels not encouraged, but envious. How does Annick take her own work seriously? Without feeling that someone is looking over her shoulder, a floating, faceless eyeball whose gaze burns judgment. Marian draws for a joke, for catharsis. To pass the time or procrastinate. She would never call it art.

"Boone's fridge is probably exposure enough."

"You embarrassed that people will see her?" Annick replies. "No cartoonist ever cared about that. Your character will pick her nose in public, and you won't even mind. You'll love her too much for that, too."

Marian is quiet. She would love to create a world, one to block her ears and rock her if this one falls apart. She doesn't have the guts.

Chapter Eighteen

Rémy's genteel email inviting her to brunch makes Marian think not of romantic getaways, but of doilies and English breakfast tea and doting aunts. Brunch, the difference between her and Rémy and more sordid adulterers, those who fornicate in bathroom stalls and seedy hotel rooms.

It was about the omelettes, they will say afterwards. The sex was entirely unexpected.

He has instructed her to go to the back entrance of the manor. No snow has fallen recently, and the garden is brown and frowsy. Crumpled vines hang limply on the trellises. She raps on the doorframe.

"Entrez," he says when he comes to the door, as though she were a formal guest, or a student who has come to his office to discuss her grades. Dressed in brown cords and a beige wool sweater, his white shirt-collar poking out, he is even more a professor at home than at work. His shiny brown loafers look recently polished. He kisses her, tasting of mint, and takes her coat and scarf and hangs them in the closet. She places her boots tidily on the mat and feels awkward in her sock feet.

He tells her that the manor was built in 1890; this apartment used to be the kitchen. She pictures servants baking bread, and bourgeois ladies ringing bells. The apartment is small, open-concept. She wonders which touches are feminine. The glass bowl filled with glass fruit on the glass coffee table? The taupe throw pillows at each end of the too-white sofa?

No photos adorn the walls or bookshelves—he must have removed them before she got here, out of decency towards her or Delphine, who apparently left this morning for her nephew's birthday party in Montreal.

He asks, "Would you like coffee or juice or both?"

"Juice. Thank you," she replies, and he sets out two glasses.

She grates cheese and chops peppers next to him at the kitchen island while he cracks eggs. He turns on the stove to preheat the pan and chatters about the curriculum committee. The curriculum committee? She hopes there is a parallel track in his mind that is thinking about what he will do to her, some part of him anticipating sweaty, creaturely pleasure. As for her, the wet ache that led her here is vanishing. In its place, she feels the urge to urinate.

The bathroom is through the bedroom. The bed is pristine—all ivory tucks and shams. Can she make love in this bed? Another woman woke up here this morning, squared the sheets before carefully folding her pyjamas or nightgown into an overnight bag. Does Rémy expect all beds to be this well arranged, does he expect the women in his life to arrange them for him? She wants to rumple something, swoop in and peck at this perfection.

In the bathroom is a beautiful old tub. She's pictured him in a narrow shower, cramped and splashy, no room for romance. She sits down to pee and notices a copy of *Ulysses* on the floor; it seems incongruous with the bottle of Head and Shoulders on the rack above the tub. Joyce as bathroom reading; *yes my mountain flower* and dandruff shampoo. Yet the book doesn't seem to have been placed there for her benefit. Its cover is frayed, the pages bent. A scholar even in his most private moments. Is this authenticity, or deep-seated pretension?

She flushes, washes her hands, and dries them on what looks like a new hand towel. Is she really about to concern herself with silverware and digestion, and wonder if her breath smells like egg? She wishes for booze or the back seat of a car, anything but desire turned to stone at another woman's table.

When she returns, she reclines on the sofa in what she hopes is a provocative position. "Tell me what it is you think I am," she says in English.

Rémy throws the whisk in the sink. "Sorry?"

"In your office a few weeks ago, you said, 'You are what you are, which complicates matters.' I want to know what I am."

"Fisher for compliments," he says. "Is this the expression?"

"No," she says.

"You're a brat," he says in French, and turns off the stove before crossing the room.

He leans down to kiss her, lips trembling. He's nervous.

She traces her hands down his legs and tugs at his shoelaces; helps him remove his shoes. "Undress me," she says, and pulls him onto the sofa.

"Wouldn't you be more comfortable—"

She places a hand on his crotch.

"It's just—the upholstery—" He gestures helplessly to the sofa.

She sighs. "Yeah, okay."

He leads her to the bedroom, and they collapse onto the bed. She shoves a fancy bolster pillow out of the way. They neck and paw at each other for a few minutes. Rémy rolls onto his elbow and makes a face, sheepish. "I don't have any condoms."

"I brought some," Marian says, and digs two out of the pocket of her jeans. She thinks, *And if I hadn't swung by the pharmacy? Would we just stop now, hold hands?*

They undress, fondling each other as they go. Before long she feels chilly, but the bedspread is tucked tight, and they would likely have to stand up again to get under it. She wriggles a little while Rémy's lips trail down her chest and navel, and his head settles between her thighs, which is gentlemanly, him putting her first, except she can only enjoy it on a theoretical level—cunnilingus just isn't her thing. Really what she's wishing for is her vibe, which is at home because it seemed weird and indecent to pack it, even though it has its own discreet travel pouch. Too late. For now, she must try to forget Rémy's tongue on her clit, and concentrate instead on the *idea* of his tongue on her clit—the idea of her *liking* his tongue on her clit—

Except that she makes the mistake of opening her eyes.

She's never before seen Rémy's head from this angle. There, right at the crown, is a bald spot. It's about a half-inch in diameter, or maybe three-quarters, and will certainly grow larger over the years. The bald spot reminds her of old men, and babies, and as she gazes through her bent knees, and watches the bald spot bob, she thinks how it looks like she's giving birth to a breech Rémy.

Half-eaten omelettes left on the table, he starts the same routine: lips trailing down her breasts and belly to her nether parts. After a minute or two he looks up, smirks. "You're faking it," he says in French.

"No, I'm not!"

"Mmhm," he says.

"Okay, fine, maybe a little."

"Some feminist." He flops onto his back beside her. "So, teach me what you like."

She blushes. She's not used to fucking in French. "It's hard to explain," she says.

"You'd better try, or I'll get bored."

"Okay. For starters, use your hand."

"Like this?"

"Yeah, except don't drag your finger . . . just—pressure."

"Better?"

"Better."

After she comes, she says, "So you think I'm a bad feminist."

"I think you showed up in my office wearing a mini skirt and talking about desire."

"A pencil skirt, I'll have you know."

"Close enough."

He disappears into the bathroom, and she hears the stream of urine hit the bowl. He emerges and retrieves his boxers on the far side of the bed. "See, that's the trouble when you espouse an ideology," he says, pulling on the boxers. "It's like being a Christian. As soon as you get drunk on a Saturday night or cheat on your taxes, you're not Christly enough. But if you don't aspire to purity, no one cares. Hypocrisy is only possible if you commit."

"That seems grossly unfair."

"Life is unfair, child."

She swats him with a bolster pillow. "Patriarchal shit."

"Ah, now see 'patriarchy' is your term, not mine. It's like God for atheists. Doesn't exist."

"I'm embarrassed to be with you."

"You would be if anyone knew."

"Touché."

"This will solve things." He pads across the room and from the tightly packed bookshelf extracts a volume, spends a minute thumbing through it. Marian tries to see the title, but it's obscured by his fingers.

He reads aloud in French: "Of the jumble of thoughts that crossed her mind, a single, harsh impression remained, as frozen as her smile: at this moment, she must bet everything she still was, all her physical charm, in a high-stakes gamble on happiness."

Marian searches the files of her mind, looking for this quotation. "Wait—don't tell me . . . Ack, I can't remember."

"Gabrielle Roy. *Bonheur d'occasion.*"

"Yes! Florentine is setting herself up to have her heart broken by the dapper Jean Levesque. She'll eventually invite him back to her place when her family isn't home . . . Poor

Florentine. Abandoned, pregnant, left to marry Jean's best friend. Not a romantic passage you've chosen. Are you giving me a warning, Professor?"

"Quite the opposite. This is intimacy. I'm sharing my shelf of wonder with you."

Marian smirks. "Your shelf of wonder?"

"Books that are wonderful. Ever since I started teaching, I've had this fantasy that I get to give a course where the only criterion for selection is the mysterious beauty of the story. Nothing else. There would be no rhyme or reason, no regard for chronology or geography or literary theory. Just books I love." He sighs dramatically. "A unicorn course, as it were. Completely impossible."

Marian dresses and examines the contents of the shelf. Camus, Marguerite Duras, Anne Hébert, Michel Tremblay, Nabokov, Stendhal, Proust, Hubert Aquin, Faulkner, Marie-Claire Blais, Cormac McCarthy, Flaubert.

"Read to me," she says.

They see each other a few times a week in December. Rémy carefully arranges their visits around Delphine's work schedule, but rarely speaks of these logistics to Marian.

He first reads to her from Marguerite Duras' *L'Amant*. Marian cries when the lovers part; cracks jokes about younger women and older men. For his part, he reminds her she's not that young and he's not that old. He reaches next for Hubert Aquin, but she refuses to let this author into bed with her. Too violent, too much of a misogynist, she tells him. He bristles, but she prevails. She asks for Cormac McCarthy instead, that old cowboy. She laughs at Rémy's accent as he reads and helps him pronounce the English.

Now she wants Anne Hébert, now Proust.

"No one ever gets past the madeleine," she says. "Anything but the madeleine."

He leafs through *Du côté de chez Swann* and reads a passage featuring mountains and rivers and beds of watercress, and the dream of a woman who will enrich the narrator with her love.

Rémy places the open book on the bed and kisses Marian's shoulder. "You're turning me into a romantic. Let's never stop doing this."

"You mean it?"

"I do."

She snuggles closer and rests her cheek on his shoulder. Maybe this relationship isn't so temporary. And why should it be, if they are happy together? She can almost see the outline of a life: the dinner conversations, engaging or sweetly banal; the choreography of familiar lovemaking, followed by the pleasures of sleep; trips to the grocery store; trips abroad. Her life with David seems distant, as though she's viewing it from the window of an airplane. Maybe she's headed towards something entirely new, and that's okay. Shouldn't she be open to all possibilities?

She flips onto her belly, and Rémy reads to her for a while longer, then with his finger spells authors' names on her back so she can guess.

"Mmm," she says. "Didn't get that one. Do it again."

When she gets home, David is in the kitchen, humming a tune she can't place and sponging the inside of the fridge.

He kisses her on the cheek. "How was the library?"

"Good." She eyes the mishmash on the counter—jars of ancient condiments and stir fry sauces, fruits and veggies in varying degrees of health. "I'm really making headway on this chapter," she lies.

"Glad to hear it."

"You seem like you're in a good mood today."

He peers into a jar of salsa and sniffs it. "You think? Yeah, I guess I am."

"That's great to see," she says, noting her own rising anxiety.

He palpates a petrified orange, tosses it in the garbage. "Want to go out tonight? Get a drink or something?"

She searches for the best before date on a jar of mustard, stalling. Places the jar back on the counter.

"Actually, I was hoping to work this evening. You know, keep the momentum going."

"Right. No problem," David says, and sticks his head back in the fridge, humming.

Chapter Nineteen

Eight and a half exams are stacked between Rémy and his chorizo sandwich, and another seven between the chorizo sandwich and a medium-sized cup of burnt coffee purchased from the new machine on the ground floor. Eight more still between the coffee and the end of French 236, "Studies in the Québec Novel," the grades of which are due by 4:30 p.m. today, December 21, to Registrar Sally Travers, whom he hates, now that he thinks about it, although he's never met her (her snide administrative emails; her strict deadlines). Hates her the same way he hates the coffee and the exams and the students who wrote them in great looping script—their inane thoughts plopped onto the page like bird droppings—all of them demonstrating in one ignorant swoop their indifference over the course of the semester not only to his discussions of narratology—fair enough!—but also to his careful and engaging explanations of palimpsest.

"Palimpsest refers to the other stories that got erased when the main historical narrative was formed," writes Denise Lillis, student #1579930, confusing the definition with that of counter-historical narratives, a concept he mentioned in passing at the beginning of the term, on his way to more relevant topics. Denise has the fat, crayonish printing of a fourth grader. She writes on every line instead of every second line, as indicated in the exam instructions, and has created a running word-count tally in the margins of her exam booklet. Total: 1008 words. Rémy has read five hundred and three of them.

He awards one and a half out of ten to question number two of Denise Lillis' exam. He won't bother to correct her unfortunate mistakes, because in all likelihood no one other than he will look at this exam, not even Sally Travers. If Ms. Lillis ever chooses to appeal her grade in FREN 236, the university will package the exam into a flimsy, yet tightly sealed envelope marked "Confidential" and deliver it to him through interdepartmental mail, allowing him three days to insert relevant commentary and corrections before she sees it.

This arrangement suited him just fine when he first started teaching at Waterton. If the students would not come to a deeper understanding of literature as a result of his reading their exam booklets, why bother marking them up? Why not slap a grade on them and keep going? Maybe even do like Denise Lillis and her pug-nosed, green-haired classmate Fiona Talbot, who, as he sits here fumbling with this crappy pen, are likely feting the term's end in someone's shag-carpeted, disco-ball dappled living room, red plastic beer cups in hand, already having forgotten the content of his course.

Happy to churn out grades and return to his research: that is how he felt in the beginning. Now, having taught for several years, having devoted too many hours to the dissemination of knowledge, he would like to bust into the vault of exams (rumoured to be somewhere in the basement of Phillips Hall), exhume those he's graded over the years, and carry them up and out, maybe into that grand, skylit common area in the environmental sciences complex, where he will magically gather his departed students and explain to them why the words in the exam booklet should matter to them, even today—

The phone rings.

"Oui âllo?" Rémy says, but a chorus of other voices chime in.

"Âllo?" says Babette.

"Normand Latour à l'appareil," says Normand.

"Oui bonjour Rémy," Adèle Faucher says, and Babette and Normand hang up on the other extensions.

Adèle asks how the grading slog is going. Rémy says it's going the same as last term and the term before.

She laughs politely. "I was wondering if we could meet in my office this afternoon. It's a delicate matter, I'm afraid."

A delicate matter. He thinks of Marian, feels the overwhelming need to stall.

"Can it wait?"

"I'll try to be brief," Adèle says, and before hanging up confirms that Rémy is free at one o'clock.

How much does Adèle guess at? He's been careful, most of the time. Lately he's been closing the door when Marian comes by his office. Is that it, the revelatory nature of a closed door? Maybe Adèle has been waiting to see if he'll come forward. Disclose.

Which is what he tried to do in the first place! Well, before Marian ended up naked in his bed. It was Marian who forbade it, Marian in her naïveté and stubborn panic. Now he's the one who will have to wear the consequences. There will be a great black mark on his file in the department office: "Undisclosed romantic relationship with a student." Who reads these files? Do they go the way of the exam booklets? Or does the dean's office get a copy? Will Jean-Louis soon be smirking in his administrative tower?

This is not the way the year was supposed to go—dragged by the ear into Adèle Faucher's office, red-faced and stuttering. He was supposed to be on top of his obligations. Now he'll have to do damage control, not let himself be stripped down and castrated. He must arm himself with pithy statements about transferring Marian to someone else's care, disclose first, before Adèle wrenches it out of him and uses the information as she pleases. Too much is at stake: his career, his public face, both of his relationships. He does not want his hand forced.

He arrives at Adèle's office seven minutes late, because he's the one in control, and because his chorizo sandwich didn't agree with him. Adèle is shaking pellets from a yellow packet into the aquarium behind her desk. The pellets sink to the bottom and her goldfish, who have been floating sleepily inside, flicker and angle their shining bodies downwards to suck at them, tail fins fluttering.

The fish glow like secrets in the blue light.

Adèle wears ugly disc earrings the same yellow as the fish food packet. They bob as she tosses the packet in the garbage. "Did you know that they only grow if they have an appropriate amount of space? Because the tank is small, the fish are small too."

"How interesting. I hadn't heard that," Rémy says. *Everyone knows that*, he thinks, as he lingers awkwardly in the middle of her office, because she hasn't yet invited him to sit. He's seen goldfish as meaty as trout in the fountains of posh office buildings in Montreal.

"Remarkable how they thrive or are stunted based on their environment."

The fish continue to suckle at the pebbles. They don't look unhappy, but how would he know what a depressed fish looks like? Maybe their little wet bodies are exploding with sadness.

Adèle presses her finger to the glass and sighs tragically. "I sometimes wonder . . ." She finally invites him to sit down, which he does, crossing his leg over his knee and leaning back to suggest that he's comfortable and relaxed.

"In fact, it's good you called," he says.

"Oh?"

"This delicate business you've referred to. I've been meaning to talk to you about it."

"Well that's convenient, then. I didn't realize you had the same idea. Makes this conversation much easier for me."

"Indeed," he agrees. "The smooth functioning of the department depends on taking care of matters efficiently."

"Aptly put."

"So, I think we understand each other. No need for alarm. It happens all the time, which is why there are protocols in place. We'll just take care of the necessary paperwork—what is that, exactly? Once it's official, Marian can choose another supervisor. I'm sure we don't have to be too elaborate. 'Contact exceeds boundaries of student-professor relationship.' That should suffice."

Adèle touches her finger to her earring and tilts her head. A gesture of feminine complicity. He's misjudged her. She's a woman who is pro-liaison, pro-romance, one who can justify the desires of others because she has desires of her own. She knows room must be made for love. Maybe she's experienced something similar. An affair with her husband's best friend. Or, in her younger days, a fling with a favourite professor.

The silence goes on too long, and slowly Rémy understands that Adèle is neither nostalgic nor approving, but at a loss for words.

"Eh bien," she says. "Eh bien. I did wonder."

The fish are done eating, and all but one have returned to their somnolent state. The lone wakeful fish puckers and stares at Rémy with one tireless black eyeball.

"Voilà," Rémy says. He fears that he's puckering as stupidly as the fish.

Adèle fiddles with her other earring. At last she speaks. Slowly, nonchalantly. "Your personal life is your personal life. I see no reason to bring the department into this. You two are adults. You can manage."

"But there are protocols," he demurs, even though he's beginning to understand that she doesn't give a damn for protocols.

"Well, perhaps. But word tends to get out about this kind of thing. Especially because of the supervisory switch. It *will* follow you. Students gossiping among themselves and all that. Plus, there's the problem of your tenure review this year. This won't serve you at all, in the long run. It truly won't." Adèle purses her lips and shakes her head. The yellow earrings bob. He half expects her to cluck her tongue.

"But that's just it. If I follow university policy, they can't hold it against me."

"True, true. But there's the trouble of public opinion. If some other female student gets it into her head that she's not safe in your classroom, if she writes a letter to the review committee, if she . . . Well, you get the idea."

"But I'm always appropriate in the classroom! That's absurd."

"Of course you are, of course. You and I both know this. Oh, I don't think there's any real risk here to your career. But you know such situations can be . . . uncomfortable." Adèle releases her earring and leans forward. "Anyway, let's not worry about that just now. I think it's settled. On the other hand, there *is* an issue of real concern that we need to discuss. Aurélie Thériault has been hospitalized for cirrhosis of the liver. No, don't call or send a card. She wants to keep things hush-hush. Made me promise not to say anything. People automatically think of her drinking." Adèle winces. "Anyway, it means we don't have a coordinator for French 102. I realize that you've already got one first-year course on your schedule, but your French 312 is under-enrolled, so we're going to cancel it and move you over to the 102. The syllabus is prepped, you just have to implement it, so to speak."

"Coordinator of French 102."

As Adèle walks him to the door, he thinks of poor Aurélie and her liver, of her husband sleeping in hospital armchairs, but also of his own skin. He is embarrassed, but safe.

The Waterton Mall in December is as horrifying as Rémy remembers, but after he has given up his luddite identity and begrudgingly bought himself a cell phone—a smartphone, no less!—and has skirted the giant Christmas tree festooned with shiny little gift-wrapped boxes, and sauntered past the kiosk selling monographed slippers, he notices the lacy orange bra on the hip-thrusting mannequin, and thinks, 1) that looks nothing like Christmas, and 2) that would look good on Marian. In the moment, he's certain that Marian will be tickled by lace the colour of a cheery gumball. But once he's got the bra home and is about to hide it behind the shoe rack in his closet, he loses confidence. What if she accuses him of treating her like a marmalade sex kitten? He scours his bookshelves and selects a copy of Anaïs Nin's *Delta of Venus* that could pass for new and nestles it in the tissue of the pink gift bag. Sex of the mind.

The next day, Marian pulls the bra out of the bag, then the book, and keeps digging. "It didn't come as a set?" she says. "No panties?"

"Um, no."

"Huh."

"Put it on."

She holds up the bra, which appears more lurid in daylight than in the inspirational lighting of the lingerie store. "You first." She dangles the bra from one taunting finger.

He deserves this.

He removes his shirt and shrugs on the bra but is too clumsy to reach back and fasten the clasp. The bra hangs flaccidly, cupping the air. "You'll miss me when you're in Thunder Bay," he says, referring to their impending separation over the Christmas break.

Marian grins. "I will. Now take it off and do what you do best."

He tosses the bra on the floor and leafs through the first few pages. "Her sex was like a giant hothouse flower," he reads, and Marian giggles and asks for more.

Not long ago, in the waiting room of a doctor's office, Rémy read an article entitled "How to Turn Her On (and On and On)." He learned that women require an average of thirty-six minutes of foreplay, and men, six. The article was referring not to bubble baths and dinner out, but foreplay of the blunt, physical sort: a lick here, a stroke there. Oooh aaah.

He never thought he would work so hard in the foreplay department, nor so unconventionally. Forget the nibble of the ear, the massage of the thigh. Marian wants to be read to—forever and ever, Amen—and he gives her what she wants—Marie-Claire Blais, Gabrielle Roy, Gustave Flaubert—he even reads to her in English, at her request, his tongue bending itself around foreign words, while his waning nether part remains tucked chastely beneath the sheet. In the beginning they fucked first, read second. Lately, only after his biceps are fatigued from holding a book, and the first signs of hoarseness creep into his throat, will she climb on top of him and work her wet magic.

Last night after his trip to the mall, at Delphine's insistence, he watched a nature program on TV about a fussy Australian species, the bowerbird, famous for its elaborate courtship rituals. The male bowerbird inhabits a permanent structure that has taken him years to build, an avian condo erected out of sticks at the base of a tree. When looking to mate, the male devotes himself to fetching attractive objects and arranging them outside his bower: flowers, berries, iridescent beetles, snail shells, colourful plastic straws. The female's decision to copulate rests solely on the artistic quality of his offerings. Are his floral arrangements symmetrical enough? Did he select the shiniest beetles? If his workmanship is sound, and his sense of style tantalizing, she will lift her tail feather and let him mount her in a flurry.

Rémy never set out to become a bowerbird. It's hard work, earning the right to copulate. Nor is the reading ritual that he displays for Marian merely a means to an end. He wants her to want him, for himself, for the words he gives her, for his dedication to story, his belonging to the literary tribe. He relishes the power of the storyteller.

If only the words he had to offer, which she devours so hungrily, were not the words of others, but his own.

Chapter Twenty

Marian opens the back door to her father's sedan, and out into
the snow jumps Kong, who marks a cedar before scrambling
up the steps to the house. An arm pushes the door open before
he reaches the top. "What a handsome Christmas doggy you
are—oh, you are, indeed!—welcome home, sweetie, I baked
you cardamom buns, and David, honey, let Robert get those
suitcases!" The arm and exclamations are her mother's, strung
together like twinkle lights.

The house smells of butter and yeast and plummy spices.
Robert hurries past Marian and David and up the stairs with
their suitcases. Some tall men lope and stoop; her father leaps.
When he comes back down, he says, "Two kids and a dog. Just
what we were missing. Did you change your hair? You did,
too, don't tell me you didn't. It was longer this time last year.
I notice these things." He removes his parka and fur hat and
leaves them on the chair in the entryway. The hat might once
have belonged to a Russian peasant.

"It's about time to put that beast down," Marian tells him.

"You can't throw a good hat out just because it's a bit worn.
You worry too much about appearances, you and your mother
both."

"Don't be fooled," David says. "When Marian's at home
studying, she wears sweats with holes in the crotch."

"A hole in the leg, thanks."

Her father's cheeks crinkle as he smiles. "This hat will make it another season yet, Muffet. You should've brought the pants home for your mother to fix."

"I made some mulled wine," Barbara calls from the kitchen. "Except I had to leave out the orange peel. Your father was in charge of buying oranges."

"Great tree, Mom," Marian says as she and David stuff their coats in the closet and her father plugs in the lights. A mishmash of ornaments glimmer against the artificial needles.

"Isn't it lovely? Your dad carried it up this morning. He did such a nice job."

"As pretty as last year," Marian says, teasing. It *is* last year's tree: at Barbara's urging, Robert threw a couple of garbage bags over it and David helped carry it down to the basement fully dressed before he and Marian caught their flight back to Waterton. Barbara said she was too busy to take all those ornaments off only to put them on again.

The cardamom buns lie on a cooling rack next to the crockpot. David is already going for his second bun. Marian has been trying to eat fewer carbs since the night of the Halloween party when she ate too many chips, but isn't about to say so in case her mother scolds her. Kong will gladly eat her share: he's ignoring his own food and crouches stealthily at David's feet, hoping a crumb will drop.

Barbara pulls some glass mugs from the cupboard. "Eat! I'll pour."

Marian shoves a doughy roll in her mouth. The phone rings, and Barbara picks up. "No, you can't speak to my mommy," she says. "She's dead." Marian smiles as she chews. She's heard her use this line before. "Yes, the lady of the house is me. Why are you bothering people on the twenty-third of December, and tell me do you have a family? Do you participate in some sort of festive tradition? Is it fair to say you wouldn't sign up for anything over the phone the day before Christmas

or Rosh Hashanah or Ramadan or whatever?" She lets loose a
few expletives and hangs up.

"Aren't you the one who's working towards a Christmas
boycott?" Robert says. "You can't fault the person, seeing as how
you're not devout yourself."

Barbara clucks her tongue. "There was never talk of any
boycott, it's a redefinition we're aiming towards, a rejigging.
You *know* that a turkey dinner means an obligation towards the
potato."

David licks his fingers and wipes them on his napkin. "I
could have done the mashing."

"We needed to do away with the hullaballoo for a couple of
years," Barbara says. "As a sort of experiment. The ideology is
too twisted."

"Amen to that," Marian said. "Praying to a brawling male
infant, born of a so-called virgin."

"You forgot to mention the glittering consumerism," David
says.

"Hold on. We're not going to become those people," Robert
says.

"Which people?" Marian asks.

"The ones with their heads so firmly up their own butts
that they can't mull some wine and enjoy a cinnamon stick."
Robert fishes one of the sticks out of the crockpot and holds
it up, dripping. "Look at this. This is festive tree bark we're
consuming. I'm not giving up my festive tree bark."

"Nor should you," David agrees.

"I don't miss the turkey," Marian says. "Last year's schnitzel
was pretty good."

"Bah, it was dry," Barbara says. "But at least it wasn't potato."

Robert gnaws on his cinnamon stick. "Can't we just enjoy
ourselves anymore?"

"We are enjoying ourselves," Barbara says, emphatic. "Who
isn't having a good time? Anyone? You see, Robert? There you

go again, stirring the pot when all you were meant to do is buy oranges."

The conversation turns to politics—the anti-abortion legislation in North Carolina and the closure of a southern Ontario automotive plant and its reopening in Indiana, where labour is cheap because the workers aren't paid a proper living wage—then on to Barbara and Robert's activist days at the University of Toronto in the seventies. Marian drifts off, inwardly smiling at the memory of Rémy decked out in a tangerine bra. When she tunes back in, David is reminiscing about his and Marian's own time in undergrad. He slips his arm around her. "So, she tells this guy, sure, you can sit down. Because she's being polite, I guess, and because there are no open tables. And he sits next to her and looks like he's making small talk, and I'm sitting further down the table with this couple we know from psych class, half listening and watching out of the corner of my eye. This was first year—we were hanging out at the Monkey's Tail. The guy tells Marian his name is Godfrey, and he runs on about how he dropped out of an art program at the college. That's what he was doing before he came to trivia night, he says—drawing. I see him pull this sketch book out of his bag and flip through it, and Marian looking on, bored, you know. After a couple of minutes she takes a pen out of her purse and yanks the sketchbook from this Godfrey guy and starts drawing. And the guy's turning redder and redder, and he's running his hand through his greasy hair. Suddenly he gets up, slams his notebook shut, and storms out. I ask her what happened. She tells me he was showing her his very own porno sketches, so she decided to take his sketchbook and draw him a cartoon. I ask what kind of cartoon. She says, one of an ugly guy with a girl who has her back to him and is whispering across the table, 'Who *is* this perv?'" David shakes with laughter.

"Tit for tat," Barbara says. "Sorry," she adds when Robert groans.

"I had completely forgotten about that guy," Marian says.

"You were wearing that striped dress I liked. It was the week you pierced your eyebrow. You were all kinds of awesome." David rubs the nape of her neck. Her skin tingles, but she wishes she could pull away.

"David's an archivist at heart," Robert says. "Your memories are in good hands, Muffet. Total recall of your salad days. That's the stuff."

Barbara removes the crockpot lid, stirs the mulled wine, and says that when they're old and senile and can't so much as hold a ladle anymore, she's counting on David to remind them of who they were. David says he'd very much like to perform that service.

The next morning, David suits up to go cross-country skiing at Kaministiquia with Robert. He tries to talk Marian into coming along, but she rolls over in bed and says she should really help her mother. He kisses her hairline, and while she's still wondering whether or not it's okay for her to enjoy this gesture, he slips out of the room, latching the door behind him. His mood has lightened these past few days. Is he putting on a show for her parents? But even in private he's affectionate and even cheerful, and he was behaving this way before they arrived. She's embarrassed to admit to herself that she's been using his withdrawal to justify her relationship with Rémy. But can she really help the way she feels now that she's spent endless afternoons in conversation with Rémy, reading with him, and yes, fucking him? And if she accepts David's affection, will she not be even more duplicitous, unbearable to herself? And if she accepts his affection and *likes* it, then what?

"Je t'aime," Rémy said to her as he held her close two days ago. "And I want to make what's between us real."

Her chest was pressed against his, and she could feel the vibration of his words move through her. "It is real. But I get what you mean. We exist in a bubble."

"Let's do something about that soon," he said, stroking her hair.

She hesitated for a moment before asking, "You would leave Delphine for me?"

"Of course," he said, as though this outcome were self-evident.

At the time, his words exuded their own internal logic, although now she has trouble imagining how she might transition from Rémy's secret lover and student to his (public) girlfriend and . . . then what? Better not to concentrate on the logistics. Too easy to panic, to assume that her identity will change in ways she could never control or predict. And her friends? What will Juliette and Patrick think of her? Will they abandon her? Will they feel she has abandoned them, taking up with her professor, lying about it?

She stares at the ceiling of her old bedroom—bright yellow like a dandelion—and tries to recapture the initial excitement she felt hearing Rémy's words. They mean that she is not really here in this room. She's drifting away from here, away from this bed and its mismatched sheets printed with posies and Greek keys. Or maybe she's not drifting, but is so deeply buried that no one can see her. It's as though she's not yet been born.

If she's not yet born, she can reinvent this life, won't need to pry pieces of it away from David. She won't wonder if she's losing a compartment of herself that she can't get at without him opening it up for her to see—and if she's ripping something irreplaceable away from him as well.

The sheets smell like David, his earthy skin. If she's buried here, he's buried with her.

She closes her eyes. It's just a bed.

Marian is watching *A Christmas Story*. David and her father are still skiing, and her mother has hurried out to buy olive oil and parsley. Kong, who got up this morning with David, now lolls

on the armchair by the window, basking in the late morning
sun. A bird flies past, and his furry eyelids flutter.

She's never asked Rémy if he likes dogs, although she often
talks to him about Kong. He did mention a cat once, but if she
remembers correctly, it wasn't his. He didn't call it by name.
She doesn't know if he likes holidays, either, or how he would
feel about this living room, this house, its mindful clutter.
Would he think it excessive, maybe even precious? Intentionally
different. Trying too hard. A faded, mounted Talking Heads
poster; an Indian yoga mat; an elegant yet disturbing papier
mâché Medusa that Marian finds impossible to dust; an
elementary school photo of Barbara, ten years old, plump
and gap-toothed, stuffed into a blue poplin dress with a daisy
appliqué at the chest. Something old, something new, although
you can't always tell which is which: an antique spool rack,
complete with thread; Robert's undergraduate diploma, cheaply
framed and hung upside down; paintings by local artists, some
naive, some well-executed; a plaque that reads "MY LAWYER
SAID I COULD;" a grouping that includes a spoon collection,
a copper peacock, and a golden plaster mould of Marian's
hand at six years old; several wall quilts featuring glittering
seashores, computer motherboards, bonsai and evergreen trees,
aliens, vines, obelisks, cogs and wheels, and Jesus. What would
Rémy do with this sensory overload? Would he gawk? Exclaim?
Perhaps he would yawn. Radical politics with a patina. Genteel
and shabby.

Maybe he would dive in, understand a subtext she doesn't,
find meaning in one of the objects that no longer register for
her because they have become too familiar. But wouldn't it be
better if he simply gazed past it all, saw a way out of this maze
of family and habit, of love defined a certain way?

The first time David came home with Marian to Thunder
Bay, he stood in front of the shiny mould of her six-year-old
hand and told Barbara that his own mother used to have
a plaster cast of his baby feet hanging in her kitchen. He

complimented Barbara's creative use of sashing in her quilts—
the way the alien toes and bonsai trees curled over the sides
of each block. His Nana was quite the sewer, he explained,
and also a rug-maker. She had an enormous loom in the attic
on which she wove strips of old clothes into colourful mats,
nicer than those made by the other ladies down the road. She
sometimes built up a bundle of scraps for years before sitting
down to make use of it.

The following Christmas, David gave Barbara and Robert
one of these mats as a Christmas gift. It had never been used; it
had been earmarked for him when his Nana died, and stayed in
storage at his mother's place. The mat was navy with slashes of
white and yellow, and it smelled of the lavender his mother had
rolled up in it to keep moths away. Barbara unfurled it in her
sewing room, beneath a large, framed poster of a beady-eyed
Shakespeare that an artist friend had painted over with glitter
so that the bard shone like a disco queen.

"Good work, Dave," Robert said, as though David had
woven the rug himself.

"Mmhm mhm," Barbara said. "Fits right in there, and, ooh,
would you look at that careful patterning. Like a drawbridge
here, and a crack of light under a door just there. Ah, I bet she
imagined things. I bet she imagined all kinds of things, your
Nana."

David loved Barbara and Robert before he even met them.
On his and Marian's first date—a Coen Brothers movie—
Marian told him about the time she'd come home from school
crying, because one of her little friends had called her family a
bunch of weirdos.

"Are we weird, Mommy?" she'd sniffled.

Barbara had hugged her tight and kissed the top of her
head. "Oh, my honey," she said. "I sure hope so."

David admires this life that Barbara and Robert have built:
kitschy and a little odd; every object a tribute, a story secreted
away. Or maybe he simply envies them like Marian envies them

now, this complicity they've built, their belief that every couple needs a Genesis story, a landscape to build on, once the choice to be together has been made.

Four years ago, she chose and married David. He is family now.

She can choose again. Can't she?

When her mother comes home from running errands, they dump a jumble of bows and two pairs of scissors on the dining room table. Marian wraps a fleece sweater by a fancy outdoor brand for David, and a canoe paddle and a couple of records for her dad (an original pressing of Television's Marquee Moon, gently used, and the reissued Springsteen 3LP box set of Darkness at the Edge of Town). She puts the finishing touches on her own gifts because her mother has grown impatient with the ribbon. While shopping for David a few days ago, in her mind's eye Marian tried to fit Rémy into the sweaters and gloves and scarves she saw in the stores. She couldn't put the pieces together: the sweaters gaped, the gloves bulged. The scarves hung on headless necks. The shirt and pants that she eventually chose for David seemed like something she'd clipped from a magazine—two-dimensional, meant for a paper doll.

David and Robert burst in, cheeks flushed from the cold and the exercise. They exclaim over the fox they saw playing with another skier's dog. "And you'll be happy to know I'm not so old yet, Babi," Robert says. "I put David through his paces and wasn't even winded." He holds his fur hat to his chest, as though paying respect to an invisible flag that they've raised in honour of male fitness.

"Men in the wild with a dog and a fox," Barbara says. "Isn't that just the sort of thing you'd see on the internet? You should have brought the camera. We could have put the pictures on Facebook."

After a dinner of grilled salmon, David sorts the gifts according to recipient. They'll open them this evening rather than in the morning, because Barbara doesn't like being reminded of Santa Claus. Robert, who has stuffed himself into the rocking chair, his long legs touching the armrests, says he doesn't see the difference—the European Santa Claus comes on Christmas Eve, anyway. Marian sips her mulled wine, reheated from yesterday but spiked with extra brandy, and wonders what Rémy is doing just now. He must be with Delphine and others, pretending like she's pretending now. This is what she tells herself, that all of Rémy's interactions with Delphine must be false, bad acting, every line of dialogue pitched too high, the timing of the delivery just a hair off. The alternative is unthinkable: that he's forgotten her, even for a moment, and will remember her only when Delphine says the wrong thing or touches him the wrong way.

"These are for you. From your mom," David says, but she already knows this, because she herself secured the pyramid of golden gifts with a white bow that afternoon. She also knows that inside the boxes are clothes that Barbara has made for her.

"So okay, it's not much of a surprise," her mother says. "Every year the same gift. But I like excuses to think about you when you're away."

This year she has dressed the thoughts in a coffee-coloured A-line skirt, a zebra-print tunic, and a cowl-necked blouse in eggplant.

"These are gorgeous," Marian says.

"They're not perfect, I'm sure, but I had a good time at it," Barbara says. "You'll try them on, and we'll tweak them. Well, now that I see them again, they're not too bad. Ah, I fussed over that piping, I tell you."

Kong stretches himself out on the discarded wrapping paper. Robert holds up his new paddle, grinning, and David sets a heavy rectangular gift in front of Marian.

"Perfect," she says. "Is it books?" She loves getting new books for Christmas, ones she doesn't need to read for her dissertation. She tears open the paper and discovers an eight-by-ten-inch digital photo frame.

There they are, Marian and David, towelling Kong after one of his baths. There again dressed for the Halloween costume party: pirate and parrot. Next, half a dozen wedding photos. And here, in the canoe with her parents . . . Marian holds the device as David shuffles through the pictures and narrates excitedly.

Unsteady, Marian stands. Stumbles up the stairs to the bathroom. Makes it only as far as the sink.

Marian leads Kong into the yard, and he empties his bladder one last time. When she comes back inside, she says she's tired. David follows her upstairs. It's their second night in her old bedroom, which her mother now uses mostly for storage. She tries to clear it out each time they come home, but only gets halfway through the job. Marian changes into her pyjamas and throws her sweater over an unplugged fan, one of three shoved in the corner.

She gets into bed and waits for David to turn out the light.

They lie there in silence.

"You didn't like the gift," he says finally.

"It was thoughtful. Really."

"I spent a lot of time figuring it out. Choosing the pictures."

"It showed." Her eyelid twitches. It's been twitching for days.

"I remember all those moments. I see them like they're right there in front of me."

"You've always been good at that. Remembering."

Marian presses her finger to her eyelid. Her body is working against her. And her mind. She can't remember. She can never remember—David has always remembered for her.

"Why are you so happy all of a sudden?"

For a while he doesn't reply. "It's good to be here," he says finally.

She waits for further explanation, but he flips over and after
a few minutes falls asleep. The moon is bright, and she watches
his back rise and fall as he breathes. For years, this was the
only back she knew. She took for granted that the skin of other
men would look just like this, stretched over sinew and muscle,
broad and smooth. This is skin; this is bone.

Rémy's back is spotted with black hairs.

How many years will it take before that back, those hairs,
become the only ones she knows?

The shop is located in a brownstone on Algoma just south of
Bay Street. Barbara and Robert own the building, and over the
years have rented out the second-floor apartment to various
tenants, most recently to a retired mill worker with a Labrador
retriever trained to clutch the knot of its poop-and-scoop bag
in its mouth. Barbara has commented to Marian that it doesn't
seem ethical, the dog carrying its own poop like that, though
she isn't sure why. The man likes his pants perfectly tailored,
however, even his jeans, and she admires this about him.

The ground floor of the building is split into adjacent
businesses. Barbara co-owns Thunder Quilts with a woman
named Alyona who used to feed Marian pastries with names
like pampushki and ponchiki. When Marian was little, Alyona
taught her how to embroider ducks and teddy bears on her
favourite backpack. The shop carries fabric and notions and
other quilting equipment, and Barbara and Alyona offer six-
week courses with titles like Log Cabin on Fire or So You Think
You Can't Quilt?

The other half of the main floor is home to Barbara's
sewing business. The lettering on the window reads *Barbara
Kristiansen | Fashion Designer*. When Marian suggested the
name change a few years back, her mother argued to keep the
word 'seamstress' instead. She said she was too short and rosy
for anything more sophisticated. Marian understood that for
her mother, the term 'fashion designer' referred to someone

sharp-eyed and sleek who performed poking-and-tugging voodoo on runway waifs. This, however, was northern sewing done by a northern seamstress: snow pants for ladies with legs too short for the store-bought ones, sturdy but flattering wool business suits, and the odd hopeful creation that squinted towards a fairer climate.

"You're the one who designs those snow pants," Marian had said. "That makes you a designer. Plus, it'll be good for business."

"Bah. Business," her mother said, but agreed it couldn't hurt.

They're here so that Barbara can alter the clothes that she gave Marian last night. She has a sewing room at home, but said she wanted to be out of Robert and David's way while they replaced a broken light fixture. While Barbara is in the back searching for a pack of straight pins, Marian lingers at the front of the shop where her mother usually receives clients. A pale blue armchair faces a curtained changing area. Marian helped her mother pick out both upholsteries when she was small, her child's hands approving of the nubby textures. Across the room and next to the window stands a three-way mirror. The shop is like a well-kept drawing room—no hint of the clutter that her mother prefers at home.

"Go change," Barbara calls.

When Marian comes out of the changing area wearing her new skirt and blouse, she stands on the riser in front of the mirror, hips squared and feet planted. Her mother bends low and pinches the waistline of the skirt. "Thought I might have got it right this time, though it's easier to take it in than let it out. You're a little skinnier than when I last saw you, but I'll ask you anyway: are you pregnant?"

"What? No!"

"Well, that's something. Was it the fish? We all heard you getting sick."

Marian blushes. "The fish was fine."

Her mother takes a piece of tailor's chalk from the windowsill, and Marian feels her draw a line at the waist of the skirt. "So you don't have food poisoning, and you're not pregnant, well that's something, what with all the booze flowing this time of year." She steps back and reaches for the straight pins. "You should tell me what's going on with David."

"Nothing's going on with David."

"Mmhm."

"You know, maybe it was the fish. Did anyone else feel a little off last night?"

"You're very coy, but I'm going to keep asking."

"Let me get through this. Please."

"Get through what?"

Marian's bare toes curl against the riser. She complains that the pinning is too tight and stares out the window. The street is near deserted. Only the man from upstairs shuffles through the snow, black dog heeling beside.

"I can ask David instead, you know," Barbara says.

"Don't bother, okay? It's just not going well."

"I can see that much," her mother says as she unpins the skirt.

"We just have no connection anymore," Marian says, editing out David's recent sweet gestures, and her ambivalence towards them. "It's all misunderstandings and resentment. He's moody and says I don't get him. I don't know what to do. Stay or go or—"

"So you haven't decided anything yet."

"Not exactly," Marian replies, trying to find the quickest way out of the conversation.

"Then do nothing." Barbara tugs at the skirt hard. Marian breathes in sharply, looks away. Outside, the man and his dog are gone.

When she turns back to the mirror, her mother is crying. Pain reflected back at her, and guilt.

"I'm supposed to tell you that I want you to be happy,"
her mother says. Her voice is even higher pitched than usual.
"I should say to you, I want you to be happy, you can leave or
not leave and it's all the same to me, or something like that?
I should say all that, I guess. The trouble is happy, *happy*, you
know? Most people know unhappy, they know *that* when
they see it. But where does that leave them?" Barbara makes a
motion to wipe her face, but notices chalk on her fingers. Her
hands dangle in the air, helpless.

"I've never seen you unhappy," Marian says.

"No, no, because if it comes near, I just push back. Hard."

"Push back," Marian says. As though it were a question of
her will giving out. Her legs prickle and the bones in her feet
hurt with cold. She wants to change back into her jeans and
hoody and put her socks on. She wants to cry, but her mother
has beat her to it, so she stands there on the riser, watching both
of them in the mirror. Without turning, she reaches behind her
to grasp her mother's hand.

Barbara moves away, and picks up the chalk again, even
though there's nothing left to mark. She says, "Have you
considered that you might lose your dog?"

"Mom, please."

Her mother examines the hemline of the skirt, tugs on the
cowlneck that doesn't need adjusting. "We should be getting
home soon," she says. "I'll just do this now. It will fit then,
won't it?"

Chapter Twenty-One

Edna peers at Marian through her bifocals. "Aren't you supposed to be downstairs with your family?"

"Oh, you know, I have so much work to do." Marian shoves a pile of books and notebooks aside and plants herself next to Edna on the bed, her back to the headboard.

"I'm loving this La Corriveau woman." Edna holds up the hardcover library book she was reading when Marian came in: Louis Fréchette's *Almanach du peuple*, published in 1913.

"You read French," Marian observes.

"I forgot my James Patterson in Waterton." Edna flips through the volume, riffling the yellow sticky notes that Marian has used to mark it up. "Fréchette is such a pervert. Look at this passage here. The gravediggers have just discovered La Corriveau's gibbet in the Pointe-Lévy cemetery." She passes Marian the book.

Marian translates as she reads aloud. "*Bands and circles and powerful rivets twist and knot artfully, following the curves of arms and legs . . .*"

Edna chuckles, shakes her head. "Nothing but a heap of rusty metal, and the narrator can supposedly tell that Marie-Josephte had a 'remarkable figure.' Who ever heard of a buxom cage?"

"Fréchette definitely goes out of his way to sexualize La Corriveau. Personally, I like the part where the werewolves come to court her."

"Oh ho ho! Courting is a polite term for it."

Marian consults a page she's flagged. "They *lie down with her and whisper in her ear. Repeatedly.*"

Edna nods approvingly. "Little minx."

"To be fair, they do offer to make an honest woman of her afterwards." Marian fans the pages of the book and the faint scent of old dust escapes. "There were werewolf trials in France in the fifteenth through seventeenth centuries. It was a subgenre of witch trials: men accused of sorcery. I imagine the stories would have travelled to New France with the settlers."

Edna picks at a cracked fingernail. "So, the werewolf is a natural partner for La Corriveau. Though she's apparently aroused by humans as well."

"And human corpses." Marian turns to the relevant passage. "She *satisfies her horrible appetite on top of newly closed graves.*"

"Rather catholic in her tastes, isn't she?"

"I'll say. It's like Fréchette was making a laundry list of creepy acts for a witch to perform. He's taken all the spicy details from the different versions of the legend and thrown them into the same pot." Marian searches her notes. "Isn't Fréchette the first writer to mention that La Corriveau kills one of the husbands by pouring molten lead in his ears?"

"Nope. That other fellow got there first." Edna extracts another volume from the pile and reads aloud from its cover page: "Philippe Aubert de Gaspé, *Les Anciens Canadiens*, 1863."

"The original literary version."

"And my personal favourite. De Gaspé is good fun. Turns the whole shebang into a drinking tale."

"Yes! That's the one where the narrator's father gets a little ambitious with the flask on his way home from town."

"He's stumbling around in the dark," Edna says as she holds out her arms and drunkenly rocks her torso, her butt still planted on the bed. "And the witch jumps out of nowhere. She mounts his back like he's a horse and she's an angry jockey."

"She wants him to take her across the river so she can dance with the witches of Île d'Orléans—"

"He refuses, so she strangles him."

"Just enough that he passes out."

"And the poor sap wakes up to an empty flask."

Marian giggles and makes a note. "Fréchette turns La Corriveau into a much darker creature. He seems bent on damning her and making her father into a saint."

Edna rolls her eyes. "The hard-done-by patriarch. An old trope!"

"You bet. Joseph Corriveau is this sweet, adoring old man, bent under the weight of his advanced age, ready to sacrifice anything for his guilty daughter. His daughter, on the other hand, is an ungrateful wretch who's bursting with glee when her father confesses in her place. Of course, she doesn't escape the scaffold in the end. He's too pious to perjure himself."

"Monstrous wolves, heroic fathers, naughty daughters . . ." Edna whistles. "It's tempting to resort to Freud here."

"I'm sure somebody has. This version is rife with fear of La Corriveau's sexuality. Fréchette calls her an 'iron-clothed vampire.' She's a thirsty harlot who imposes her over-abundant desire on the community." Marian closes the book and sets it aside. "To be fair, she doesn't limit herself to sex. Sometimes she just blusters around making noise and scaring people."

"But her wanting too much sex crops up in other versions, too," Edna says. "I got through a bit of the Victor-Lévy Beaulieu this morning." She shuffles the pile of books, taps the cover of the 1976 play. "It's ridiculous. In this one, La Corriveau kills her first husband because he's lazy and impotent and won't knock her up. Grounds for murder, my ass! Laughable, if you ask me."

"It is," Marian agrees. "But the play is supposed to be a serious engagement with the legend and with Québec folklore generally. Beaulieu, in the introduction, proselytizes about the importance of the oral tradition within Québec culture. The text is really just one long series of *québécismes*."

"Translation, please," Edna says.

"Words and structures that are specific to Québec French," Marian clarifies. "Remember, this was the seventies, when the question of Québec national identity was at the forefront. And language had a huge role to play. By staging the oral legend of La Corriveau, Beaulieu was trying to reaffirm his people's cultural sovereignty."

Edna snakes a finger into her bonnet to scratch her temple. "Well, all I'm saying is that he doesn't know how to write women. His La Corriveau is a baby-crazy harlot. She kills her first husband to free herself up for relations with this fellow named Ti-Oui. Goes on and on about how she needs a man's strong hand to stroke her lady parts. But Ti-Oui ends up ignoring her. Prefers to sleep in the stable rather than in her bed. So he doesn't make the cut, either."

"She's quite the man-eater," Marian says.

"She's irritating, is what she is! A horny housewife-turned-psycho. Not exactly a complex character." Edna snorts. "You never can trust a man to write properly about witches."

Marian fiddles with her pen, weaving it through her fingers. "This version of La Corriveau is sex-crazed, but abstinent. Willing to kill just to have babies. Nattering about housework and kitchens. She seems to be a warped blend of different figures: the virgin mother of the Catholic tradition, the Québécois *mère de famille* who valued her large family above all else, and the scary, over-sexed witch."

"You're the expert," Edna replies.

Marian flips open her spiral notebook, jots down a few key words. "I would say that the text demonstrates ambivalence towards woman's traditional role as nurturer, her reproductive power, and her potential as desiring subject."

"Lalala," Edna says, and puts her fingers in her ears. "Jargon-lover."

"Sorry," Marian says, sincere. She doesn't want to sound uppity. "I guess Anne Hébert is the corrective to all this."

"I didn't read Hébert."

"In her play *La Cage*, she makes it clear that La Corriveau is the victim of a patriarchal system. She's aiming towards a feminist rebirth and even gives La Corriveau a new name. Ludivine."

"Which means?"

"The etymology is 'friendly or welcoming people.'"

"Ironic, I suppose."

"Sure," Marian says. "And the irony cuts both ways: it's the English who try La Corriveau—Ludivine in this version—in their court, but it's the Québécois who transform her into a witch over the centuries."

"Everyone played their part."

"But the name 'Lu*divine*' also has the more obvious connotation of the divine, of saving or being saved. Anne Hébert is the first to save La Corriveau outright. The play presents an alternate literary history. Ludivine kills her husband by accident—he abandons her for a stretch to go hunting, and when he comes back, she takes him for a stranger breaking into the house and shoots him. She's charged with murder, like in all the other versions, but she's saved by Fate when the judge who is about to sentence her drops dead."

"What do you make of all this?"

Marian doodles in her notebook while she thinks. "The legend of La Corriveau is elastic," she says after a minute or two. "It stretches itself to encompass the values of each era. Nineteenth-century misogyny and puritanism, twentieth century feminism, you name it. That much seems obvious. But what is more interesting is how Marie-Josephte Corriveau constantly regenerates herself. How she makes people want to reinvent her. She just has—" Marian waves her hands up by her head.

Edna grins. "A certain *je ne sais quoi*?"

"Je *sais* quoi," Marian says. "She kicks spectral ass. Her story inspires infinite interpretations, as though she's too tenacious to disappear. She's a dark muse who inserts herself into every era—elbows her way in and won't leave artists alone."

"I like a stubborn ghost," Edna says as she gets up from the bed and smooths her dress. "I should buy this woman a beer sometime. See what she's been up to lately."

Marian picks up the Hébert play and begins rereading the first act. Edna plucks a tissue from the box on the bedside table and vigorously blows her nose. She goes to the window and comments on the blue jay visiting the bird feeder, throws her dirty tissue in the garbage bin and stands over Marian, staring, until Marian looks up.

"Yes?" Marian says.

"Did you really think I was going to leave without prodding you about your life?"

"I was hoping."

"You're up here obsessing over La Corriveau so that you don't have to think about the mess you're in."

"That's true."

"But it's impossible, isn't it? Avoiding thought."

Marian reluctantly closes her book. "I guess."

Edna paces the room, shuffling across the hardwood in her stocking feet. "The disapproval. Your mom's denial. It hurts. What kid wants to be disapproved of?"

"It's not great, that's for sure."

Edna leans down and blows dust off one of the fans in the corner. "But that's not all, is it?"

Marian sighs. "My mom and dad love him so much. And I can see him how *they* see him—this great guy—" She breaks off, swallows. "And David doesn't deserve to be lied to. Except I can't tell him! I can't tell him about Rémy. He isn't depressed anymore, he's happier than he's been in months. How do I tell him?"

Edna plugs the fan into an outlet and fiddles with its buttons. It hacks and whirls to life. "I'd like to make a joke about shit hitting this," she says.

"For God's sake."

"Okay, okay, I won't. But I really want to."

"I appreciate your restraint. Are we done here?"

Edna looks surprised at Marian's testiness. "I was just trying to help. Lighten the mood again now that you've divulged."

"Your levity is noted," Marian says. "I think I'll take Kong for his walk."

Chapter Twenty-Two

Rémy pushes through the turnstile at Saint-Laurent station and takes the escalator down to the Honoré-Beaugrand platform, passing on the left as though in a terrible hurry. He's got time—he's not meeting Delphine at the botanical gardens until eleven—but he likes to navigate with a sense of urgency. It makes him feel like he's an essential part of the city, however small. Montreal needs him as much as he needs her. He hasn't moved away, not really—he still belongs to its crowds and jumble of faces and languages and, most of all, to its unpretentious French. Vowels and consonants dropped as though everyone is too busy living their lives to keep track.

In the long corridor, a man in a suit plays Vivaldi's "L'Iverno" on the violin, his instrument case splayed on the floor in front of him. Rémy stops to listen, and the people he passed on the escalator now pass him. The violinist's chin is nuzzled into his instrument and his mouth hangs open a bit, moving like that of a child learning to read. Rémy tosses a couple of dollars into the case; another generous donor has left a gold-wrapped condom. Beside the case are a bottle of Orangina and a small brown paper bag, its top and corners neatly folded. As he hurries once again towards the platform, Rémy imagines the bag contains a fresh bagel, crusted on both sides with sesame seeds, and wishes he had a similar one in his possession. Such a bag would mean he had just come from St-Viateur Café, his afternoon snack in hand after having lingered over morning espresso and the *traditionnel*: cream cheese on one side of the bagel; on the other, lox and capers haloed with white onion. He would have taken a bite of the cream cheese side before lining it up over the lox and pressing down so that the cheese rose up through the hole in the middle, crowned with capers, then cut the bagel in perfect halves with the special knife that lay on the side of his plate, and finished the first half slowly, knowing there was still more to come.

All this he would have done had he not chosen books over bagels, as there wasn't time for both this morning. After browsing for an hour at Gallimard, he came away with several treasures: Marc Augé's *Le Métro revisité*, because the title and topic could not be more perfect for this day; a couple of recent releases in Québec literature (for its empathy, *Le jeune homme sans avenir* by Marie-Claire Blais; for its contribution to the Catholic imaginary, *Le Christ obèse* by Larry Tremblay); finally, he selected a French translation of *Anna Karenina*, because he has never read it, may never read it, but is ashamed not to have a copy of it reposing on his shelf. He now enjoys the heft of the familiar red plastic bag as he aligns himself with the other commuters along the platform. He's often complained to both Delphine and Marian about the lack of bookstores in Waterton. There's only one independent shop, and they don't carry French volumes. He takes advantage of Gallimard's online catalogue instead. When he arrives at work and Lucie hands him the books he's ordered, he feels both elated they're finally his, and regretful they came to him without the help of serendipity. He found these books, and not the other way around.

The ground rumbles. He and the other commuters inch towards the tracks; the train emerges from the tunnel, ushered into the station by a rush of air and noise. He's convinced that in the moment before it slows, everyone on the platform is thinking the same thought: it would be so easy to step forward and drop into the path of this train. By how many people has this philosophical musing multiplied over the years? An infinite number since the métro was first built.

The train stops, and Rémy boards. The pole he grips is hot from the hands of strangers. The train pushes off and gathers speed, a thrust of glass and steel. Only one direction possible. A relief at a time of year where he feels pulled every which way. Though so far, despite the bloat of kitsch and visiting, Christmas has been pleasant, familiar. He ate two turkey dinners: one in the afternoon at his mother's place in Notre-Dame-De-Grace—which is where he and Delphine are staying, and where his grandfather lives—and another at Delphine's brother's in the evening. He won the game of *belote* that his in-laws force them to play every year. Olivier, their one-year-old, clutched at Rémy's cards with wet baby fingers, which Rémy didn't mind, though he washed his hands afterwards. At his mother's house, he opened presents and listened to his aunts bicker over burnt tourtière, then escaped to the living room with his grandfather. He drank scotch with Papi before joining Delphine in bed.

If he feels unsettled, it's because he doesn't feel unsettled enough. He has one woman here and one there, and is functioning as though this weren't one too many. He recalls his promise to Marian to 'make things real' between them. Comfortably vague. He's less comfortable with the elliptical response he gave to her question: "You would leave Delphine for me?" "Of course," he replied, which wasn't disingenuous, because she posed the question in the conditional, and the conditional and future tenses are worlds apart. But he's not stupid. He knows that she, unlike him, probably isn't busy analyzing the grammar of his statement.

For now, a break. He loves Marian—he wouldn't have told her as much if he didn't—but is relieved that there's a structure in place that, for the moment, has nothing to do with her. And 'love' is a slippery word. For example, he can't say definitively that he doesn't love Delphine. Only that his love for Delphine has been rendered problematic, has been buried by this new overlay of love for Marian. He's happy to be away, not to have to go into the office, where, in the manner of a cat, Marian might as well have rubbed her pretty nose against the furniture. She's that present for him when he's trying to concentrate.

It's mostly at night that he wishes she were here with him. That's when the memory of her scent makes him hard, and he thinks that if he could, he would bury his face in every crevice of her body. Legs, underarms. The nights are what make him think that he could divide this life in half, share with her the part that falls to him, and pass her dissertation project on to someone else, despite Adèle Faucher's warnings. That arrangement would be for the best, because he would no longer be mixing pleasure with pleasure, and business would have nothing to do with it.

A robotic female voice announces Pie-IX station. He exits and finds Delphine waiting for him at street level, just inside the doors to the station. She's excited for him when he tells her about his book purchases, and he tries to look interested while she shows him the sleepers she bought for Olivier. Not that he dislikes Olivier or the idea of babies and children. It's just that he imagines the issue of his loins being like the children in Renaissance portraits—miniature adults. He pictures himself siring an eight-year-old savant.

He and Delphine cross the snow-covered grounds to the botanical garden's reception area, where they pay twelve dollars for admission and another dollar to stuff their coats into lockers. Rémy tells her that he feels like a tourist in his own city. She says the gardens aren't just for tourists or they wouldn't offer yearly passes. She would like to have such a pass one day if they ever move back here. Rémy catches himself nodding as she says this, as though it were the most natural outcome in the world. Delphine wonders aloud if her friend Isabelle might be able to get them one at a discount. Isabelle works at the garden and will be meeting them in a few minutes, once they have had some time to wander around. Rémy isn't sure why his brief presence here is necessary, but he felt too guilty about everything else to pose the question to Delphine yesterday when she was making plans.

They skip the geraniums and cacti and go straight to the tropical greenhouses. Delphine remarks on the air, fat with oxygen. She says it helps her whole body relax, but what Rémy feels here is energy and exertion. How many plants have been dug up and hauled from all corners of the world and forced into the sophisticated beds of this glass house, along whose lock-stone pathways they now stroll, and whose grapefruit and banana trees have displaced whatever indigenous plants must have once grown here? All this he wonders detachedly, because he has no special fondness for indigenous flora. He admires man-made vigour.

A chrome stairwell and walkway provide an overhead view, and Rémy climbs and finds himself at eye level with a pineapple. Below, Delphine reads an information panel. She's far away, in another world and quite content.

Would it be possible to separate from her gently, quietly, without disturbing anyone? If he works hard enough to make it look natural, inevitable, and if he finds her a way to reconnect with her roots, here, in this city they both love, maybe she won't feel it as much. And neither would he.

From his vantage point, Rémy can see Isabelle successfully sneaking up on Delphine from behind, even though Isabelle is as pregnant as they come and thus easy to spot. She grabs Delphine, who lets out a happy shriek.

"Don't ask me how I am," Isabelle says to Rémy once he has made his way down from the tops of the pineapple trees. "The answer is hungry, cranky, generally inhuman. There is a parasite living in my body. I can't wait to be rid of it."

"And here I was thinking you had a glow."

"That's the gas."

Delphine smooths Isabelle's hair and tucks it behind her ears. "I think you look great."

"Tell Luc that." Isabelle rocks back on her heels and with her hands supports her lower back. "He keeps calling me 'La Grosse Femme d'à côté.'"

Rémy chuckles at this literary reference. "Not bad, that one."

"He should be kinder to the host."

Isabelle and Luc are in the midst of a move out to Saint-Jérôme, where they've bought a split-level with a pool. The conversation turns to the joys of packing boxes when you can scarcely touch your own toes. Rémy and Delphine offer to help, but Isabelle says that most of the work is already done. Before Rémy leaves the two women—Isabelle has taken the afternoon off, and they plan to shop the Boxing Week sales together at Simon's—he searches Delphine's face and the tone of her voice for evidence that she resents him for not putting a baby under the Christmas tree. Delphine, however, seems perfectly content. She follows her pregnant friend through the flora after kissing him goodbye.

That evening, Delphine takes Isabelle out to a late movie, and Rémy stays in with his grandfather. Papi is in the kitchen now, rinsing the glasses. Rémy tried to get up and take care of this himself, but Papi said a man shouldn't let his guest handle an empty glass, and Rémy didn't argue. He rarely argues, in fact. He feels flimsy next to his grandfather, who at eighty-nine is firm and capable, and who moved in with his daughter after his wife's death four years ago not out of need, but by choice. He certainly could have continued living in his house in Gagnon, except that most of his buddies had already passed away, and without Jeanne around, he was feeling bored. Plus, he doesn't like to cook for himself. He knew that moving in with Thérèse would put an end to eating scrambled eggs five nights a week, and that Rémy's aunt Carole and her wife, Kasia, would invite him over to their place for Sunday dinners.

When Marian asked Rémy about his family—they were lying in bed together, she playing with his chest hair, he enjoying it—he'd launched into the story of his grandfather's head. "Papi worked for an iron ore company. He fell down a mining shaft in 1973. Fractured his cranium and had to have a bar fixed to his skull for a time to right the injury. He called it a halo, I think."

"Holy shit. How do they do a procedure like that?"

"No idea. All I know is that the bar stuck out eight inches from the top of his head because the doctor ran out of time that day. Apparently Papi was supposed to go back a couple of weeks later so the doctor could remove the excess. But that wasn't soon enough for him. So when they discharged him, he pulled into the lot of the local garage and fetched the pliers from the back of his truck and tried to nip it off himself. The kid who was working the gas pump was watching the whole time, wide-eyed with horror. When the pliers didn't work, Papi went at the bar with a hacksaw, and when that failed, he asked the kid to blast it off with the shop's blowtorch."

"You're making this up."

"Je te jure. If you don't do it, he said, I'll have to do it myself, and you don't want to be responsible because you refused to give a neighbour a hand, do you? *Non, monsieur.* The kid fired up the blowtorch and sheared off the upper half of the metal bar, bawling the whole time. Papi came home with a few less inches of steel to him and not a single hair from the neck up. There's a patch on his eyebrow that never grew back."

"Your grandmother must have been beside herself."

"She slapped him and sent him off to bed, then phoned the garage to give the manager an earful."

Rémy would like to introduce Papi to Marian. But why can't he imagine the three of them in the same room together? Because she's Anglophone? Because she's not Delphine?

His grandfather comes back now, an orange plastic cup in his hand, and sits squarely on the sofa opposite Rémy.

"You're bothered tonight," he says.

"Tonight more than any other night?"

His grandfather works his jaw a little and spits tobacco into the cup. "Well. What is it?"

"Work."

"Work doesn't wear a face that long."

"It does now."

"Do I need to pour another drink?"

"Maybe. No."

"Then talk."

Rémy swears under his breath.

"That bad?"

"Worse."

"Love or money?"

"Do I have to choose?"

"Smartass."

"Fine," Rémy says. "I'm in love with my grad student." He stops himself from adding, "In a complicated and problematic way that I have yet to fully analyze."

"You knock the girl up? No? Though that wouldn't be the end of the world these days, either." Papi lifts the cup to his mouth and spits. "Well, you're not married yet."

"My *student*," Rémy repeats, almost hoping to be scolded.

"I heard you the first time. All I'm saying is you want what you want. But why this one, is what I want to know."

"She's pretty," Rémy says, and realizes how lame this sounds. "Smart. She loves books."

He stops here. His description sounds like a grocery list.

He doesn't mention that Marian is Anglophone.

"Seems simple to me."

"Somehow I knew you would say that."

"Spend some time busting up the ground and sorting it. Then you understand the rest of life's not much different."

"That's reductive."

"Big word." His grandfather glares and spits. "Reductive, you say. Night or day, a hole in the ground doesn't care when and how you work it, and neither should you. You get what you came for. If you want it. If you work to get at it."

"I'm working."

"You are. I see that. Maybe time to work something different then."

Rémy rolls his eyes.

Papi snorts in response. "When I wasn't drilling, I blew things up. Tonnes upon tonnes of *terrain mort* to blast and sort through, all to get at a bit of ore. Dead ground, Rémy. And inside it, exactly what we came looking for. That red earth everywhere. My vehicle upholstery turned red. My clothes the colour of dried blood. My fingers stained, and your grandmother joking that I needed to stop carrying my trade to bed. Even my snot was rusty."

"Yes, well. I'm too buried in my own rusty snot to see my way out of this."

"There you go." Papi rests the tobacco cup on his knee. "That dead ground stuck to me for years. But the mineral we dug up fed six children. It paid for your grandmother's sunroom and the family's trips to Maine. You have to be ready to blast and sort. But you get what you came for." Papi nods his head definitively, rises, and makes his way down the hall to bed.

Rémy looks at his own reflection laid over the darkness that has fallen beyond the living room window. He wants to be more like his grandfather, straight up and down like the beam in his skull, so confident which way is up. Which way is out.

His mother comes downstairs for a glass of water. She's wearing her bathrobe with the frayed sleeves, the one she's had since he was a teenager. He wonders what she's heard.

"Your father had that expression on his face sometimes," she says.

"Before you left?"

"The times I stayed."

Chapter Twenty-Three

jeudi 29 décembre 2011 15 h 19
Objet : coucou
De : Rémy Leblanc <leblanc_remy17@mailgratuit.fr>
À : Marian Kristiansen <m_kristiansen82@bestmail.com>

Ma belle Marie,
Just a little note to let you know that all is well here. I've been
drinking Talisker, shopping for books and listening to my
grandfather's pep talks regarding relationships. "You must be
ready to blast and sort," he told me last night when I confessed
to him the full weight of my difficulties. He has a flare for
allegory. He's curmudgeonly but romantic, and he seems to be
rooting for us.
    I've been thinking of you, wondering what you're up to,
hoping you're doing well despite all. As you know, it's been
difficult for me to write to you, as there are always people
about. Do let me know how your visit with your family is going.
    Je t'embrasse,
    Rémy

Thursday, December 29, 2011 at 6:27 PM
Subject: Re: coucou
To: Rémy Leblanc <leblanc_remy17@mailgratuit.fr>
From: Marian Kristiansen <m_kristiansen82@bestmail.com>

Hello, my dear. Let's not talk about my family. I could go for a
little escapism just now. Your grandfather is right—there are
many good reasons to torch your current life for your graduate
student. I'll name a few:

- Playing fast and loose with cliché must be better than
belote (what's belote?)

- Graduate students know how to have fun in Jacuzzis and
elsewhere

- It's the only way to get back the books you've lent her

- It's our department's turn for a scandal (German went last
year)

And of course, the newest, most compelling reason:

- Your granddad told you to

Start the flame. I'll bring the marshmallows.

Love,

M.

vendredi 30 décembre 2011 7 h 15
Objet : [Aucun objet]
De : Rémy Leblanc <leblanc_remy17@mailgratuit.fr>
À : Marian Kristiansen <m_kristiansen82@bestmail.com>

I've always enjoyed your sense of humour. Torches and
marshmallows? The fires have been a little more serious over
my way, but not to worry, all is under control.

Let me explain. I'm sure I've expressed to you my concern
that D. needs to know a little bit about what I'm feeling these
days. It's not fair to keep her completely in the dark. I'm happy
to say that we talked last night, and I think it went well. I didn't
mention you. No need to complicate matters, at least not
immediately. I know you'll understand. Suffice to say that D.
and I discussed a lot of the relationship "disconnects" we've
experienced since moving to Waterton five years ago. She's
convinced that many of our problems stem from the move, and

I would have to agree. It *is* harder to breathe in that Anglo town. (Not that some of its inhabitants aren't lovely!)

To make a long story short, we've found ourselves a pied-à-terre here in Montréal. We have it all worked out. D. can get a job here, either at another dentist's office, or maybe at the jardin bo (she has a contact there). As for me, I can commute back and forth (Monday-Thursday in Waterton, Thursday-Sunday in Montréal). It's only a two-and-a-half-hour drive.

I hope your visit with your family is still going well, though I fear there is tension under the surface, given your reference to "escapism." We will have ample time to talk about whatever is bothering you when we're both back in town. In the meantime, hang in there. I'm thinking of you.

Friday, December 30, 2013 at 10:04 AM
Subject: Re: [Aucun objet]
To: Rémy Leblanc <leblanc_remy17@mailgratuit.fr>
From: Marian Kristiansen <m_kristiansen82@bestmail.com>

Rémy, I read and reread your email and still don't know what to say. You're buying a place with Delphine? You must be kidding. Only two weeks ago, you were talking about making our relationship "real." Or did I imagine it?

I'm profoundly confused.

vendredi 30 décembre 2011 18 h 21
Objet : Rép.: Re: [Aucun objet]
De : Rémy Leblanc <leblanc_remy17@mailgratuit.fr>
À : Marian Kristiansen <m_kristiansen82@bestmail.com>

Chérie, I see that I wasn't clear enough in my message. I've worried you, and to make matters worse, I've been away from my email all day. To answer your question, of course I'm not buying property with D.—that would be foolish. We're renting, obviously. A couple we know are moving out of a cute little apartment—setting up in the suburbs, etc. etc.—and we're taking over the lease. We've just come back from there. D. has pointed out that a move to Montréal would give our relationship a fair chance, and I didn't have the heart to tell her that I am not so sure. Anyway, she's right in certain ways. We used to be happy here, maybe because of our separate routines, who knows. She says I owe her this much—a try, that is—and she's right. Of course, it's unlikely that there will be some sort of miraculous reconciliation between us, but I have nothing to lose, since I really would like to see her set up here. After all, this is her home, and I know you'll understand that this is a step in the right direction.

Did you get any dissertation work done over the break?

Friday, December 30, 2011 at 6:46 PM
Subject: Re: Rép.: Re: [Aucun objet]
To: Rémy Leblanc <leblanc_remy17@mailgratuit.fr>
From: Marian Kristiansen <m_kristiansen82@bestmail.com>

"Unlikely"? Perhaps I shouldn't be surprised. You never have said when you plan on leaving her. And now this morning's email.

So, either you're further in, or you're phasing Delphine out. Neither makes any sense. Coming from you of all people. Aren't you always the one expounding the virtues of logic? What am I supposed to do with this information?

vendredi 30 décembre 2011 19 h 33
Objet : Rép.: Re: Rép.: Re : [Aucun objet]
De : Rémy Leblanc <leblanc_remy17@mailgratuit.fr>
À : Marian Kristiansen <m_kristiansen82@bestmail.com>

Logic, Marian, involves due process, and above all, clarity. You're not seeing things clearly. "Phasing D. out." What a crude suggestion. I'll let it pass since I'm certain that you're speaking

out of frustration and desire and don't mean to be harsh. I
can tell that it's been too long since we've seen each other.
The distance has led to an unfortunate misunderstanding.
Nonetheless, I will say that I see no trouble in helping D. renew
her life here. The move will also give me a chance to reconnect
with the city.

Email is obviously not the best medium for this discussion.
Are you back in Waterton? Can you meet me at the office
tomorrow at, say, 3 p.m.? I would have you over to my place,
but when I come back tomorrow afternoon, D. will be with me.
As you can imagine, she'll need to give notice at work and
arrange for the move.

Rémy stays up late, stalking his email account, but by the
time he goes to bed, Marian still hasn't responded. When he
wakes up in the morning, his muscles ache, as though the
battle he's fought in the past twenty-four hours were physical.
He groans and stretches out onto Delphine's side of the bed.
She's already headed out for a swim at the downtown YMCA,
using a gift card that Isabelle gave her. He half remembers her
crawling over him and kissing him on the cheek. Does Marian
know how to be sweet like this, even when things aren't easy?
Why does she not know how to make allowances for life's
complications? Can this skill be taught?

And yet, does Delphine not hide behind this sweetness, use
it to throw him off her scent, to pretend that everything is fine?
For example, the swimming. This is her third morning at the
pool since they arrived in Montreal four days ago, which would
be unremarkable enough, except that she's gone out for a run
every evening as well. She's not replacing her obsessive exercise
regime. She's augmenting it.

He pushes these thoughts away—deep into the pre-coffee
fog of his brain—and pulls on sweatpants and wool socks
and readies himself to face other human beings. Papi, still in
his pyjamas, is snoozing in his favourite chair in the living

room. Rémy's aunt Carole and Kasia, who live a short drive away in Plateau Mont-Royal, sit at the kitchen table with his mother. There was talk yesterday about peanut butter and bacon crêpes—a childhood favourite—but the women don't seem to be in any hurry to start cooking. Kasia yawns over her mug, and Carole rubs her neck. Thérèse offers Rémy coffee but doesn't press him to talk. She knows not to bother him in the morning.

He sips his coffee in the living room while his laptop boots up. Papi snores softly, his hand twitching.

No email from Marian. He rereads the messages in his "Sent" folder. Perfectly reasonable replies. Why hasn't she written back?

In the kitchen, the women speak in voices low enough to be conspiratorial and loud enough that he can hear. This is how his mother and Aunt Carole have long communicated with him. It started when he was a teenager, right after his parents' separation, because he would disappear to his room or a friend's house if they tried to tell him something important. He didn't want to be hammered with reality. The only way to get through to him was surreptitiously. He could see through it, even then, but didn't mind because it meant he didn't have to justify himself or tell them to fuck off. Kasia joined their little theatre when she moved in with Carole, and he doesn't mind that, either. What's the difference between two women talking in his direction and three?

He experiences their floating words as a radio play of which he is the star:

THÉRÈSE: I always said he'd come home. Didn't I say that?

CAROLE: You did say that, though saying it doesn't make it come true.

KASIA: He never met people there.

THÉRÈSE: He didn't need anybody.

CAROLE: I don't know about that. One always needs people.

KASIA: I think he could have worked on his English more. If he took lessons, like I did, that might have helped.

THÉRÈSE: He's too busy for that. Look at him, working away in there! Always working. Besides, his English is good enough.

KASIA: I don't know . . . there's more to it than just getting by.

THÉRÈSE: They hired him to teach French. So, he speaks French. What more does he need?

CAROLE: Is it really a question of either/or?

THÉRÈSE: Sure it is. It's a worldview, as they say. First he learns English. Then he comes home with some Anglophone. Before long I've got grandbabies I can't understand.

CAROLE: I think Delphine would notice that!

KASIA: Babies are babies, and you'd love them in English or Farsi or any other language. That's what I hear, anyway.

THÉRÈSE: I'd love them even better in French.

KASIA: Is this about language, or blood? Not everyone can be *pure laine,* and not everybody needs to be. Some of us couldn't be that if we tried.

CAROLE: She's not talking about you, sweetie. We love you the way you are. *I* love you the way you are.

THÉRÈSE: Oh, honey. You know you've always been welcome here. I mean it. But we're not talking about that. We're not talking about individuals. Individuals are okay most of the time. But then they form groups. If father weren't busy napping, he'd agree with me.

CAROLE: No doubt. Doesn't make you right.

THÉRÈSE: Impossible to be wrong about my own opinion.

CAROLE: Yet somehow you manage it.

THÉRÈSE: What are we arguing about?

CAROLE: Roots. Who to sleep with.

KASIA: Who not to, rather.

THÉRÈSE: He should get married already, once the move is
    done. Do something definitive.

CAROLE: You're one to talk. *You* never got married.

THÉRÈSE: I never got engaged either.

KASIA: People do that. You see it all the time. They get engaged,
    and life happens, and then nothing happens.

CAROLE: You would have dumped me if I tried that.

KASIA: Probably. It was an excuse to carry a bouquet.

CAROLE: I would have bought you a bouquet.

KASIA: And you did, see?

THÉRÈSE: I could have married Paul. At that time, people just
    didn't get married anymore. It meant going to church.

CAROLE: Last I heard, the church that Mother and Father got
    married in was turned into a needle exchange clinic.

THÉRÈSE: Now weddings are *à la mode* again. Bouquets.
    Dresses. Toasts to the bride and groom. If I met Paul today
    . . . saved me the trouble of a divorce, anyway.

CAROLE: Divorce. Now *that* would have been definitive. It's
    a whole lot harder to waffle back and forth once you're
    divorced.

THÉRÈSE: It wasn't just me! You know it wasn't just me. Paul
    couldn't make up his mind, either. One minute he wanted
    me out. The next he wanted me to stay.

CAROLE: If you threaten to go, sometimes they tell you to go. If
    you tell them you're staying, they say, Okay, stay.

THÉRÈSE: He could have gone. He could have done it himself.

CAROLE: Men don't leave unless they have somewhere to go.

THÉRÈSE: Women either. Sometimes.

KASIA: I'd leave if it were bad, just for the *possibility* of
    somewhere to go.

CAROLE: Is that the same?

KASIA: Except for the details, I think it is. More coffee?

THÉRÈSE: Always.

[Silence]

CAROLE: Is Delphine out running?

THÉRÈSE: Swimming.

KASIA: She swims now, too?

THÉRÈSE: Appears so.

CAROLE: Did she eat before she left?

THÉRÈSE: The Shreddies box was on the counter. Rémy doesn't like cereal.

CAROLE: No bowl in the sink, though.

THÉRÈSE: Nope, no bowl.

KASIA: Are you going to do like him and watch her at every meal, then pretend that's not what you're doing?

CAROLE: She hasn't eaten much these past couple of days.

THÉRÈSE: I hope she's not sick again. No, if she were sick again, he would've made her an appointment with Dr. Pelletier.

CAROLE: It's Christmas. Dr. Pelletier is off like the rest of us. [Pause] Maybe we should say something.

KASIA: You are saying something.

THÉRÈSE: Mon trésor, can you hear us?

RÉMY: What's that?

THÉRÈSE: So, you hear us.

He did notice the cereal box waiting for him when he got up. Delphine wants him to believe in her appetite. He's not fooled. She's been counting her calories, stubbornly and quietly, as though the right number will reduce her anxiety. And yes, he's been counting them with her. Two accomplices, mathematically

168

precise in their actions and reactions. The abandoned dish, still full. His prodding: Why don't you try a bite or two of my pasta? Her concession: Okay, but just one.

Looking back at the chronology of her illness, he feels both guilty and confused. When he'd just finished his PhD and was teaching five classes as an adjunct at McGill and l'Université du Québec à Rimouski, too exhausted and bitter to give Delphine the time of day, she remained cheerful, cajoling, the picture of health.

"Do you need to be so fucking happy all the time?" he'd said to her as she arranged a bouquet of cheap flowers she'd bought at the Provigo.

She centred the vase on their crappy kitchen table. "We can't both go under, can we?" she said, and told him about the little girl whose teeth she had cleaned that afternoon. The girl got through the fluoride part of her visit by imagining that the trays were alien gums—they would give her access to inter-planetary secrets.

Rémy left the apartment in a huff and drank alone at the Irish bar around the corner, but the experience wasn't nearly as cathartic as it looked in the movies. He just felt tired and pathetic. When he crept guiltily into bed at two a.m., Delphine wished him goodnight and told him she'd already set the alarm.

It was only once he'd signed the contract for his tenure-track job at Waterton and wanted to make love and make plans and make the most of their time left in Montreal that Delphine withdrew into hunger. It was as though during those gruelling two years, he'd eaten through what was good in her, and now she wanted nothing to do with him or herself. When she fainted in the supply room at work that spring, she weighed one hundred and seven pounds. Body mass index: seventeen. The emergency room doctor who treated her and ordered tests—a man whose presence made the nurses stand up straighter— diagnosed her with hypokalemia.

"Low potassium," he explained when Rémy asked what that was.

"Like bananas," Rémy said, stupidly.

"Like what keeps cells and muscles running properly," the doctor said. "No arrhythmia coming up on the EKG, though."

Rémy waited for him to go on.

"An irregular heartbeat," the doctor said. "The heart can't do its job properly, because it doesn't have enough nutritional support. Anyway, she'll be fine enough in a few hours. The IV will do its work, and we'll likely discharge her this evening. After that, she'll need to take potassium supplements. She should see a counsellor or psychiatrist. We don't do referrals here. You'll have to talk to your family doctor about that."

Delphine lay under the mint-coloured linens and blinked sleepily as she ran her fingers over the IV tubes at her wrist. "I don't mind taking supplements," she said. "But I don't know about the counsellor. I'll just eat a little more."

"Yes, you will eat more," Rémy said. "But you are going to see someone."

"I'll think about it."

Neither Delphine nor Rémy had a family doctor. When Delphine's boss called that night to see how she was, he gave Rémy the number of a physician colleague who had a special interest in eating disorders. Delphine was able to see Dr. Pelletier right away, and he prescribed anti-depressants and atypical antipsychotics for mood and appetite. Rémy felt both nervous and protective seeing those pill bottles resting on the kitchen counter afterwards. The physician also referred her to a psychologist, and Rémy drove Delphine to her first appointment and waited in the car to make sure she went in and stayed for the full session. She came out an hour later looking tired.

"Was it okay?" he asked.

"Sure. I mean, I'd go back, I guess."

"What did she ask about?"

"Work and relationships and all that. Fifty minutes goes by pretty quickly."

"What did you tell her?"

"A bunch of stuff. Nothing in particular."

"I mean, we're fine, right?"

"Yes, chéri. We're fine."

It was February when Rémy signed his tenure-track contract, and March when Delphine collapsed. They moved to Waterton in July, and by then, her anorexia was under control. In the few months that followed, she insisted on driving herself to her appointments. She never spoke about what happened there. Rémy began to resent the intimate conversations she was having with this stranger. What did she say when ensconced in that cozy green loveseat? How often did she reach for the Kleenex box, conveniently but unobtrusively placed on the coffee table in front of her? (She had never described the office to him, and yet he was convinced that these details were exact.) She must have talked about her mother's depression when she was a little girl, and her death from ovarian cancer when Delphine was twelve. But that's not what Delphine implied. She mentioned 'relationships.' Did the psychologist think him responsible for her condition?

Condition, Rémy thinks as his mother, Carole and Kasia bang around in the kitchen and accuse each other of being underfoot. The scent of melted butter wafts his way. How can Delphine be so satisfied closing her mouth around nothing? And how does he know just how far to push, how many bites is too many? Is this what control tastes like? Who controls whom? Are they not out of control, both of them? For the past few weeks, weight has been dropping off her body at a steady pace. He doesn't need to call Dr. Pelletier, though. Not yet. He refuses to become the enemy in Delphine's eyes. Once it sinks in for her that they've signed a lease, she'll plan for the move and distract herself with rituals that don't relate to food. Shopping, nesting. Throw cushions and area rugs.

In his email message to Marian yesterday morning, he said that his talk with Delphine went well. Indeed. He talked; Delphine listened. Say something! he thought at the time. When your fiancé tells you that he's feeling detached and alienated, you say something. 'Detached,' 'alienated.' Professor words. Why does he always sound like such an ass? Why can't he talk—*think*—like a normal person? Marian makes fun of him for it. "Bien sûr, Rémy Leblanc, PhD," she said once, pronouncing the letters of the degree title in English. (He had just described to her his suspicion that his new lower back spasms were a psychosomatic symptom of his double life.) She's a hypocrite to make fun of him. In a few years, she'll be just like him. She, too, will come to see her emotions through the lens of big words and big theories.

Feelings of alienation, and an awareness of how those feelings make up a veritable *discourse*: he was predestined for all of this. "I bet you've got a word for everything. Even your own bullshit," a CÉGEP teacher once said to him in response to a paper he wrote. It was the year he turned seventeen. He and his mother had moved out six months prior and his father was about to relocate to Louisiana to be with a woman he'd met in Florida on vacation. Rémy spent most of that year getting high with a girl who gave lazy blowjobs and went by the name of Lennie. In the paper he handed in to the CÉGEP teacher, he eloquently argued that Jacques Ferron must have written his novel *L'Amélanchier* while experimenting with opiates. Something about 'creative impetus' and 'pharmaceutical enlightenment.' Or was it 'pharmaceutical enactment'? Ferron was a psychiatric doctor as well as a novelist, and he would have had access to such drugs. As for Rémy, he would have needed something harder than pot to take the edge off his parents' split and arrive at an enlightened place far, far away. Maybe he needs some of that pot now. Maybe Marian needs some of it. *Chill the fuck out.* There's some ordinary language, something Lennie would have said. *Think of someone other than yourself.*

He's talking to Marian.

Maybe she'd wish he were talking to himself. (Her prolonged silence makes him wonder just what she is thinking.)

If he wanted to chill the fuck out, he wouldn't even know who to ask anymore. Lennie got kicked out of school after a locker raid, and the last time he smoked a joint was at Carole and Kasia's wedding a couple of years ago, when Kasia's ex-boyfriend, a clown named Philippe, gave him one as a peace offering after he'd insulted Rémy's wing-tipped shoes. The clown asked Delphine if she, too, wanted to step out for a joint, but she declined. Didn't want to get the munchies, Rémy thought then.

Rémy and Philippe smoked next to a lamppost outside the reception hall. Moths fluttered above their heads.

"You know, Philippe," Rémy remembers saying, "That's the most beautiful wedding I've ever seen. Can't you just tell they really love each other? As in, *really* love each other?"

Philippe took a long drag. "Don't I know it, man. She never looked at me like that."

"It gets me thinking about how lucky I am. You want to know how lucky I am?"

Philippe exhaled and nodded gravely and stared up at the moths.

"I've got someone who thinks I'm the whole world. I mean, she'd lie down on train tracks for me. If there were train tracks somewhere close by. You know."

Stinking of pot and wine, Philippe gripped his shoulder and leaned in close. "You better do something about that, man. Do it *right*."

The impulse to get married was still there a few months later, when Rémy wasn't stoned and in the company of a clown. That's when he proposed, over an expensive dinner at Laloux, meant to compensate for the fact that he hadn't bought a ring. Delphine's glee was almost embarrassing. Almost.

"You proposed? Really," his mother had said when he told her. "Where did you learn to do a thing like that?"

"Congratulations," his dad said when he phoned him in Louisiana. "You'll probably do okay."

"That's it?" Rémy said.

A long pause. "She seems reasonable."

Reasonable. This is what he needs now. Maybe his mother was on to something the other day. Maybe it's cultural. Marian can study the literature all she wants; she'll never be *québécoise*. Are his people more reasonable than hers, something to do with the French rhetorical tradition? Do he and Marian fight because they're speaking the same language, but from different registers? What if there's a cultural shorthand that can't be learned, one that's dyed in the wool?

His mother calls out. "Breakfast!"

Papi snorts and shuffles into the kitchen. Rémy follows. As his mother serves them crêpes, Delphine comes in. She drops her duffle bag in the hall and sinks into the chair next to Papi, spent. Rémy's mother asks her if she wants a crêpe. She offers to leave off the bacon and peanut butter.

"I've already eaten," Delphine says. "Later, maybe?"

Papi pours maple syrup over his plate. It pools at the edges. "Eat something."

"No, really, I'm fine."

Papi shoves his plate in front of Delphine. It knocks over her empty juice glass.

She smooths her damp hair and rights the glass.

"If you don't eat, you'll die," Papi says, and Delphine laughs nervously.

Kasia raises her hand to her throat.

Rémy stabs his crêpe. "Didn't you . . . she said she wasn't hungry." He can't look his grandfather in the eye.

Delphine takes Papi's fork and knife and cuts off an oozy chunk of crêpe and shoves it in her mouth. Syrup drips down her chin. She dabs at it with Papi's napkin. "These are so good. You were right to insist. What was I thinking?"

Papi asks his daughter for another crêpe with extra bacon. She brings it to him and says there is more where that came from.

Chapter Twenty-Four

He should have known that the building would be freezing. The administration has turned the heat down for the Christmas break to save money. He received an email to this effect and deleted it.

As he reaches the top of the stairwell, he exhales a puff of air—he can't quite see his breath. The door to the grad student office is closed; no light shines under it. He peers into the computer lab across the hall. Marian is there, hunched over, her back to him. She wears a clingy blue sweater. Not chosen for its warmth, he's sure. He considers offering her his coat but thinks better of it. Chivalry is for men who show up on time.

She closes the web browser she's looking at, but doesn't turn around. "I was just on my email, checking to see if plans had changed." Her voice is flat.

He hovers behind her, places his hands on the back of her chair, but doesn't dare touch her yet. "There was holiday traffic leaving Montreal. I didn't think it would be a problem. Marie. Je suis désolé."

"You sound it, at least."

"I am," he insists.

"David thinks I'm at Roast," she says, and he wonders what she wants him to make of this. That there's someone else at home wanting her?

But she's here, isn't she? Shivering in that little sweater.

"These plans of yours," she says.

He looks around uncomfortably, feeling as though the blank screens of the computer monitors are surveilling them. He says, "My office?"

She follows him and he closes the door behind them. She goes over to the radiator and places her hands on its grate before turning to face him and crossing her arms. Rémy fiddles with the knob on the thermostat. He listens for the hiss of the radiator. Nothing.

"Where's Colette?"

"Who?"

"Our plant."

"I brought her home for the break."

This lie seems to satisfy. Evidence he cares about the plant. Has not accidentally killed it by leaving it too close to the drafty window.

"The apartment," he says. "It doesn't mean anything."

She pretends to ignore him and occupies herself with the sleeves of her sweater, which she tugs over her hands to form mittens. He remembers an old space heater somewhere at the bottom of the storage closet and decides to leave it where it is.

"Hypocrite," he says quietly.

Her eyebrows twitch and her eyes widen. "So, we're throwing insults now."

"You haven't left David yet."

"You want me to go first? Is that it?"

"Why not?"

Her hands emerge from her sleeves like small, furless animals. They seem to gnaw at each other as she fidgets.

She says, "How else am I supposed to know you're serious?"

The anger has receded from her voice, and fear has crept in. For a moment he considers letting well enough alone.

He says, "You know what I think? You like it this way. You like that I have Delphine. Because it makes me the bad guy and means you don't have to do anything about David."

She mutters something bitter in English that he doesn't understand.

"At least I have a valid reason," he says.

She looks at him with a glint of interest, waits for him to continue.

A *reason*? Idiot. He has no plan beyond this word.

"Never mind," he says.

"No, don't do that. What is it?"

"Forget it. I didn't mean anything."

"But you *did*."

He stalls, circles the room. Comes back. "Delphine has—"

"Yes," Marian says, eagerly but cautiously, as the though the rest of his sentence could set everything right, but only against all odds.

He takes another lap around the room. He feels like a trapped animal. "It's that I can't leave Delphine until after the appointment."

"Appointment," Marian repeats, slowly.

"At the end of February. I can't talk about it. Out of respect. Discretion."

He waits to see the effect of this vague statement, this invention. She seems to absorb it in stages. Suspicion passes first over her face, then a hint of doubt: maybe she's been wrong to judge so harshly. Maybe the appointment is real, and its cause life-threatening. He knows what he wants her to think: it must be medical, dire. And it is, isn't it? Delphine's anorexia. But he also wants her not to believe him. He has offered Delphine up as collateral, and now wishes to protect her from crude hypotheses, from his betrayal.

He calculates. "If it were David, you would do the same."

David the talisman. She won't let him threaten her husband's wellbeing, even hypothetically. Will she?

She slouches against the radiator.

He waits.

"Okay," she says finally, and when he moves near, she lets
him hold her.

"Last night I dreamed we slept the night together," she says.

The drama, he thinks once she has left. And also: the banality.
He understands now how Flaubert felt about Emma Bovary.
The vulgarity—the ordinariness—of this character made
Flaubert nauseous. He wrote as much in a letter to Louise Colet.
His own creation, sickening.

Rémy tries to be objective. Is this affair still pleasurable? Or
is he simply addicted to its intensity, its secret highs and lows?
Does addiction rule out real connection? He's heard people talk
about being in love with love, which is a trite explanation that
misses the crucial point. It's a question of angle of vision. To
love is to focus on the sexy, the quirky, the serendipitous; until
sexy goes stale and lurid, quirky exasperates, and serendipitous
proves itself unlucky.

A real writer would use this material, he thinks as he hauls
out the space heater, brushes its dust off his fingers and onto
his trousers, and plugs it into the wall outlet near Colette's old
spot. Sort the melodrama, and write himself, only better: more
capable of change and revelation.

The cuckold cuckolded. This is the story he chooses to write.
A way of deflecting his guilt about Delphine. But also a way
to transpose, to deepen the themes of his own life: guilt and
betrayal and the gnawing anxiety of relationships. Art and even
death, why not?

"Nuit blanche," Rémy writes, and centres this title at the top
of an otherwise blank screen. *Sleepless Night.*

The story opens with a bang on the door in the night. The
main character, Vincent, a professor of literature (too close to
home) . . . philosophy (too abstract) . . . Vincent, a professor of
history, blindly shuffles across the apartment to the peephole.
His drunk neighbour's bald head *glares* at him (good word!)

under the fluorescent lights. "The outside door," the neighbour shouts. "You left the outside door open again. It's not safe!"

Here Rémy pauses. From which corner of his unconscious does this neighbour issue? The neighbour must be a symbol of invasion. Or primeval competition. A bit of David, perhaps?

Stop it, he thinks now. Stop analyzing your own story. The neighbour exists, full stop.

A bang on the door . . . an accusation . . . the conflict is crackling.

"You hear me?" the neighbour bellows.

Will Vincent tell the neighbour to fuck off? They seem to have preassigned roles to play. Antagonists.

No. This time, Rémy realizes, Vincent just wants it to end.

"Look, I'm really sorry," Vincent says through the door, sounding sincere, contrite. "It won't happen again."

Silence.

More conflict, or?

An unexpected armistice.

"Ah. Well—goodnight!" the neighbour exclaims, and through the peephole Vincent watches him cross the hallway and slump against the door to his own apartment. Vincent hears a woman's voice, at once angry and pleading. The neighbour's girlfriend.

"Again!" The girlfriend shouts, worried, angry. "Four in the morning. Where were you?"

Vincent's own girlfriend—Daphné—is sitting up in bed. Who is Daphné, what type of woman? A depressive painter, Rémy decides. But he can't just plop a woman into Vincent's bed mid-scene, so he goes back to the first paragraph and inserts the painter girlfriend there. Now she, too, has been disturbed by the bang of the neighbour's fist on the door.

"You know it's his girlfriend who leaves the door open," Daphné says as Vincent lies back down. "Why don't you just tell him?"

Vincent resets the alarm on his cell to ring later and places it back on the nightstand. "Who wants to be told?"

(This is it—the crux, the foreshadowing. Secrets, discovery. Willful denial.)

Now a little bit of backstory—no, no, not too much, just enough to raise questions in the reader's mind. How to segue? Thoughts about the lease on their apartment, which is due to be renewed. They should move, bury old traumas, but of course they won't. Inertia reigns.

Rémy writes: They've lived here almost three years now, if that's the way you count. Another way to count is in events: one dissertation defense (his), three art shows (hers), eleven adjunct gigs (his), one ongoing depression (hers), one miscarriage (hers? theirs?), one suicide attempt (hers).

Miscarriage? A metaphor for the artistic process, no doubt. (Here he chases away a series of feminist objections that Marian would certainly make. Male appropriation of female reproduction. Metaphors that shroud men's historical control of women's bodies.)

And what about the suicide? Is it too obviously a condensation and displacement of Delphine's anorexia? Rémy shudders, gnaws on guilt, deliberates. No, the connection will be evident only to him.

More characters wander onto the scene. An artistic pair who maintain an ambiguous relationship. Sometimes a couple, sometimes not. Tristan and Yvonne. They share workspace with Daphné, a loft, where they also live together in artistic squalor. This is the scene of the crime (read: suicide attempt). After the miscarriage, the reader learns, Daphné tried to hang herself from the rafters of the loft.

Who finds her, who saves her? Tristan. Skinny as his hipster jeans, he nonetheless fetches a ladder and heroically carries Daphné down.

Rémy writes: The three of them—Yvonne, Tristan, Daphné—now refer to the incident in jest, Yvonne telling

Daphné she would strangle her all over again for spilling a can of brush oil; Daphné telling Tristan he'd better not put on weight because what if she needs him to climb another ladder? Vincent is smart enough to know this is their way of coping, but he isn't relaxed enough to be a part of it. He adds their conspiracy to the wad of resentment that he chews on his long drives to and from Chicoutimi, where he is teaching three courses as an adjunct this term. L'Université du Québec à Chicoutimi, l'UQAC, both in its long form and short, to him sounds like expectorate.

(Waterton, Waterton, Rémy thinks. My own personal purgatory.)

Now for more intrusions, betrayals: Vincent often comes home and finds Yvonne and Tristan slumped at each end of the sofa, Daphné stretched out between them, her head resting on one lap and her feet on the other. They always greet him as though they've been talking about him, so he has begun listening at the door before entering the apartment. His fingers warm the metal of his keys as he anticipates winding, intimate narratives from Daphné, confessions protected by his absence and the dim lamplight of the apartment and the undulation of voices and traffic from the street below. He waits for Daphné to recount their fights that skip like dark stones and sink, unresolved. Like two nights ago, when he refused to watch a documentary on the polar ice caps, and she lay on the sofa and watched it alone, her hands folded over her stomach, a protective, habitual gesture now, while he sat at his computer desk, feigning work.

(Delphine and her nature videos. They appear in their darkest form.)

Vincent lurks outside the apartment, ear to the door. No voices this time—only fado music and silence. He enters, dripping from the rain. On the sofa, Yvonne and Tristan, the space between them empty. They lift their wine glasses to their mouths, almost in unison. Another glass waits on the coffee table before them, still brimming. Daphné has gone out to buy . . . pomegranate. Yvonne offers the wine to Vincent. He wedges himself between them on the sofa, wishing there were another place to sit.

"Uneventful," Vincent says, when they ask him about the drive from Chicoutimi in the pouring rain.

Now with a cerebral pleasure that is almost physical, Rémy types the following:

Great, slow globs of rain slap the sidewalk outside the Pavillon des Arts. Vincent is thinking he'll make it before the skies burst, but they light up, crash, pour. He doesn't know the girl in the orange rain boots. She grips the handle of her umbrella like *this*, the wind is blowing that hard. Where is he headed? The parking lot, just there. She walks with him, holds the umbrella high, speaks the digits of her phone number clearly and calmly before she hurries away. The wiper blades thrash while he fumbles with his cell phone and hopes to God he remembers—

Daphné enters, her hair and jacket dripping on the linoleum. Now Rémy must get rid of Yvonne and Tristan—he writes them out of the scene with what he considers insufficient flair. (He'll deal with it in a later draft.) Daphné stabs at her pomegranate, waves the knife around as she talks, invites Vincent to an event at the loft—some sort of impromptu show . . . a dollar art sale, Rémy decides. Of course, Vincent invents an excuse. Daphné peers into the gouged pomegranate shell, looks up, smiles. "You don't want to go to the loft because I tried to hang myself there."

Vincent drinks. "Ever heard of a euphemism?"

"It's my throat."

Perfect. Now to bring the neighbour subplot back. Vincent must meet the neighbour's girlfriend. She will be sympathetic, empathic. Plain. The reader will wonder about the potential for sex. Of course, that would be too obvious.

Vincent goes out for a drink alone. He forgets his keys and now he's locked out of the apartment. He slumps, his back resting against the door. The neighbour girlfriend comes home. She's wearing a brown food service uniform. She says, "Lucky the downstairs door was open, eh?" She goes inside and returns with rosehip tea for him in a butterfly mug.

Now, an exchange regarding happiness. (Gently, gently, Rémy thinks. Don't hammer the themes too hard.)

"Wait—" Vincent says, and the woman does.

"Do you remember being happy?"

The woman pulls her cardigan over her chest and crosses her arms.

Vincent laughs, uncomfortable. "Stupid question. It's late. I'm sorry."

"You can keep the mug," the neighbour woman says, her tone bright. "We've got plenty."

The fluorescent lights buzz and click and voices waft from the other apartments. Vincent dozes, his head resting on the doorframe. A bump to his leg wakes him. His bald neighbour towers over him, swaying a little. Vincent blinks at him warily.

The neighbour snorts. "They're such a pain in the ass, right? Christ."

It takes Vincent a moment to understand. "Tell me about it," he says. He closes his eyes and waits for the man to leave. When he opens them again the butterfly mug is gone. The apartment across the hall is silent.

New scene. How much time has passed? An hour? A week? It doesn't matter. What matters is that Vincent texts the umbrella girl. This exchange is devoid of literary appeal. It pains Rémy to squeeze his main character's impressive scholarly mind into one-hundred-and-forty-character blips. Clichéd advances punctuated by smiley faces.

The girl's name is Mara. Rémy cannot help himself. He'll rename both her and Daphné in a later draft. Of course, Mara is Anglophone.

Vincent takes Mara for dinner at a bistro in Chicoutimi. He learns that she's studying Management at the University of Toronto and is on exchange at l'UQAC to learn French. She's nineteen years old. (So much younger than Marian! That much more illicit!)

In Rémy's mind, despite her nineteen years, Mara looks like Marian, but the reader doesn't need to know this. The reader only sees what's on the page. So Rémy gives her dark brown eyes (Marian's are blue), and bird-like ways (Marian is too curvy to be bird-like).

Dinner does not lead to sex, but Mara tells Vincent that next time, they will spend the night together.

Now for another chance encounter, another character. Can Rémy pull it off? Does this make for too many characters, too many coincidences? The reader may think the story unfocused, or contrived. But Rémy is committed to the structure—he must persevere.

A knock on the doorframe of Vincent's derelict office in the basement of the Pavillon des Arts. The middle-aged man in the unfashionable jean jacket has the look of a mature student: nervous, wanting to make something of the second half of his life now that the first half has proven unsatisfactory. But no—it turns out he is looking to collect his daughter's assignment. Vincent is dismissive—he can't give out student work. Against university policy. But the man, whose name evokes honesty, simplicity—Amable (too old fashioned), Matthieu (too Biblical), Gérard (perfect!)—Gérard Leclerc is looking for . . . Camille Leclerc's assignment.

I'm sorry, Monsieur Leclerc, Vincent says, but I can't give out your daughter's work.

Now, for the reader, the gap between Gérard Leclerc's puzzling need and Vincent's lack of understanding grows palpable. Over a few excruciating lines of dialogue, it all becomes clear, but too slowly for poor Vincent. We learn that Camille Leclerc was killed in a car accident, that Vincent was her favourite professor, and that Gérard Leclerc has come looking for the girl's last piece of writing.

Vincent cannot remember Camille Leclerc, but now her name, at least, rings a bell . . . the subject heading of an email from the dean's office that he never opened. Embarrassment, awkwardness.

The conversation continues. Gérard Leclerc, we learn, was on the phone with his daughter when she died. His wife blames him for the accident. Everyone knows it's unsafe to drive while holding a cell phone—illegal, after all.

Now, a startling epiphany! (Gently, gently, Rémy thinks again. Elegance in invisible.) This man's pain resonates. Vincent feels loss ripple through him. He wants to give this grieving father an offering, and so he thumbs through a folder of graded assignments. "It's just a reader response paper," he says. "But she wrote it. It's hers."

As Gérard's face melts with relief and gratitude, Vincent feels ashamed. Whatever comments he has written on the paper will be terse and discouraging, as always.

"Thank you for—" Gérard breaks off.

"She was a very good student," Vincent says.

Cut to the next scene. Vincent meets Mara outside the Pavillon sportif. Her ponytail is wet. Her black yoga pants conform appealingly to her thighs, but Vincent briefly feels as though he's picking up a daughter from ballet or gymnastics. He checks them into a bed and breakfast—no, an inn (verisimilitude!—who goes to a B&B to have sex?). Once in their room, he says he must make a phone call. Mara is unfazed—the girl is eerily devoid of jealousy. (Would that Marian were so stoic!) She says she needs to take a shower, anyway. When she asks to borrow some shampoo, Vincent tells her that toiletries are provided.

"Right. Like a hotel," Mara says, and while Rémy is enjoying her subtly naive ways, enjoying his own skill at creating her subtly naive ways, Vincent accepts a kiss from

Mara, who strokes both sides of his face with her thumbs, and closes the bathroom door behind her.

Now for the finale. Can Rémy bring it home?

Vincent dials, bursting with the need to talk to Daphné about Gérard Leclerc. The reader comprehends perfectly: suddenly, unexpectedly, he understands loss.

Daphné doesn't pick up.

When Mara gets out of the shower, he is lying fully clothed on the Chintz bedspread with his shoes still on, crying. Mara spoons him, still wrapped in a towel, and while the dampness transfers to the back of his clothes, she tells him he's a good man. After a long while, she rises, dresses in silence and zips her belongings into her bag. Before slipping out, she turns off the light.

Vincent's cell rings several times before he realizes in which dark room he's been sleeping. He sits up and finds the phone in the pocket of the pants he's still wearing. The caller ID reads Daphné.

Static on the line. Voices. Slowly it becomes clear that Daphné didn't mean to call him. She must have accidentally pressed the button—

"—no I didn't put it there," Daphné is saying. She sounds giddy, perhaps drunk.

"Then where?" a man says.

"I don't know. Look in the drawer."

Seconds pass. "Found it," the man says.

The man, Vincent realizes, is Tristan. The object they are searching for, a box of condoms.

Silence on the line. Now the neighbour makes his final appearance.

"Ugh, not again," Daphné says after a moment. "Just ignore him. He'll stop pounding eventually."

"Dude's obnoxious. I don't know why you don't just move."

"Me neither. Come here."

"I'm here."

A first draft. Rémy unplugs the space heater, locks up, and heads out into the cold. For a bracing moment he is Vincent; he has turned away and closed his eyes just in time. When he opens them, he's never slept with the student in the orange rain boots, never pulled condoms from an unfamiliar drawer, has only lain there on the sofa behind Delphine, his hand on her belly, silently crying as the screen flickers and the ice melts.

Chapter Twenty-Five

Cancer, Marian thinks. Delphine must have cancer.

Except you can't just ship a cancer patient off to another city, even if that city is Montreal. Good luck and Godspeed, cancer patient. Nice knowing you. Here's a moderately comfortable apartment close to the métro. Enjoy what's left of your life.

Surgery, then? Knee replacement. Tonsillectomy. Triple bypass. But why would these require 'discretion'? Something intimate, then. Abortion? (Marian shudders.) Something embarrassing. Hemorrhoidectomy.

He said 'appointment.' Not procedure, not operation. Appointment.

Therapy?

Optometrist. Manicure. Cat groomer.

He's faking it. Liar. But what about Marian? What's her excuse? Is she not the same? Has she told David? Has she confessed? Some days her conscience is pulled so tight it could snap.

Hasn't yet, though, has it?

Everybody hurts people. Cruelty is in how long you make it last.

"They fired me," David says, which is not the answer she is expecting when she asks him what is wrong, after coming home to find him gripping the remote and blinking at the muted TV set.

She shoos Kong away but doesn't go over to David, just slouches awkwardly in the middle of the living room. "No," she says.

"What do you mean, No?"

"They can't do that."

"Oh, but they can."

"You're so good at your job!"

"I hate to disillusion you, but actually, that's not true."

"They probably just wanted to save money. It's always about money."

"Not this time."

"Well, what then?"

"Where have you been the past few months?"

"Here. School. What kind of question is that?"

"You don't get it."

"I know I don't get it! That's why I'm asking."

"Edna," he says quietly.

Marian sighs, her exasperation tinged with guilt. "Not this funeral business again. I said I was sorry. I haven't got a special time machine, David. I can't go back to that moment and go with you to the funeral." But even as she speaks, she sees on his face she's missing something. He won't even look at her. And she shouldn't be annoyed at him when he's just lost his job. But why has he chosen this moment to dig his finger into an old wound?

"Would *you* want to go back there? If you were me?"

It takes her a moment to realize that he's talking about work.

"The Acorn House," she says, stupidly. "Because Edna— because you—"

His tears are already welling over. He never cries, and she doesn't know how to process what she's witnessing.

"I can't stand being there," he says, avoiding her gaze, thumping the remote against his thigh. "I can't fucking stand it. It's as though I can smell her. Everywhere." He laughs bitterly.

"She didn't even stink yet! She was only dead a couple of hours. But it's like death just crawled up my nostrils and stayed."

Marian knows she should go over to him, wrap her arms around him, but she's like a marionette whose puppeteer is off taking a piss somewhere. Her limbs are not her own.

"And I just keep thinking—over and over—" David shakes his head.

She waits for him to finish. When he doesn't, she says, "Thinking what?"

"I mean, you're off doing God knows what." He points angrily in the direction of the window with the remote. Throws it down on the sofa. "No, I'm pretty sure I know what, but let's not get into that."

Marian winces, hopes he doesn't mean what she thinks he means. As though hope were an antidote against him knowing.

David grinds his knuckles to his chin, then stares at his hand and violently shakes it as if this nervous tic were responsible for his anger. "And all the while I'm thinking: people die alone. Without anyone. They live their lives alone, they work at a crappy tourist site, cash their pay cheque, go home to an empty apartment . . . and it kills them. Because nothing has meaning."

Marian retroactively pieces together the past six months. The nightmares, the apathy about getting to work on time. The reprieve from his depression when he was on vacation in Thunder Bay over Christmas, and away from the Acorn House.

"The board," she says cautiously, "when they fired you— what were their grounds?"

"Oh, you know. Not showing up. Not doing anything at all when I did show up. Not answering calls, not returning messages. Letting the raccoons in." A crackly laugh.

"Maybe they'll change their minds," Marian says. "Maybe if you explain—"

"That I can't do the job anymore?" David interrupts.

"Okay," Marian says. "I see that. I do. But it's going to be okay. We'll find you another job. At another historical site, or—"

"Enough," David says. "Would it kill you, just for once, to be okay with things *not being okay*?"

Marian looks away. "I never say the right thing."

"Nope," David says. "You certainly don't. When my parents split, you told me it was better for them to be apart, to not be at each other's throats anymore. Then you dragged me to the Toronto Zoo to look at the llamas and giraffes. When I was working that string of shitty restaurant jobs, you told me it wasn't so bad, that at least we were together." David exhales, shakes his head. "Easy for you to say. You were the one collecting a fat scholarship and taking seminars on Marie-Claire Blais and Camus."

"I just wanted you to feel better again," Marian says.

"Maybe. Or is it that *you* didn't want to feel shitty?"

Marian doesn't reply. She picks up a stack of junk mail from the bookshelf and leafs through it without seeing it, hands shaking, holding back tears. She drops a flyer on the floor and leaves it there. So she's as bad as her mother. Push back hard, her mother told her when she said she wasn't happy with David. As though emotions were nothing but willpower.

David rubs his eyes in exhaustion. "You haven't told me who."

"Who," Marian repeats. She understands but takes the time she needs for the name to travel from her brain down into her mouth. Once she spits it out, she won't be able to take it back.

"Rémy," she says, meeting his gaze. At the very least, she can look him in the eye.

"Rémy. Of course." David springs from the sofa and paces the living room. Kong skitters away and crouches at a safe distance.

"It started at the conference—well, not exactly—it was after that—in the fall, I guess—"

"Shut up! Just shut up. I didn't ask."

"God, oh God. I'm so sorry."

"Stop it! Quit crying! You hear me? *You* don't get to cry."

"Okay! I'll stop. Don't you want to know why?"

"Do I want to know why, she asks. There is no *why*, Marian. What do you think this is? Some essay you're writing? Rémy. Good old Rémy."

Over by the muted TV, the dog whimpers. "Come here, honey," Marian says, but Kong drops his jaw to pant.

"That's perfect. Now you muster up some empathy. Now you care about someone other than yourself."

"That's mean."

"It's mean, all right." David hiccups. "What could you possibly have done to deserve it?"

"Okay, I get it. Call me a bitch. Call me a whore."

"No." He holds up his hands, as though to say, *Stop*, or *I surrender*. "You're not going to turn me into some asshole. The world is already full of assholes."

Kong mewls like a sick calf.

"What the hell?" Marian says.

"Ah, Jesus."

The dog is advancing towards the kitchen in a squat. He rocks on his haunches and drops three symmetrical turds as he goes.

A strange noise issues from David's throat, half hoot, half sob. "There's shit on the living room floor, Marian," he says. "You see that? *Shit on the floor.*"

"I see it."

She finds a plastic bag and spirits the turds away, then spritzes and scrubs while David cradles the dog.

"I really love you, you know," he says.

Chapter Twenty-Six

Marian calls Juliette and explains the whole mess through gulping sobs. When she describes the part about Rémy, there is a long silence on the other end of the phone.

"You there?" Marian asks. "Of course you're there."

"I think my mind just left my body."

"Well, let me know when it returns."

"Okay, I'm good." Pause. "When you make a mistake, you make it big, don't you?"

"I know," Marian whines. "Shut up. Do you think I'm an idiot?"

"No, honey. Rémy's the idiot."

Marian knows better than to defend him. "David asked me to leave," she says.

"No surprise there. Pack your things. There's room here for you."

"Down the hatch." Juliette's fingers hover above Marian's face.

Marian cranes her neck and opens her mouth like a baby bird ready for a worm. In drops a Swedish berry.

"Do you want to talk some more?"

Marian rests her cheek on her friend's leg as she wanly chews her gummy. "I feel like I've done nothing but talk these past couple of days."

Juliette nods. "TV or movie?"

"Who cares?"

"TV, then." Juliette flicks through a few channels and settles on Radio-Canada. She places the remote on the futon and, for a few minutes, pets Marian's head like she's an oversized cat. On the screen, a swarm of student protestors has blocked the Jacques Cartier bridge in Montreal. Police officers force the students backwards with pepper spray and riot shields.

"Funny how most protest footage ends up looking the same," Juliette says. "No matter where it takes place or what the cause."

"Pepper spray makes for good television," Marian observes. "I admire the students—I really do—but I can't help feeling like they live on another planet."

"Because their tuition is so much less than ours?"

"Exactly!" Marian exclaims, eager to get worked up about something other than her love life. "We paid over six K last year. Even with the hikes, Québec students will still only pay thirty-eight hundred dollars a year."

"True," Juliette says. "But if it's all relative, you could make the argument the other way, too—in France, tuition is basically free. University is treated as a democratic right. The idea is that when education costs too much, it ends up being accessible only to those who pay."

"I guess I'm just jealous."

"That's the rational response, frankly. Is my tongue red?"

"No. Surprisingly. Mine?"

"Nope."

Marian reaches for another gummy. "It's like a topic for a debate team. How much is an education worth to the collective? To the individual? What percentage should the student pay? And the taxpayer? Who benefits the most? Right now, the Québec taxpayer is footing most of the bill."

"That's as it should be. Otherwise inequalities just grow."

"I get that everyone benefits from an educated society. But should tuition really be frozen for forty years? Seems like maybe it's time to play catch-up."

"I don't know," Juliette says. "I wonder if the forty-year streak is almost the point. There's a tradition of access to education that dates back to the Quiet Revolution. Why let politicians mess with that? Anyway, our Québec peers put us to shame. When the Waterton Admin slashed budgets all over campus, there was hardly a whimper. Other than the petition in the fall that went nowhere."

"We've definitely underperformed at protesting."

"Agreed."

Marian shifts to look up at her friend, tears in her eyes. "It's hard work trying not to be sad."

Juliette nods and pets her head. "Feelings. They'll come for you one way or another. Should we offer them a glass of rosé?"

"Might as well let them wallow," Marian says, and Juliette gets up to fetch the wine.

Chapter Twenty-Seven

Rémy is intimately acquainted with all the shades of Marian's mopey existence. She sleeps on Juliette's lumpy futon with Juliette, who snores but is not a blanket-hog, and when she wakes up, she 'looks at' her dissertation. After she's done looking at it—she must not like what she sees, because she hasn't submitted any new work to him in several months—she comes to his office to sigh and smile bravely and describe to him her unmoored existence, and occasionally cry. Some days he even listens while she goes on about David. The experience is both pleasurable and repugnant—it's like picking at someone else's scab. (Rémy is part voyeur. He has always known this about himself.) Marian says she feels unnerved by her husband's detached civility towards her—it's as though he's bundled all his emotions into one courteous little ball. He delivers her mail to her once a week, coolly arranges her visits with the dog, and inquires after the well-being of her parents.

Rémy both admires and is troubled by David's behaviour. Such quiet dignity! Why does he not feel angry and castrated? He should curse and drink scotch and go down swinging his wounded ego. He should plot murder—*murders*, plural, for both Marian and Rémy must rightly die—and imagine every detail of his subsequent arrest and incarceration. He should obsess over the words he will use to describe his raging pain to his prison therapist, that sturdy depository of his guilty conscience.

Rémy prefers this fantasy version of David to the real one, the David who seems to be mastering the trick at which Rémy is failing: compartmentalization. Packing a few things to move to the Montreal apartment is stirring up a grand confusion in Rémy regarding Marian, Delphine, and the institution of love. He is overwhelmed by the open cardboard box in front him that contains slotted spoons, a paper towel holder, spice shakers, and a gravy boat that, to his knowledge, has never been used. What are these objects doing here? Do they have meaning? The gravy boat he has just wrapped in a couple of pages from Tuesday's *Le Devoir*, to which he has now resubscribed. He was careful to use the "Monde" section and not the front page, because he's hoarding the daily coverage of the student strikes. Sweet distraction from his own problems! In response to the Liberals' university tuition hike, Québec students are banging pots and pans in a great cacophonous symphony of solidarity. At least thirty-six thousand of them on strike so far, and the movement shows no sign of relenting. *Les manifs casseroles*. This is the difference between Québec and Canada, Rémy thinks: people *bother*. They don't just grumble and say, What a shame. They cut up boxes like the one in front of him now, and instead of docking gravy boats in them, they make picket signs to point towards the sky, and flash their symbolic red squares, and generally stomp around. They honour the legacy of their parents and grandparents who fought for access to education during the Quiet Revolution. Who fought and won! They make noise while the rest of the country looks on in indifference or anger or incomprehension. (Rémy knows damn well that his own indignation is righteous. He knows and revels in it.) Those Quebeckers, the English are thinking: always demanding something beyond their due. Or so suggests the worst of the Canadian media, which might as well be run by American Republicans. Where did facts disappear to? Does a seventy-five percent increase in tuition over five years not merit a conversation? You can't just shove the increase down people's throats. Rémy imagines himself being interviewed by one of those English-Canadian TV personalities, like the one with the receding silver-blonde hair. "Say what you will regarding the increases," Rémy tells Lloyd Robertson as he leans back in his chair, relaxing into airtime and studio space, occupying intellectual territory. "It's not a question of money. It's a question of democracy. We voted these parliamentary representatives in. They are there to represent *us*. If they stop acting in the interests of the people, civil disobedience is the only answer."

The fantasy fizzles and vanishes into one of the cardboard boxes. Rémy looks down at his hands, which are stained with ink from the newspaper sheets he has been handling. If he were working in Québec, if he were these students' professor, would he picket with them? Of course he would. But he's here in Waterton with this mess, waiting for a new tape gun because the other one broke, and Delphine is not yet home from the office supply store. He is in desperate need of adhesive.

"Where the hell—"

It takes him six rings to find the phone. (In a laundry basket, under a wok.)

"You didn't call last week," Papi says.

Rémy apologizes and says he's been busy.

"I could die tomorrow." Papi pauses to spit tobacco. "I don't say this to make you feel bad. It's the other way around. If I don't wake up tomorrow, you'll be thinking, Tabarnak, I should have called."

"You're right. I should have called."

"Mhm."

"I've been wondering how things are going over there," Rémy says. "I mean with the strikes."

"Those casseroles are music to my ears."

"You getting around okay?"

"Your mother is following the protests on Twitter. We try not to be in the car when the kids hit the streets in the evening.

That works out okay. For the most part they're nice enough to schedule their rabble-rousing." Papi coughs. "Kasia crocheted me a little red square to pin onto my jacket. She swears up and down it's not girly. I have my doubts. I wear it anyway."

"Ask her to make me one."

"She already has. Says she'll tack it on you when you come around." Another pause to spit. "And the move? You got your junk sorted out?"

"*Getting* my junk sorted out. Present tense."

"Your mother's making me sort through my old clothes here, too. She's spring cleaning. I don't care for it, but she's running a duster over me all the same."

"Good to know we're in solidarity."

"How's Delphine? She eating?"

"Some." Rémy pauses. "Not really."

"That's a problem."

"You say it as though I don't know."

"It bears repeating."

"Apparently."

"You still conquering the English?"

So he's guessed at Marian's background.

"Franchement," Rémy says.

"A joke, a joke. But that woman at work. The story there."

"I've got to go."

"Ouais. You call me next time."

Rémy hangs up, gazes helplessly at the clutter of the move: piles of clothes, books, DVDs, plastic bags of utensils, a bin containing toiletries, clothes hangers, and a power cord. How complicated everything feels! How enmeshed. Impossible to sort. David knows about him and Marian. So do Juliette and Patrick, no doubt. David is not the problem; Juliette and Patrick are. Now that Rémy is coordinating French 102—Aurélie Thériault has taken her medical leave—he will be running weekly meetings with them until the end of the year. He's held two of these meetings already, during which he thought of little else other than what *they* were thinking about him. Each time it seems to him they leave his office as quickly as possible, the elephant in the room following them out the door. Does Patrick hate him? He's one of David's closest friends—Marian has told Rémy this. Does he think Rémy an adulterous pervert for seducing his married grad student? If so, how dare he judge a situation he knows nothing about? And Juliette, who has already seen him in his swimming trunks: hairy-chested, stripped of his academic dressings. Can she now accurately picture the bulge and blush of his more private anatomy? Has she heard about the sighs and groans he makes in bed? He is certain that women talk; they aren't like men. A man can't stand the thought of a buddy picturing his lover nude. A woman, on the other hand . . . Juliette must know, then, that there hasn't been as much opportunity lately for groaning. He's only had Marian over once in the past couple of weeks, while Delphine was working her last shift at Dr. Gauvin's office.

"You feel different," he made the mistake of saying to her.

"Like I left my husband?" She propped herself up on her elbow and glared.

"Your husband kicked you out," he said. "And your books and your dog are still there."

She rolled so that her back was to him, and he thought how she was poutier, touchier, and no longer as arousing as she once was. Even so, he read to her that day, found a passage from Marie-Claire Blais to hang between them in the bedroom air. But the session had no electric intensity, and dissolved into an almost paternal snuggle. He's grown increasingly conscious of Marian's age, of the nine years between them and the fact that she's still a student. He finds himself correcting her French as though to make himself feel superior.

As for Delphine, she's suddenly sharper, more focused, and thus less herself. Less herself, or more? It's as though her filters have eroded and are letting through raw content. Gone is the Delphine who only posed questions on a diagonal. Ever since they took that walk at Arrow Point—since she'd wanted to know why, exactly, he'd asked her to marry him—she's been evolving into another creature. Increasingly, she refers to past and present pain without euphemism. Just the other day, she began an anecdote by saying, "When I was in the hospital with my anorexia," as though the disorder were some friend from college with whom she'd taken a boozy vacation. Yesterday she commented that he seemed tense, and that maybe he should see a counsellor.

Is this shift in her meant to accuse, to menace? Has she guessed at his relationship with Marian? Is she using up her ammunition on her way out of town? Yet there's nothing self-satisfied in her tone, no hint that she takes pleasure in the shock value of her words. It's as though she's sorting strange truths as she goes. 'Here is our baggage,' she seems to say. 'I wonder where we should put it all now?'

He would applaud this straightforwardness if, behind his back, she hadn't stopped eating. She's lost a size since Christmas and thinks she's hiding it well beneath leggings and bold tunic sweaters. Striped, multi-coloured, paisley even. Anything to distract from what's beneath. She only undresses when it's dark or when he's out of the room, and starves herself when he's not looking. This morning as he was leaving for work, she was making herself peanut butter toast. When he threw out the broken tape roll, he noticed the untouched toast, buried in the corner of the garbage bin.

From what he can tell, she eats only yogurt in mini containers and pureed soup. When she's done putting the soup through the blender, she offers him some—"ginger-carrot bisque," she calls it—and he declines. Is she asking him to be a co-conspirator? Next, will he be expected to commune over the mini yogurts that she goes through at a rate of several packs a week? The thought of the yogurt makes his stomach turn: it's not the taste she likes, but the precision. *50 svelte calories per serving.* Airy white font over blue sky.

"Delphine is sick," he says aloud.

He leaps up and kicks the cardboard box. "Delphine is sick!" he yells. He collapses back onto the sofa, pulls the coriander shaker out of the box and cups it in his hands.

This afternoon, this day. What has he done with it? Ruminated. Sprinkled his thoughts into boxes. Shook them all out, as though through the holes of a spice shaker.

And what's wrong with that? Why so much emphasis on *action*?

Rémy pictures Flaubert hunched over his writing desk, ink on his fingertips; Flaubert removing a comma in the morning, putting it back again in the afternoon. He pictures Proust, madeleine suspended between lip and teacup, a world of memory whirling within.

Contemplation ≠ indecision. (This could be his motto, his own useless picket sign.)

Thought *is* action!

Liar.

A car door slams, and a minute later Delphine chirps at him about the confusing signage that marks the aisles of the office supply store. She passes him a plastic bag that contains the tape gun and some labels for the boxes. Hands on her hips, she surveys the kitchen. She says, "I'm taking the blender."

He imagines the carrot-ginger bisque. Her body shrinking. The body he has held over the years and watched transform for better and worse. The body he has loved, feared, made a part of him.

His decision to stay with Delphine is physical; it precedes thought. Emanates from his cells.

"Please don't," he says.

Tells his cells: *You made this decision. Now own it.*

Chapter Twenty-Eight

Marian should have peed at Roast, but hindsight only exists now, in line at the student services kiosk in the foyer of the athletic complex, where she's waiting to renew her bus pass before the kiosk closes at five p.m. One person in front of her, three behind her. She's luckier than some, and the line has to move eventually—that's the line's one job. Still, a couple of large mocha lattes in a row: not exactly a conservative choice on her part. She could admit defeat, go find a bathroom and walk the twenty minutes back to Juliette's—bus pass be damned—but the temperature outside has dropped fifteen degrees since this morning, and unlike the guy in front of her, who's sporting a furry Yukon hat, she has nothing to cover her ears, having lost her toque somewhere between the cafeteria, the library, and the café.

The girl who is being helped right now wants to buy tickets for a basketball game. Whose idea was it to have the bus pass counter deal with sports tickets as well? Is there no hierarchy of needs? The credit card machine isn't working, and the girl isn't impressed. She needs tickets for herself and her parents for this weekend. Her boyfriend is a point guard.

The basketball groupie tells the woman behind the counter to forget about the chip already. "Would you just key in the numbers? Please? Thanks very much."

Marian has cash. If the basketball groupie stepped aside, and the guy in the Yukon hat took pity on her, she could buy her bus pass in sixty seconds flat and go find a bathroom.

Another two people queue up behind her. If she leaves now, she certainly won't be able to renew her pass before the kiosk closes. Which, okay, she could pay the two dollars and seventy-five cents for the single fare. But that would feel like a moral failure, and there's the sunk cost to consider. She's already spent nineteen minutes in this line. Later tonight she'll have to spend nineteen fewer minutes trolling the Internet or playing around on Facebook just to make up for it. And if she has to come back tomorrow in addition?

She turns to the undergrad girl behind her, whose blue leather jacket marks her as an Engineering student. "Not exactly efficient service today," Marian says.

The girl looks up from her cell, alarmed that a stranger has plucked her from her pixels. "The employee is doing her best," she says, presumably wanting to show that she's made of more patient stuff than both Marian and the basketball groupie. "Relax."

Marian suppresses snarky instincts and fishes her own cell out of her pocket. Still no email from Rémy. She hasn't heard from him in over a day. Admittedly, twenty-six hours isn't that long—the sun and moon have only had time to trade places twice in that period. But still, a whole day? Where is he?

At home. At work. At the grocery store. Does it matter? Not emailing her, that's for sure.

In a meeting. In the bathtub. On the can.

If only Marian herself were on the can.

"Is there a manager or someone else who can help me?" the basketball groupie asks.

"Nope. Just me," the kiosk worker replies flatly.

Marian tears the attention of the engineering student away from her smartphone a second time.

"I need to go to the bathroom. Would you mind saving my spot?"

The girl surveys the scene, her eyes running the length of the line. "Yeah, no, sorry. That would be unfair to everyone else."

"Your sense of equity is touching," Marian says, and the girl makes a show of rolling her eyes.

Marian edges past the Yukon hat guy and shoulders in next to the basketball groupie in order to address the woman behind the counter. "Sorry to interrupt. Can you please tell me where the nearest bathroom is?"

"The locker rooms are to your left and down one level," the woman says, not looking up from the credit card machine. "You'll need your student card."

Marian thanks her and hurries along the dank corridor that stinks of bleach, sweat, and cement. Its postered walls depict human silhouettes in postures of exertion or triumph: dangling off a cliff face, slogging up a sand dune, cresting a ridge. NEVER GIVE UP. She passes another kiosk where a mother is enrolling her young daughter in swim classes. The girl crosses one leg over the other and pinches her face, evidently concentrating hard on holding her urine. *I hear you, little sister,* Marian thinks as she powers by, impressed by her own speed, as spry as anyone who ever starred in a motivational poster. Maybe she's an athlete after all. Champion pee walker.

With her student card she swipes herself through the gym's turnstile and follows the arrow that points her down to the locker rooms. On the stairwell she's held up by three young women who descend in slow motion, texting their boyfriends or mothers or maybe even each other, who knows. That Marian is nipping at their heels like an antsy puppy doesn't faze them— doesn't even register. They exist only virtually, and Marian has the misfortune of existing in the world of flesh and blood and full bladders. She unzips her down coat, which is making her sweat, and counts to sixteen-Mississippi as she shuffles down the stairs behind the trio of texters, resisting the urge to kick their calves.

The basement level of the athletic complex is a windowless labyrinth—a Soviet bunker that reeks of chlorine. A young lifeguard flip-flops towards Marian, munching on cheese doodles, and above her head beckons the skirted icon that signals relief. Marian laughs in gratitude. The lifeguard shoots her a look of confusion mixed with post-adolescent disdain. But Marian is too busy praying to the bathroom gods to care—please let there be no line-up, no swarm of water polo players ridding themselves of sport drinks, no Aquafit ladies emptying their bladders before performing transabdominal twists in the pool.

She heaves the door wide and startles a mother with babe-in-arms. The mother turns her body and thus her child away from Marian, avoiding such an uncivilized and insensitive person, one who neglects to navigate the world in anticipation of babies-on-board. No matter! Because Marian has almost completed her obstacle course: a mop bucket and a handful of women in various states of undress are all that stand between her and her goal.

"CAUTION: WET FLOOR," a yellow sign warns her. She advances without caution and whacks her knee on one of the long, wooden benches that run the length of the locker bay. Silently swearing, she evades the breasts of a corpulent woman who applies deodorant with unusual vigour, and manoeuvres around the hips of another, towel-clad, woman, bent over and rooting around in the bottom of a locker. But just when she thinks she's in the clear—when the bathroom stalls are but ten feet away—the towel-clad woman draws herself up and spins around, brandishing a hairbrush. In order to avoid a collision with her elbow, Marian pivots, rocks, and helplessly gropes the air. The woman's mouth pops open in surprise, the hairbrush springs from her hand and wings across the locker bay, and Marian, mid-fall, understands that she herself is about to make contact with one hard surface or another. She decides to aim for the bench rather than the floor, torques her body and lands squarely, miraculously—but not without abuse to the flesh over her sitz bones—in an upright posture on the bench.

The hairbrush skids across the tile and settles bristles-up in a puddle. The towel drops.

Both Marian and the naked woman are shocked stupid.

When Marian was a child, she would come to the pool for swimming lessons or a classmate's birthday party, and stare at the female bodies on display in the change room: the scrawls of pubic hair, the slash of stretch marks, the browned and wrinkled skin like that of a cooked turkey neck, the smattering of moles and age spots, and especially the fat: cellulite, meaty breasts, underarm waddles, thighs like pizza dough. Revolting, the idea that over time, she, too, would bloat, stretch out like tired leather, engorge, discolour. That she might grow fat or reptilian. Worse, that she might get used to such ugliness, find it normal. Now that she has her own stretch marks and fleshy thighs, and has grown up and out, and masturbated and fucked and read Luce Irigaray, the tightly contained pre-pubescent body that once surveyed public change rooms in giggling disgust seems a pale prototype of what a body should be: messy, aching, spreading, flawed.

The naked woman lifts a protective, futile arm to her chest. From her seated position, Marian is level with the hand that can't quite shield both tiny breasts, can't hide the prominent ribcage just below. Her eyes are drawn downward, as though by gravity, to the impossibly small waist, the jutting hipbones and atrophied thighs.

Shit, shit, you're staring, she thinks. Jesus, stop it! What's wrong with you? Let this anorexic woman alone!

She looks up, wincing.

Looks up into Delphine's eyes.

"Oh," she says.

Repeats herself: Oh.

Confusion and embarrassment move across Delphine's face. She shakes her head free of Marian's stare, reaches down— her arms slender and breakable like the bough of a tree—and snatches the towel from the floor. Clutches it in front of herself as though it were a child's blanket.

Something wet seeps through Marian's jeans.

No.

Not possible to be sweating in a down coat in front of Delphine's naked body—her naked, anorexic body—while she *pisses* herself.

Except that her bladder is still burning.

She rocks onto one hip, looks down. A wet bathing suit peeks out from beneath her thigh. Yellow racing stripes over black.

She rises gingerly, makes an apologetic gesture over the swimsuit. Delphine angles around her, scoops up the wet garment, and grips it against her chest along with the towel. Backs up against the lockers to get a better look at Marian.

"Ah, la Petite," she breathes.

"Yes."

"I didn't recognize you."

"I was looking for the bathroom."

"You were headed the right way." Delphine points to the stalls. "There."

How long does Marian remain hunched in the metal stall? Long enough to urinate forcefully, then wait for the change room to be still. Long enough to cry in silent waves.

La Petite, she whispers, thinking of Delphine's body, so frail.

Little One.

Chapter Twenty-Nine

He waits three days before emailing Marian. Ignores her increasingly frantic queries. Finally proposes a café in the north end, outside the campus orbit. There will be strangers gabbing, espresso machines whirring. Hummus and cucumber sandwich orders being taken and delivered. Marian's stages of grief will be lived out quietly and respectfully before his eyes, under halogen lights. Shock. Denial. Bargaining. Anger. Sadness.

He isn't so naive as to foresee Acceptance.

"Sure, I can meet," she writes back. "I'll see you at The Pint at eight p.m."

The campus pub.

He is magnanimous, big enough to let her have her way one last time.

Her nose is already in the plastic menu when he arrives. She debates aloud the merits of the bacon burger and the chocolate lava cake. Orders an IPL, cancels it for bourbon.

He orders himself an espresso.

Feels the pressure at his temples, affects an air of calm.

"You should really try this," Marian says.

A forkful of lava cake hovers between them. He shakes his head and it retreats. Chocolate oozes and just misses her pink sweater. It lands on the edge of the table. He's never seen her wear pink before. Where did she get this sweater with the sleeves like bat wings?

She is both feminine and powerful. She glows like dark matter.

A bearded server asks if they ordered a pound of buffalo wings. Rémy solemnly shakes his head and the server moves on.

The lights dim. Marian licks gooey chocolate off the tines of her fork. She sniffs and imbibes her bourbon.

"Well, then. I suppose you're wondering why we're here," he says, in the tone of a man who has already cleared his throat.

"You're wondering how my dissertation is going?" She sounds innocent, sincere, like a student asking a question in class.

He looks away. "Not exactly, no."

"Hm. I suppose not."

"So, you do see."

She takes another bite of cake and stares at him as she chews. Across the room a student in a Leafs jersey guffaws. A group of professors and grad students raise their pints to a successful thesis defense. A herd of engineering students sets up for a game of quarters.

"Well. We've both been enriched by this," Rémy says. "It came upon us suddenly and we reacted in the most human way. The question now is how do we proceed?" He falters. He had a script but has forgotten most of it. What remains sounds ludicrous.

He fingers his dainty espresso cup, observes Marian's hostile consumption of cake, her pouty lips around the tines of her fork, her pink-cheeked face, at once cherubic and sulphurous. Her curves push defiantly against this new sweater. He remembers her laughing and blushing at his ribald readings of Anaïs Nin. Coaching him on how to make her come.

Even as he resolves to stay on course, firm in his conviction that *this must end*, he surprises himself with a partial erection, pictures himself tunnelling towards—but never quite arriving at—the inevitable dead end. Soft moist ridges leading nowhere.

He reaches across the table, grasps her glass of bourbon. Must end, he thinks as he takes a drink. Must.

But not necessarily today.

Why today? Why not another day? What difference?

This realization, brilliant in its simplicity, is like a valve opening. It spews relief.

Chapter Thirty

Is she free Tuesday?

Strictly speaking, she is free. Free as a bird, or a fish, or a bear, or any other animal—avian, piscine, mammalian, you name it—free as any creature free of a Tuesday.

"You're joking," she says.

"Why joking?"

"No, really."

"I think I'll have some of that cake after all." He saunters to the bar to order.

She came here at Juliette's bidding, in Juliette's sweater, because she more or less agreed with her friend that she had no choice. In the history of the world, getting dumped has rarely been optional.

After three excruciating days of silence from Rémy—three days spent going over and over with Juliette her unalloyed sadness at seeing Delphine's naked body, and her anger at herself for placing her own body where it didn't belong, and her desire to be absolved of this guilt and return to a state of *not knowing,* and her anger at Rémy for ignoring her, and her simple, irreducible and humiliating desire simply to be with him—Rémy's email inviting her to coffee pierced her inbox. She closed her laptop and buried herself in the blankets of her friend's futon. She said, "I'm unglued."

"Yup," Juliette said. "Where are your jeans?"

Marian was wearing pyjama pants and the tangerine bra Rémy bought her. "Who cares?"

"You do."

Marian pointed feebly to a pile of dirty clothes by the closet. Juliette grabbed them and tossed them to her and dug through a couple of drawers. She placed a magenta sweater and a blush compact on Marian's stomach. "You've got to look alive. Well, then pretend!"

"He's dragging me to a café we've never even been to. Eight kilometres from campus."

Juliette nodded. "It's insulting and transparent. Tell him you'll meet him at The Pint. You shouldn't have to take a taxi to get dumped."

"Will you come with me?"

"I'll walk you there. You can come and get me at the library afterwards. Up with you! Before I get annoyed."

They arrived at the pub almost an hour early. Domestic drafts were on special.

"I don't even know how to act," Marian said, holding fast to her second beer.

"You could play the role of the cool bitch," Juliette said.

"Or the survivor."

"You could weep."

"I could scream."

"No matter what, the result will be the same."

Except it wasn't the same, because Rémy changed course. She saw it on his face, she could practically smell it, the shift from righteous to cowardly.

He heads back in her direction with his plateful of cake. Where does he get off, not emailing her for three days, steering her here—unwilling vessel that she is—only to let go of the oars and declare the whole thing a recreational paddle? She came here to get dumped, goddammit. Why has he taken this away from her, the humiliation for which she has waited sleeplessly?

Because he's phasing her out. Or, worse, because he's doing nothing at all.

In her mind's eye, Delphine clutches a towel, hides her tiny breasts, vanishes.

Nuh-uh, she thinks. No way. It's not happening this way. Don't you ever come near me again.

"I opted for Turtle cheesecake," he says as he sits back down.

She shakes her head and immediately sets her voice dial to LOUD. "I can't believe you would do this to me *here*," she says in English.

Rémy unfurls the fork and knife from his rolled paper napkin. "Pardon?" he says in French.

She cranks up the volume. "Here, in front of all these people. Didn't you love me *at all*? Even the tiniest bit?"

Now heads are turning, including Rémy's—he's looking to see who's looking.

"Marian, I don't know what you're—"

"Did I not mean *anything* to you?" she screeches, enjoying her crescendo.

All eyes are on them now. Pints are put down, conversations dropped.

Now she half-shouts, half-wails. "I was your student. You used to read me stories in bed. And now you just abandon me like some tired pet? Some plaything? Some Playboy bunny, with books as well as tits?"

Snickers and smirks from around the bar.

"Ostie de criss keep your voice down," Rémy hisses.

"I suppose you'll want your things back," she continues hysterically. She reaches into Juliette's sweater and performs a swift, acrobatic gesture she learned long ago at summer camp.

In a flash she has removed the tangerine bra. She flings it across the table and one cup dangles provocatively over Rémy's lap.

"Take it," she howls. "I sure as hell don't need it anymore."

Rémy frantically shoves the tangerine cups aside, those lacy orange globes of his choosing. Clumsily he gathers his jacket, keys, wallet. The vein at his temple is likely to burst.

"Je m'en vais," he says, breathless, and sprints across the bar.

She follows him to the exit. "That's not what you said when you had your hand on my clit!"

Chapter Thirty-One

For several weeks Marian holes up in Juliette's basement apartment. She reads *L'Assommoir* and *Maus* and Lynda Barry comics. She draws scaffolds and gibbets, hatchets and dung forks. Marie-Josephte Corriveau raises both arms over her sleeping abuser, her grip on the hatchet firm. Dodier, curled on his side, his face mashed into the pillow, snores lightly. Marie-Josephte traces a swift arc through the air and drives the dull blade into his skull.

Sometimes, in the place of Dodier's sleeping body, Marian draws Rémy's. On his back, patches of black hair. The wooden handle of the hatchet warms under Marian's grip. Rémy snores as the blade swoops down.

"We could kill him," Juliette says when Marian shows her the drawings. "But then we'd have to touch his remains."

"Can't we just open the door and leave him to be eaten by wolves?"

"A less dignified animal. Raccoons or maybe skunks."

"Skunks are cute."

"But they love garbage."

Marian nods. "Circle of life."

When she's done plotting murder, she obsesses over the details of the past few months, forsakes all social invitations—none of which come from Patrick, who seems to be avoiding her—drinks a little too much, sobers up, wakes up optimistic, crashes again. David was right. She didn't know how to relate to him when he was sad—couldn't cajole him out of his dark

moods—so she bailed. Abandoned him because she didn't want
to get dragged down with him. Now look at her. David's gone,
and Rémy's gone—good riddance!—and she can't pull herself
out of her funk to save her pathetic life. She's a shitty person
who lies around thinking about what a shitty person she is,
which really just means that she's still wrapped up in her own
problems, in her own stupid feelings. Which in turn means
she's no less self-centred than she was a few months ago.

Every day, sometimes twice, she talks to her mother. At
first, Barbara asks regularly how things are going with David.
What she really means is how are things going *without* David.
Marian pretends not to understand this nuance and tells her
that if she is so interested in David's well-being, she should
maybe consider calling him herself.

"I don't want to go behind your back, but if you think it's
okay," Barbara says, not missing a beat. "I just want to know
everyone is *okay.*"

"From what I can tell, he's all right." Which is not a lie.
Most of Marian's awkward conversations with David have
revolved around dog care and Marian's visitation rights.

"So, I can call?" Barbara asks.

"I would prefer that, yeah."

"You're sure?"

"I'm sure."

Barbara phones David every few days, and out of loyalty
calls Marian to tell her before immediately moving on to her
usual sort of news: her quilting shop's upcoming class schedule;
the slight rise in Robert's cholesterol (something to keep an eye
on; nothing to worry about); her recent project selling reusable
cloth menstrual pads on Etsy. She asks Marian to help her
name the pad styles. "Pelvic Pride." "Amsterdam." She checks
if Marian would like a new tablecloth. (That Marian no longer
has a full-time table seems not to have occurred to her.) She
calls to ask which Frenchwoman sang that song about bells. In
this seemingly trivial manner, she confirms that her daughter

hasn't tossed a bottle of pills down her throat in the night. She is present without being pesky, afraid that if she pushes too hard, further emotional toxins will spurt out and poison their already strained relationship.

These vapid yet vital conversations with her mother are all Marian seems to accomplish in a day. They structure an otherwise shapeless existence, one devoid of familiar tasks or roles. She is no longer a wife or a mistress. She can't in good conscience call herself a student, as she hasn't worked on her dissertation since December. At the very least, she is somebody's daughter. Someone wants to talk to her.

The day after Rémy fled the bar, Marian received a curt email from him. He had spoken to Adèle Faucher. "I have officially stepped down as your supervisor," he wrote, as though this were a noble deed accomplished after a lengthy, efficacious term in office. Marian never heard from Adèle. The department chair apparently can't be bothered to deal with her. Marian is confused by this silence but doesn't know what to do about it. Juliette is enraged, and threatens to call the dean of students or human rights or whoever the hell is supposed to deal with these problems. Who *is* supposed to deal with them? The Student Handbook doesn't say.

When Juliette stops ranting to take a breath, Marian points out that the hot tub was kind of her idea.

Arched eyebrows. "Are you calling me a hypocrite?"

"Yes, but I love you for it," Marian says quickly, wanting to keep her friend on her side.

Juliette continues to rail against the broken-down, dead power, patriarchal bureaucracy that refuses to be held responsible for its own excrement. She's talking about Rémy, but Marian's thoughts jump to her own treatment of David.

She thinks, The excrement is me.

After a month, Juliette begins nagging Marian to poke her nose outside, but Marian can't picture herself going anywhere other than her old apartment to walk Kong when David happens to be out. The world is no longer a safe place. If she goes out, she will also have to see *people*, people who will ask her how she is, and when they ask, she'll have to smile and say she's fine. Once alone again, this 'fine' will clatter through her brain, and she will be left listening to a dissonant echo: *I am not fine.*

When she says no thanks, she'd rather not go out just then, Juliette threatens to kick her out, and says that she has to make an effort or else *that's it.* "I mean it," she says. Marian can't see how she could possibly mean it, but is only ninety percent sure and understands that she should probably pretend a little. The futon she shares with her friend need not become another bed of resentment.

She says, "It's been a while since I had good slice of cake."

They spend the morning at Java House. Juliette works on her dissertation, and Marian reads the Feminist Philosophers blog on her cell phone until her mother calls.

"Suicide watch," Marian says to Juliette before she picks up.

"Glad there are two of us on that." Juliette searches her bag for her gloves. She has to teach a class on campus in an hour. On her way out of the café, Juliette stops to chat with Boone. He's just come in with Annick, who waves at Marian before ordering and settling with her coffee at a table by the window. Marian understands that she will have to say hello. She tells her mother she'll call her back.

Boone places his own order and comes over smiling at Marian, a small carton of chocolate milk in hand. "Mary-Anne from French. How goes it?"

She tries to look cheerful. "Fine, thanks."

"You are out of cake and company, and we have an extra seat."

"I'll say a quick hello. I was just heading out."

"You were not. You were licking the last of that cake sauce off your finger. Yes, I saw you. But don't be embarrassed."

"I wouldn't dream of it."

"I'll carry your jacket and purse for you. I am chivalrous that way." Boone crosses the café and deposits her belongings at the table where Annick is sitting. Marian follows him over, not wanting to be rude.

Annick greets her in French as they sit down. "We were just talking about you," she continues in English. "Oh, not like that. What secrets are you hiding? Wait, don't tell us. Boone takes himself for a man of mystery. He doesn't like to be upstaged."

Boone laughs. "See how Annick flatters me. She credits me with a bigger ego than I in fact possess."

"Not ego," Annick says. "Dramatic flair."

"Just to prove Annick wrong," Boone says, "I will forgo theatrics and get to the point. You do comics, Mary-Anne, and that is what we happen to need just now."

"Is this like the drawing game from a few months ago? You still owe me a map, from what I recall."

"This is much more serious business."

"Why do I have my doubts?"

"I imagine that is my fault. I am too mischievous. It gives the impression that I may pull a rabbit out of my shoe at any time. Today I do not jest, however."

"What kind of comics?"

"Any kind," Annick says. "We're starting our own grassroots press. Comics written by women. We're calling it FemmeInk. We want you to propose a manuscript."

"What does Boone have to do with it?"

Boone grins. "You underestimate me because of my sex. I'm an ally, Mary-Anne."

"I'm flattered, really, but I don't think I can take on a project like that just now."

Annick leans in. Her hand is warm on Marian's arm. "It's a start. It's always a good time for that."

"I'll think about it, how about that?"

"You already think too much. Look at that furrowed brow."
Boone scrunches up his face.

"That bad, huh?"

"Awful," Annick says.

"I'll think about it," Marian says again. "Really."

Chapter Thirty-Two

"Move over."

"Mm?

"You're hogging the bed," Edna says. "Scooch."

Marian sits up, kicks her legs free of Juliette's sheets, which are twisted around her shins. She slides over to make room for Edna and tugs the duvet back over her hips. It's mid-morning—the sun pokes through the slats of the blinds.

"Where's Juliette?" Marian asks.

Edna fiddles with the sleeves of her dusty rose dress. "Dunno. School, probably."

"Did she make coffee before she left?"

"Geez Louise, child. Do you ever do anything for yourself?"

"Not lately."

"That's pathetic."

"It is." Marian sighs pathetically.

"Tell me why you're moping."

"My life is in pieces over here."

"That's right. Because you smashed it into teeny tiny bits and flung them around like a monkey slinging poop."

"Okay, okay. I screwed up."

"Yup."

"And I'm a bad person."

"That's probably true."

"Hey! Aren't you here to make me feel better?"

"Not in the slightest."

"Well, what, then?"

"I'm here to ask: *What do you want?*"

"Can we have some coffee first?"

Edna adjusts her bonnet, crosses her arms over her chest. Whistles a cheerful tune that Marian doesn't recognize. "Still waiting," she says while Marian's head fills with contradicting, half-formed thoughts.

"I don't know if I want to finish this PhD," Marian says finally, and it's like a bubble inside her has popped. She lays her head down on Edna's lap. "I need a break from it, to figure out where to go next. Do I transfer to another university? Another department? Do I drop out? All I know for sure is that I want to try that comics project. As for the rest . . ." She exhales helplessly into the duvet cover.

Edna pats her head. "That's perfect, dear," she says. "That'll do just fine. Now, I take mine with a splash of cream and two sugars. Since you offered."

Marian and David dangle their legs over the rock ledge as they eat gelato, jackets zipped tight. Seagulls screech overhead. A few weeks from now the Saint Lawrence will be buttoned with sailboats. For now, rivulets darken its slowly melting surface.

"Romantic," David says. "If you don't count the breaking up."

"It's like a first date in reverse," Marian says. "Awkward for all the wrong reasons."

David smiles tightly. He looks new to her, foreign. His jawline is slimmer than she remembered and his shoulders broader. He wears a new softshell jacket she doesn't recognize. In the past she would have picked out this jacket with him, weighed the pros and cons of its scuba hood and extra-long sleeves. It wouldn't have found its way into his closet and onto his body without her knowing.

"What have you been up to?" she asks. Small talk, but not just. She wants evidence of his uninterrupted rhythms and routines. Confirmation he is still himself.

He scrapes the edge of his gelato cup with his spoon and after a moment smiles shyly. "I'm heading back to school." He tells her that he's applied to Waterton to do a master's degree in Canadian history. If he likes the program, he'll continue on to the PhD.

This news surprises her, and yet is inevitable.

"You were working to support us," she says, recognizing the full weight of his sacrifice even as she says it. "While I was studying."

He confirms her words with his silence.

"And now I'm taking leave from school."

"You have your reasons," David says, not sounding bitter, but resigned.

She observes his face in profile—aquiline, softened by sadness—and tries to picture him doing a PhD, and later finding a position as a professor. A position like Rémy's. In a few years, David, too, will be educated and articulate in that specialized way that demands admiration.

"What will you research?" she asks.

"Honestly, I'm not sure yet. Labour relations, maybe." He pauses, smiles shyly. "It's not a burning desire to study a particular period or subject. I just want to ask questions. Find meaning."

Marian remembers his frustrated sobs when he told her that he had lost his job, how he said he couldn't stand to be alone with Edna's death.

Working at a crappy tourist site, he'd said. Dying alone.

She touches his shoulder. "It's never about a single set of questions," she says. "Only about the process of asking them." She pauses, tries to find the words. "Whatever your project, it's going to mean something."

They share the silence that follows.

"David, you've got to know that I'm sorry," she says, the words rushing out of her. "I'm sorry I didn't understand. And for all the stupid—" She breaks off.

"I need you to come and get your stuff from the apartment," he says calmly, meeting her gaze. "It's too hard for me, looking at it all the time."

"That's fair," she says, and swallows the mess of emotion that has risen in her throat.

"Have you been following the demonstrations in Québec?" he asks, changing the subject.

"A little bit. Honestly, I haven't been doing much. It's been an effort to get out of bed."

He flicks her with his spoon. "Now you know what it feels like, huh? Try setting the alarm."

An elderly woman approaches the shore with her golden retriever. Seagulls scatter and shriek. "I've got to go soon," David says. "I'm meeting Patrick for a game of squash."

The mention of Patrick's name stings. Marian hasn't seen him since she's been staying at Juliette's. She misses him.

"I think Patrick's mad at me," she says.

David presses his lips together. "Everybody's losing something here."

Chapter Thirty-Three

Students are sprawled on the library steps in T-shirts and tiny skirts. They sip lattes and smoothies and call out to friends who cruise by on bicycles. As per the electronic reader board affixed to the environmental sciences complex, it is 4:11 p.m. and the temperature is seventeen degrees Celsius. But there's a psychological conversion to be made: seventeen degrees in March feels like thirty degrees in June. Clothing goes flying; patios teem. The winter's been long, and everyone knows this is only spring's preview: in a few days, snow and cold will blow through for one last hurrah.

Rémy, as he makes his way past the smoothie drinkers on his way to Jean-Louis' office, rolls up his shirtsleeves and takes these unseasonably warm temperatures as welcome symbolism, a sign that he is going to be okay, that he has come out of this disturbing affair with Marian mostly unscathed and a wiser and better man. True, he still has nightmares featuring her orange bra cups, her loud and ludicrous accusations, but he's confident the pub drama will fade in time. No colleagues were present to witness his humiliation that day, and he has now rid himself of that borderline personality, that sphinx—that psychopath!—and reestablished the normal order of his universe.

Oh, he's not letting himself off the hook. He admits to himself that he enabled the bra tossing by purchasing the offensive object. But to buy a gift is *not* to invite having it thrown back in his face in public. Complete disregard for the social code—the workings of a deranged mind! He should have seen it in her earlier. Her intense attachment to him, the cartoons, the accusatory emails. He must have been blinded by Eros. Yes, Eros. He clings to the dignity of the ancient Greek term. A phenomenon that great men deemed worthy of study. Plato, Freud, Jung. Impossible to call the experience *love*, which, he now understands, implies a shared complexity that can only be understood over time. Nor would he describe the affair as a simple lapse of judgment, a lusty charge led by his . . .

Bygones.

He rounds his least favourite corner of campus, glowers at the giant construction hole, site of the future multi-million-dollar student centre, dormant and covered in grimy tarps. He enjoys a few breaths of indignation but then lets his resentment evaporate in the faux-spring air. If the university administrators want to piss away money, let them. He, Rémy, soon to be promoted to associate professor of French, is letting go of old grudges.

He felt a smug jolt of confidence a few hours ago when he received Jean-Louis' email asking if he would be available to come to his office, and maybe out for a drink afterwards. The departmental tenure committee sent his file up to the dean's office last week with a positive evaluation. Now he's waiting for the administration's rubber stamp. At first, he worried whether Marian would make trouble for him, but he's heard no noise from that direction. She's made herself scarce since the bra incident. He thought he glimpsed her profile a few weeks ago as he was walking home, and a city bus roared past, she inside. He hasn't seen her at the department. She must be avoiding him. At least she is sane enough to feel ashamed. In his more charitable moments he wishes her well, doesn't pray for her to be struck by lightning. After all, the girl needs help. Counselling, at the very least. Medication, too, ideally.

He climbs the steps of the administration building, is swept through its revolving doors, and crosses the vestibule. He shares the elevator with a white-capped catering employee and her cart of muffins and sliced fruit. They exit together on the fifth floor. Employee and cart glide past him and continue down the hall. Opposite the elevator is the glassed-in reception area that frames the various deans' offices. There are at least four deans that Rémy knows of in this building: dean of social sciences, dean of arts (alias Jean-Louis), dean of research, dean of students, and the various associate deans who seem to multiply annually. Rémy presents himself to the slim and well-tailored "Executive Coordinator to the Dean of Arts"—or so reads the Waterton-logoed nameplate on her desk—and mourns the demise of the title SECRETARY, which, now that it is becoming extinct, to him seems simple and dignified. The executive coordinator smiles widely but mechanically, taps on a closed door, pokes her head in and announces Rémy's presence. Opens the door wide for him to walk through.

"Jean-Louis."

"Rémy."

Bisous, bisous.

Jean-Louis sports an unremarkable blazer and trousers, but his shoes are orange and pink wingtips that appear handmade. Italian, surely. Rémy is jealous of the shoes, or of the confident cheekiness they express. Pink! He acknowledges in himself a girlish and therefore infuriating urge to ask where Jean-Louis bought them. Of course, he refrains.

"Nice office," he says instead.

"As long as there's room for my books, I'm happy." Jean-Louis shows Rémy his new La Pléiade edition of Paul Claudel's plays, which just arrived in the mail, before motioning to a couple of wingback armchairs near the window. The chairs are angled around a glass coffee table; beneath the furniture arrangement is a sheepskin rug. The kind of set-up that aims to put one at ease—not an office, but somebody's living room.

Rémy chooses the chair by the window, and watches Jean-Louis subtly hike up the legs of his trousers as he sits. Not the type of man to wear out a garment at the knees. But why should he? Has he not earned his position here? Has he not played by the institution's rules? Publications, politicking, grant-snagging. The sacred triumvirate.

They exchange small talk in French—the protests in Montreal, the weather—before Jean-Louis signals a change in topic by leaning forward and resting his elbows on his thighs, hands outstretched and clasped. An intimate posture, like he just might bow his head and pray. For whom?

Rémy is afraid he knows. He reels back through Jean-Louis' email in his mind. Was there anything to suggest bad news?

"I just want to say how there are things I can't change," Jean-Louis intones. He doesn't quite make eye contact, yet somehow aims his gaze directly at Rémy's face. "Things that come down from above. From the president. From the board of governors."

The invocation of gods higher up, the abnegation of responsibility—Rémy's fears confirmed. He's not here for congratulations and a rubber stamp. He briefly fantasizes about jumping out the window to his right. "The president and board don't involve themselves in tenure cases," he says instead, and thinks, *That's your job.*

Jean-Louis nods slowly, not so much in agreement as in acknowledgement that Rémy's words exist. They have vibrated through the air and reached his own eardrums. And yet there is something sympathetic in this nod, as though it's not only Rémy's words that exist for Jean-Louis, but Rémy himself.

"That's true, they don't get too involved. Not strictly speaking, no." Jean-Louis gently shakes his folded hands—a single knotted fist bobbing in a gesture of powerlessness, both false and sincere. Mostly sincere. If he believes himself to be powerless, then that's how it is. In such matters, attitude is outcome. And yet, isn't he the one with the fancy office, the one with the shoes?

Jean-Louis seems to have lost his train of thought; he pontificates on the structure of university governance. Rémy glances out the window. The dead grass of the rugby field smudges the landscape brown, and along Waterton Drive cars perform their rush-hour crawl. Beyond it all the Saint Lawrence naps prettily under a bonnet of unmelted ice.

"The university is in a difficult position," Jean-Louis is saying. "Building projects. Enrollment pressures. Budgetary difficulties." The quiet neutrality of his tone suggests that he doesn't agree with the workings of the institutional machine but would never be caught on record saying so. Certainly not today. "The board members are talking about program prioritization, about research dollars, about raising the university's profile by funnelling resources into larger departments and initiatives in order to—"

"Accouche," Rémy says. Spit it out.

Jean-Louis does not startle or harden at this, as Rémy would have expected. He looks Rémy sincerely and dolefully in the eye. "The Office of the Dean has rejected your application for tenure and promotion on the grounds that you have an insufficient research record."

Rémy absorbs his friend's statement slowly, through layers of meaning. The subtext is clear: Rémy is being fired because, like any employee, he costs money, and because his department is small and irrelevant, and the university doesn't want to invest in it anymore. His research deficiencies are a convenient excuse for the bean counters to buy fewer beans. And between the bean counters and Rémy is Jean-Louis, who, even though shrouded in admin-speak, has been more honest with him than is appropriate from his position as dean.

Rémy floats somewhere above himself and Jean-Louis and this whole conversation. In shock, he recognizes. It doesn't hurt yet. From his detached position he admires his old comrade, who is suffering through a meeting he was not obligated to set up, and a conversation that never should have taken place, because it shows cracks in the system, dissension within the ranks. An official letter, cleanly and coldly dispatched, would have done the job. "Nous avons le regret de vous informer . . ."

Gracious on Jean-Louis' part to invite him here, to give him the pieces he needs to understand that merit has little to do with the rejection of his tenure case. And yet, how easy it must be for him to act magnanimously. So little at stake for Jean-Louis: a few minutes of discomfort, nothing more. And by enduring these few awkward minutes is he saving himself from a longer bout of guilt? Is he playing the role of the decent guy stuck between a rock and a hard place?

"Please let me buy you a beer," Jean-Louis says.

The easy graciousness of success.

Rémy hesitates. It is failure and humiliation that test the limits of one's character.

"I prefer to drink alone," he says.

And so he does. But after downing that second generous glass of scotch and leaving a cryptic message on Delphine's voicemail—tonight, he's hibernating and won't be disturbed—a sneaking suspicion catches up with him: he is dousing himself in old clichés. The unemployed man, drinking himself into further oblivion. The drunk (erstwhile) humanist. He recaps the bottle and contemplates ways to appear less pathetic to himself, only to conclude that maybe what he needs is not to be less pathetic, but *more*—so thoroughly buried in pathos that he pops out on the side of catharsis.

Art. Art will save him. He has nothing; he has everything. He is not too drunk to write. He plunges himself into the manuscript he banged out two months ago, that story of an adjunct instructor whose girlfriend tried to hang herself from the rafters, who engages in an affair with a nineteen-year-old student, and who is cuckolded in the end. After six and a half hours of tortured labour shot through with coffee and honey roasted peanuts, he fears that the story is a flop, a funhouse mirror reflecting his own sad foibles in grotesque proportions. Who will read it?

He drinks some more, and time and event become nebulous. He holds his head in his hands, and curses Marian, the gods, ambition, mediocrity, Jean-Louis, Flaubert, Waterton, and his empty fridge. He falls asleep on the sofa, wakes up four hours later, pisses like a rhino, dabs with a hand towel at the smudge of drool on the sofa cushion, forks tuna fish into his mouth straight out of the can, cancels his classes 'due to illness,' and points his hatchback and his wounded soul in the direction of Montreal.

Chapter Thirty-Four

Clusters of protestors hoot and chant their way up Rue Saint-Hubert, stragglers on their way to join the march that already grinds into motion at Place du Canada and will soon head east on Rue Sherbrooke. Rémy has tuned in to the radio a few minutes too late for this information to prove useful. He now feels the melodramatic urge to bang his head against the top of the steering wheel. No escape—he's just another log in the logjam.

The students sport red clothing of all kinds, T-shirts or bandanas or boots, their cheeks branded red with face paint. A woman pirouettes past in a red spandex unitard. She wields a small Québec flag on a dowel, the kind that proliferates on Saint-Jean-Baptiste. Rémy strains his neck in order to read the bobbing picket signs. *Nous ne reculerons pas. J'ai honte de ma patrie. Le savoir au pouvoir. Ensemble bloquons la hausse.* And simply: *NON.* He pulls out his cell phone and laboriously—he is not yet skilled with its virtual keyboard—taps out a text message to Delphine to let her know he is stuck in traffic. He hits "send" only to discover that cell service is down.

For the third time, the radio announcer advises motorists to stay out of the downtown core. If only. Bumper to angry bumper, all engines turned off—it's like a ferry ride across hell. Nothing to do but wait. The driver of the silver SUV in front of Rémy's own vehicle—a businessman in a grey suit—leaves his door ajar and slowly paces between the lanes of traffic, smoking a cigarette. Rémy smiles at him in solidarity. The owner of a black Hyundai two cars back, a woman in thigh-high leather boots, has slipped into the dépanneur on the corner and emerges now with a sack of beef jerky. Rémy watches in the rearview mirror as she leans against the hood of her vehicle and gnaws on the jerky, pausing at intervals to stab anxiously at her cell phone.

The businessman wanders over and motions for Rémy to roll down his window.

"You need a cigarette?" he asks in English, then poses the question again in accented French. A friendly offering. Two strangers marooned together on this urban island.

Rémy shakes his head. "Thanks, though," he says in French, and the man continues in that language.

"I guess you didn't get the traffic tweets either."

"Don't the students usually hit the streets in the evening?"

The man takes a long, squinting drag. "Yeah. But today's march started at one."

Rémy nods as though this were news to him. He glances at the clock on the dash for what must be the fiftieth time. It's 1:26.

"Going to be here a while," he says, a way of resigning himself to his fate.

The man drops his cigarette butt and mashes it into the asphalt with his heel. "I've got a mobile office," he says. "Could be worse." He saunters back to his car, apparently unaware that cell service is out.

Rémy leaves his window down. The air is even warmer than it was yesterday in Waterton. The temperature must be somewhere in the mid-twenties. Warm enough for many of the students to be out in shorts and T-shirts, and for Rémy— underslept, road-weary, emotionally chewed up—to be lulled into a trance for several minutes despite the activity around him. He dozes with his eyes open and his fingertips resting on the wheel; snaps to attention when a girl decked out like Cat-in-the-Hat reaches into the car and dangles in front of his nose a red felt square on a safety pin. He blinks dumbly at first, but once she skips away, he gathers the energy to affix the symbol to the pocket of his shirt, all the while aware of a cruel irony: masses of students who care deeply about higher education, about their right to access a world that he has just lost.

Now, inexplicably, the silver SUV piloted by the friendly businessman inches forward, and Rémy scrambles to start the ignition. Tap the gas, brake, wait. As he hiccups forward, frustration dukes it out with fatigue for supremacy over his emotional state. Twenty minutes pass before he sees an open parking spot on his right. Half a spot, really—the rest of it is part of a loading zone. He'll take his chances—he's yet to see a parking enforcement officer today. The loading zone means that he can manoeuvre his car into the space despite the traffic jam. Without engaging in conscious thought—responding to a vague but pressing psychological urge—he tugs the parking brake, grabs his jacket from the back seat and locks up. He heads in the opposite direction of his and Delphine's apartment on Saint-Denis, first cutting west on Maisonneuve and eventually north on Rue Saint-Urbain, aiming to intersect the march.

The din of the crowd crescendos as he nears Rue Sherbrooke. Two police cruisers seal traffic on one side of the intersection, and on the other lock the protestors into their chosen route. Several officers stand at the ready, their bodies pivoting mechanically as they observe all sides of the action. Beyond them is the throng—a crimson, many-legged caterpillar with picket signs for antennae. It's the sixth week of the protests, and for the SPVM, crowd control has become half the job. Two weeks ago, riot officers ignited controversy when they deployed tear gas and stun grenades against students who occupied the Loto-Québec building. The students were vying for the attention of the Québec universities' rectors and principals, whose offices are located there. A couple of officers eye Rémy, impassive, thumbs hooked into the belt loops or pockets of their black trousers. Rémy ducks his head submissively, and they allow him to slip through the barricade and dissolve into the crowd.

He is now a cell within the shouting, undulating organism that has consumed the city. A woman who marches alongside Rémy slaps at the bongo drums that hang by a strap around her neck, her downbeat marking the protestors' pace. Ahead, a father bends down to allow his son to climb his shoulders. The man straightens, and from this godly vantage point the boy twists his body to stare in fascination at the bongo player, his mouth hanging open to reveal that he has recently lost a tooth. The boy's older sister, who marches a few paces ahead, thrusts a metallic pinwheel into the air like a beacon. It twirls in slow motion, tossing light from its pointed tips. "Ouvrez les yeux!" an androgynous voice shouts over a loudspeaker. Two women to Rémy's right pull off onto the sidewalk to touch up the hearts and squares that they've drawn on each other's cheeks with a tube of lipstick. Next to them a street vendor is making a killing selling bottled water from a cooler on wheels.

Clouds shroud the sky and spit rain. A horse joins the throng, a helmeted police officer astride its muscled back. Horse and officer appear authoritative but benign—Rémy can't help but think of trips to the farm or carriage rides through Vieux-Montréal.

"Hey, how about a picture with your horse?" a young man yells in English. His naked torso is solid red above his brown jeans, as though he himself were a brush dipped in paint.

The riding officer doesn't even turn his head, and the horse's hooves plod forward, stamping out the young man's request. On the other side of the animal, a wiry young woman is texting, not looking about her but somehow keeping out of the horse's way. Rémy taps the power button of his own cell phone. Service is up and running and he manages to send his message to Delphine. From her, no word.

The rain intensifies, smearing the asphalt black, and the protestors take refuge under hoods, protest signs, umbrellas.

Rémy canopies his head with his jacket and trudges forward in this manner for a quarter hour or so before the rain ceases and the sun elbows through the clouds.

At the intersection of Sherbrooke and Saint-Dominique, a man rocks rhythmically from heel to toe. He looks to be in his forties and wears a mismatched suit and a pilled winter scarf. What is left of his hair is parted an inch above one ear and combed over his gleaming scalp. He holds a white plastic grocery bag that dangles at his thigh. From the bag he frantically draws pamphlets that he wags at the protestors, his whole body leaning into the motion like a sapling tipped by the wind. A fervent evangelical tract, no doubt. Parables that speak of the bread of life, the light of the world, thieves and robbers and shepherds. After several rejections in a row, the man gestures wildly and shouts something that is drowned out by the atonal trumpeting of a plastic horn. A young woman in red overalls takes pity on him: without slowing her pace, she accepts a tract and jams it in her purse.

Rémy draws near, unable to skirt the zealot because of the density of the crowd. The man performs the same frantic gesture: plunges his hand into the bag, fishes out his offering, and lifts himself onto his tiptoes, extending his arm well beyond the slanting trunk of his body. With the tract he pokes Rémy's shirtsleeve.

Startled, Rémy makes eye contact.

"I have written a story," the man says in English, his French accent so heavy that it's painful even to Rémy's ears. "Will you read it?" His tone is both pleading and accusatory.

Rémy peers down at the tract—white A4 papers, halved and stapled together. "Théâtre des morts," the title page reads.

He's mildly surprised. There are worse titles.

"Désolé mon gars," he says, and turns away.

"No," the man says, and grabs his sleeve. The plastic bag knocks against Rémy's thigh.

Rémy recoils and twists his arm free, his annoyance tinged with fear. "I said that I'm not interested."

The man blinks rapidly, as though he has something caught in his eye, or is about to cry. Instead, he shouts above the discordant buzz of the crowd. He draws out the words as though they were a battle call.

"I AM HOMME-LETTE!"

Rémy looks around for the nearest cop.

"Not listening, not listening," the man mumbles, and squints at his booklet as though trying to read what he should do next.

When he cries out again, Rémy finally understands.

"I AM HAMLET!"

A loud silence falls. Protestors flow around them, and Rémy peers into the man's face, which is round and fixed in an expression of frustration and pride and desire for recognition.

Rémy grasps the booklet, and slowly the man relinquishes his hold on it.

"Prince of Denmark, are you?" Rémy says, idly flipping through the booklet. "Master of your own dark theatre?"

The man first remains motionless, then cautiously nods.

"Needy?" Rémy says. He folds the booklet in thirds and shoves it into his pocket. "Solipsistic? Angry, are you. Wounded. Obsessed."

The man holds his plastic bag high above his head—a gesture that has meaning only for him.

Deep in Rémy's gut something gargantuan roils: pity, anger, awe.

I am Hamlet. Will you read me?

The dark thing inside Rémy tows him under and he hears its weird, underwater voice—his own distorted voice. *I exist—look at me. Look at me—I exist.*

What bubbles to the surface erupts as laughter.

Rémy holds his belly, doubles over and gazes up at the man, apology in his eyes, unable to stop this breathless heaving release, or the tears streaming down his burning cheeks. He wipes at his face, streaks his hand with the snot that drips from his nose.

The plastic bag drops to the man's feet. His mouth opens in surprise like that of a child, and his outstretched, empty palms seem to weigh the air. Slowly, the O of his mouth flattens and distorts as though in pain; stretches into a wavering smile. He reaches up and clutches his combover with both hands. Finally, he, too, laughs—tentatively and soundlessly, then with full force—a strident, staccato of a laugh.

Rémy dries his eyes. "I will read you," he says.

The man nods vigorously as though this is just as it should be.

Rémy leaves the man to his evangelism—his plastic bag, his slanting offering—and thinks how he will describe this moment to Delphine. But even as this thought arrives, it is subsumed into another that is only half-formed: he has not heard from her in over two days.

Dread propels Rémy down Rue Saint-Dominique and along Rue Ontario. He tries to remember the details of his last phone conversation with Delphine three nights ago. Did she sound sick? No, chipper—loving her new job at the Jardin botanique, enjoying a yoga studio that had cropped up two blocks away. And he, overwhelmed by grading and course prep, and busy flushing the last vestiges of Marian from his system, didn't ask how she was feeling, or if she had been eating. Now as he weaves around obstacles—most of them human—his right leg cramps and his sprint slows to a helpless trot while the simulator in his mind churns out gruesome prophecies. Delphine, collapsed on the floor of the apartment. Delphine, too weak to get to the phone. Delphine, dead.

It isn't until he rounds the corner of Saint-Denis that he realizes that he has left the keys to the apartment in the cup holder of his car. Nausea, panic. How could he be so stupid? He looks about him, bewildered and furious with himself. The

Latin Quarter hums indifferently—smartly dressed women stroll past, dangling pretty shopping bags; a shopkeeper caresses a headless mannequin; a flock of teenagers migrate from the French fry joint, wafting behind them the cloying smell of grease. His thoughts are garbled. It seems to him that he is many kilometres from his car. No—he walked west for fifteen minutes in order to join the march. Rue Saint-Hubert is only a couple blocks away. He calls up the image of his car in the loading zone, the young woman leaning in the open window to give him a felted red square. It's as though he has travelled along a giant Möbius strip. He's lived a year since that moment; he's barely had time to blink.

An apparition flickers into focus. Delphine walks towards him on the opposite side of the street. A grocery bag dangles from one arm, and a brilliant, cellophane-wrapped bouquet blooms from the other.

Why does he tuck himself inside the doorway of the fry joint? What prevents him from calling out to her? Is it his embarrassment at his own melodramatic fantasies? Or does he sense some bad omen in her vigorous stride, her strong grip? Her back is to him now as she climbs the cast-iron staircase, rests the groceries on the landing, and lets herself into the apartment.

A minute later a text message chirps.

J'allais t'appeler ce soir. Il faut pas venir.

Don't come.

The text is a stone in his gut. The flowers, the groceries. His own arrival a day early. She has someone else. The only logical explanation.

He stations himself at a window table of the fry joint, orders a grilled cheese sandwich. Unabashedly resolves to stalk her.

When dusk falls his patience is rewarded—finally he can see her through the kitchen window. She has uncorked a bottle of wine and her head bops subtly to a music he can't hear. He tries to guess. Boris Vian? Radiohead?

When she finally sits down at the kitchen island to eat, she is alone. She tears the lid off her mini yogurt, dips the spoon inside, hesitates for a full minute before raising it to her lips.

He presses the buzzer. That she told him not to come is irrelevant. He's already here.

She exhales warily as she lets him in. Returns to the kitchen and fiddles with the gerbera bouquet that she's arranged in a vase on the kitchen island. An unfamiliar bluegrass song twangs from the speakers in the living room.

He follows her but keeps his distance; leans back against the counter near the sink. Pooled water seeps through the base of his shirt. "I called. And texted."

"I know," she says, her voice detached and almost cheerful. She extracts a flower from the arrangement and with a pair of scissors clips a chunk off the bottom of its stem before nesting it back in the vase.

"I thought something had happened to you."

"I'm doing really well, actually."

"I see that," Rémy says. "You look well."

And she does. Her cheeks are slightly flushed from the glass of wine she's just finished. She's wearing a new purple dress and appears to have put on the barest bit of weight over the past couple of weeks.

"It's kind of you to say so." She rotates the bouquet and pokes at a few stems, making the arrangement less symmetrical. "So pretty," she mutters as she gives the vase one last turn. "There can never be enough flowers." She gazes around the kitchen as though looking for something else to do; pulls some heirloom tomatoes from the fridge. He steps aside as she moves to the sink to wash them, her back to him. She hums along to the bluegrass tune, and he senses that if she could have him spirited away from her on the strains of the mandolin, she would.

"It feels so right to be here," he gushes with a sincerity that ends up sounding false to his own ears. "You wouldn't believe the past few hours. The traffic, the protest. People everywhere. There was this man . . ." He babbles for too long while she dries the tomatoes with a paper towel and waits politely for him to finish. He paces the kitchen and describes to her in detail the hooting energy of the crowd, the man who called himself Hamlet. The tract—still in his pocket—and the gasping laughter. "It was like I was meant to be there to witness it all. The defiance of the people, this need to make history and really take control. The profound humanity. There's a story here, I'm sure of it—a powerful story—"

"And you're the one to tell it." Delphine pulls out a cutting board and paring knife and begins whittling one of the tomatoes.

"I mean, that's what I felt. I guess I'm not describing it well." Already the power of the last few hours is dissipating, as though he's trying to recall a vivid dream that is further and further submerged by the effort of conscious thought and the weight of her indifference.

"You know, it's amazing," Delphine says as she works away at the tomato flesh, not looking up. "Just think of how far he had to come, that man with the pamphlet. Think of all that had to happen just for you to find him. The wretched upbringing. Mental health problems from an early age. Addiction, probably. Never able to hold down a job. Couldn't pay the rent. Sleeps under a tarp, or in a shelter if he's lucky. Gets mugged and beaten up once in a while. Eats breakfast and dinner at one of the missions. And in between, yells at strangers on the street corner."

"I have no doubt his life is wretched," Rémy says. "I really do understand that."

She sets aside this first tomato—now fashioned it into a stout, spiky flower—and grabs another. Zigzags her knife to create the same crenellated top. "It's so lucky that you were there to see him," she continues. "So lucky you were there to finally hear him."

"It was real. There was this connection." Rémy hesitates in the face of her sarcasm, no longer certain.

"Oh, we're all real around you, chéri. Yet somehow very real people and events only exist if you're looking at them and you need them. We're just a colourful backdrop for your ego." She shoves a lock of hair out of her eyes. Looks down angrily at her fingers, which are covered in juice. "Have you ever thought that no one wants to be your shitty muse?"

"Come on," he says, aiming to keep his voice low and gentle. "That's unfair."

"Oh, we're playing fair now, are we?" She shakes her head and continues carving. "Forgive me, I didn't know. It's so hard to tell these days. Tell me: is it *fair* to have to read a story about your stupid, banal infidelity? To wake up to a drunken email attachment and be expected to read your sick ego right down to the last word? What do you think of my handiwork here, by the way?" With the paring knife she gestures to the elegant tomatoes. "Is it up to the quality of your pomegranate scene? Or should I wave the knife around a little? Like this? Maybe hold it up to my throat? Am I giving you enough to work with? Or will you let me know in the middle of the night when you've had one too many?"

After a long and effortful search, he locates his drunk self in his memory and traces the actions of this foreign person over the course of last night. It's horrifyingly plausible, what she's saying. That he emailed her his semi-autobiographical story. That he asked her to read it. That he sought her validation and praise.

He may even have emailed her twice because the first time he forgot to append the attachment.

Delphine laughs softly. "*Mara*," she says. "*Daphné*. It's one thing to have to look the other way while you live out your midlife crisis. It's another to be asked to hold it up as art."

"I don't know what you're implying." He trails off. Why bother trying to deny the affair? It's clear that Delphine has travelled to a realm beyond wheedling and negotiation. For a moment he wonders how much she knows, but in the end is forced to admit that his actions over the past few months, like those of every other adulterer in history, must not have been as cagey and invisible as he thought. She has probably known for some time.

"I lost my job," he says, offering his misfortune as penance for his stupidity. "They didn't tenure me." He waits for her to soften.

"Can't say I'm surprised. Your behaviour with that student is absurd."

"Wait, that's not what I meant," he says, regretting his strategy. "It was a cost saving measure."

Delphine shrugs. "I've always thought the universe had a way of evening things out."

"Look, you have every right to be upset."

"Upset? Upset. I left my job and friends here in Montreal and followed you to Waterton. I left my doctors and my psychologist and my favourite run on St. Helen's. And you seduced your student and deposited me right back here as though I'd never left. Like I'd tripped and fallen backwards into a time warp."

"I didn't seduce anyone. I'm not saying I'm not guilty, but there was context—"

Delphine tosses the paring knife in the sink and rinses her hands. "The context is that you abused your power over that girl."

He grips the counter. "Marian was a consenting adult. *Is* a consenting adult."

"Right, she had *agency*. Isn't that what you academics call it?"

"That's the gist of it. Yes."

"Even though you were her professor."

"This isn't some sixteen-year-old we're talking about. I'm not her homeroom teacher."

"You honestly believe that she could freely consent to a relationship with her professor."

"I do."

"Funny, my therapist doesn't think so."

He tries to ignore this introduction of a higher power into the conversation, an invisible arbitrator who sees only one side of the story. "She knew perfectly well what she was doing."

"I have no doubt that she *thought* she knew what she was doing. But do you really think that girl would have loved you if you were her equal? If you were just another grad student muddling your way through the program? Or would she have run the other way because you're a narcissistic mess?"

"Ad hominum attacks are beneath you, Delphine."

"Oh, not today they're not. Remember: you came to me. You can leave any time. But here's the real question: would *you* have loved *her* if she wasn't your student? Picture it, just for a moment. Imagine that she's not some caged little bird who has no choice but to come to your office asking for advice and approval. Do you still want her when she's not weaker than you? When you have no power over her? Have you ever wanted to be with your equal? Or do you always need someone smaller?"

"I can see we have some issues to work through."

She holds up her hand. Enough. "Would you have loved *me* if I weren't ill? If I didn't need steering and monitoring and controlling?"

He burns with anger and the shame of a recognition that is still only barely conscious. "I don't even know what to say."

"Not to worry, your actions speak volumes. You rushed here to save me! So gallant. Let's be clear: I may need saving, but you are not the person for the job. I have friends and family and professionals who are far better equipped. And I do have the will to live, despite what you may think."

"Of course you do. I've never doubted it." He circles the island and moves to caress her face, but she jerks back as though a hideous spider has just dropped into her path.

He backs away a few inches. "I know you still love me."

"So confident. My God." She crosses the apartment and opens the door wide. Leaves it ajar for him.

"Wait," he says, but already she's in the living room turning up the music, a couple of notches at first and then a few more, enough that he would have to raise his voice to be heard.

Chapter Thirty-Five

She shares the house with five other student artists. Large,
Victorian, three blocks from downtown. On the front lawn
is a stainless-steel sculpture of a hound. Indian saris curtain
the front windows. Her bedroom is small and narrow: space
enough for a single bed, a dresser, and her new drafting table,
which she has placed beneath the dormer window. In French:
chambre des bonnes. Maid's room. Kong, when he comes to
stay, sleeps at the end of the bed, his chin resting on her foot.
The room is all wood—wide-planked hardwood floor, pine
panelling on the walls and ceiling. Outside, a sugar maple
rustles and tosses sunlight. A treehouse where anything can
happen.

She spends her mornings alone with her graphic novel: *Marie-
Jo Corriveau.* She'll open the story with her title character being
deposited at Barnum's American Museum in New York, and
later drop some of the salient bits of Marie-Jo's past into the
narrative via flashback: the trial, the gibbeting, the theft of her
cage from the Pointe-Lévy cemetery, and finally, the murder.
But Marian wants the momentum of the narrative to stay in the
present—she plans to tap the weird, heady energy of Barnum's
museum. Marie-Jo will befriend a fellow freak, a pantomimist
or a fire-eater. She and the fire-eater will set out to look for
Marie-Jo's three children. Breaking with the old misogynist
stories of sorcery, Marie-Jo will travel the continent on a quest
to find love, family, and herself.

On the drafting table lie loose sheets of Bristol board and
a small tear-away notebook of the same. Marian is learning
to work like other cartoonists and draw her comics much
larger than the final printed size. At first, she only dared
begin if she thought small and used the notebook, but now
she enjoys the expansiveness of the larger page. To the top
corner of her drafting table she's glued a small, lidless box
that contains the tools of her trade: various rulers, a lettering
guide, pencils and erasers, India ink, nib and Micron pens, a
few watercolour brushes, and opaque white ink for correcting
mistakes. These objects comfort her, give her purpose. She's not
yet skilled enough to use the nib pens or watercolour brushes
for inking, but she practices with them a few minutes each
day. She doodles characters or abstract forms, dips a brush
into the India ink and runs it over the pencilled drawings. It
will take her years, she knows, before she masters the delicate
manoeuvres of brushwork—the elegant, pressure-free dip and
trace; the controlled, swooping lines that give life to the best
comics. She's patient, aware of what she lacks: countless hours
spent at the drafting table. (Craft, she's come to believe, is a
synonym for doggedness.) For her Marie-Jo comic, she trusts
the Micron pens, their varying widths and degrees of wear: the
smooth point of the new nibs, best for finer work, or the more
ragged and unreliable point of the old nibs, which she uses to
colour in large swathes of black.

Sitting down to her project day after day, Marian feels the
slow, deep joy of progress. Already she can trace change in her
art. Before beginning the book, her cartoons were carefree,
almost slapdash—she expected nothing from them. She was
not an Artist and went straight to work with whatever pen and
paper happened to be lying around. It was like doing cartwheels
in the backyard as a child: a breathless, spontaneous trajectory.
The more serious two-stage process of pencilling and inking
has changed her approach to comics, and instilled in her an
awe of those who do it all day, every day. After the creative high

of the initial sketch, the real work begins: hours spent inking. At best, she finds the task meditative—arm moving, thoughts drifting. At worst, it is excruciating: mechanical in a way that fatigues brain and muscles alike. When she grew frustrated and complained to Annick about the process, Annick invited her to the FemmeInk office, located downtown above the indie bookstore. She brewed Marian some strong coffee, fed her a brownie, and sat her down at a lightbox while she herself bent over her desk, quietly sketching some of her own cartoons. In this way she initiated Marian into a community of solitude, of practice.

This is how their tribe passes the hours, black line by black line.

Marian hasn't told Annick what happened to her this past year, although she may have heard about it through other channels. Annick knows that Marian is separated from her husband—this much she's talked about. Marian is happy to keep her relationship with Annick professional. What they have in common is their craft. Now and then Annick comments on Marian's technique and helps her to gesture towards the real without being a slave to it. A cartoon tree is the essence of a tree, not the tree itself. The two women share an investment in spare drawing and a suspicion of hyper-realism. Purity is in the line carefully chosen and cleanly executed. They shun comics featuring Barbie-like figures, globular breasts, and impossibly round buttocks. Cartoon should never be caricature. Even the superhuman should evoke what's human.

In the afternoon, once she's done dreaming up frames and painstakingly etching them onto the page, Marian opens the door of her bedroom onto the noisy creativity of the ARTus students who live in the other rooms of the house: Boone, Georgia, Finn, Jessica, Raff. In the huge living room downstairs, the collective hosts art shows, concerts, small theatre productions. Marian accepted the position of treasurer when she moved in, and she spends some time each day walking the few blocks to and from the bank, keeping track of the float, or balancing spreadsheets. It turns out that even though she doesn't consider herself organized, she's more organized than some, and these menial tasks keep her busy, prevent her from brooding about the break-up of her marriage. They also make her feel like she's gesturing towards having a real job, and isn't entirely spoiled, living off her parents' generosity. They deposit a modest sum into her bank account each week, enough that she can get by if she shops at the discount grocery store. Once she's completed the first draft of her graphic novel, she'll look for a job, something in government or tourism, any position where French is an asset.

This afternoon, rather than run errands, she's bringing her first and second chapters over to FemmeInk to scan. She'll see her careful lines metamorphose into pixels before making their way back into print, transposed. She and Boone plan to walk over to FemmeInk together. He'll be working on the press's first catalogue. She hears his quick, heavy footsteps on the stairs.

"You're ready, Mary-Anne," he says when she answers his knock. Not a question but a statement. He flashes his friendly teeth, and she feels the tingle of happiness.

She's ready.

Acknowledgements

People

I am indebted to the insightful, smart and funny Caroline
Adderson and Zsuzsi Gartner for their mentorship on early
drafts of this novel. Thank you both for letting me be the
dumbest person in the room.

Annabel Lyon provided invaluable expertise and
encouragement when my manuscript was in its infancy. Thank
you, Annabel.

I owe a debt of gratitude to Monica Dutt and Judith
Peranson, who provided answers to the various medical
questions that the novel addresses. I have tried very hard not to
bend out of shape the excellent information they provided.

Kristi Karathanassis is the best research assistant who ever
lived. This novel would have been substantially worse without
her. Likewise, my friend Sarah Jacoba lent me her critical eye
when it was most required.

The team at University of Calgary Press worked tirelessly
on this book. In particular, I am grateful to series editor Aritha
van Herk, copyeditor Naomi K. Lewis, and press staff Helen
Hajnoczky, Brian Scrivener, Melina Cusano, Alison Cobra, and
Kyle Flemmer.

A version of "Great Historical Curiosity" appeared in *Geist*
110 (Fall 2018), and I was the beneficiary of the careful editing and
professionalism of AnnMarie MacKinnon and Michal Kozlowski.

To my colleagues at Huron University College: you are the
most generous and open-minded intellectuals I've met. Thank
you for letting me be creative for a living when you easily could
have insisted otherwise.

My family has fiercely supported my work since the
beginning. Thank you, Mom, Dad and Karina.

To my husband John: you are the perfect reader and partner. Thank you for everything.

Prose

For details on the life of Marie-Josephte Corriveau and the history of her gibbet, Catherine Ferland and Dave Corriveau's *La Corriveau: de l'histoire à la légende* (Septentrion, 2014) proved invaluable. Likewise, Nicole Guilbault's anthology *Il était cent fois La Corriveau* (Nuit Blanche, 1995) revealed to me the many literary incarnations of this spectacular figure. A. H. Saxon's *P.T. Barnum: The Legend and the Man* (Columbia University Press, 1989) opened up the wonderfully bizarre corners of P. T. Barnum's American Museum.

In chapter twenty-one, Marian quotes Louis Fréchette's *Almanach du people* (Librairie Beauchemin, 1913); the translation from the original French is mine. Marian and Edna also discuss the following works: Philippe Aubert de Gaspé's *Les Anciens Canadiens* (Desbarats et Derbishire, 1863); Victor-Lévy Beaulieu's *Ma Corriveau suivi de La sorcellerie en finale sexuée* (VLB, 1976); Anne Hébert's *La Cage, suivi de L'Île de la Demoiselle* (Boréal, 1990).

The brief Gabrielle Roy quotations in chapter eight are from *Bonheur d'occasion* (Boréal, 2009); I've also translated into English another quotation from Roy's novel in chapter eighteen. The jargon that Rémy writes on the board in chapter eight is from Gérard Genette's *Figures III* (Seuil, 1972). The psychoanalytic theory that Marian and Rémy discuss in chapter ten is from Jacques Lacan's *Four Fundamental Concepts of Psychoanalysis* (WW Norton, 1998). James Joyce's *Ulysses* (Shakespeare and Company, 1922) is briefly quoted in chapters fifteen and eighteen. I paraphrase a few lines of Proust's *Du côté de chez Swann* (Bernard Grasset, 1913) in chapter eighteen. Rémy reads a snippet from Anaïs Nin's *Delta of Venus* (Harcourt Brace Jovanovich, 1977) in chapter nineteen.

Photography by Jon Munn

ANDREA KING holds a PhD in French Studies and is an associate professor at Huron University College in London, Ontario, where she teaches French and creative writing. Her fiction has appeared in *Geist* magazine.

BRAVE & BRILLIANT SERIES

Series Editor:
Aritha van Herk, Professor, English, University of Calgary
ISSN 2371-7238 (print) ISSN 2371-7246 (online)

Brave & Brilliant encompasses fiction, poetry, and everything in between and beyond. Bold and lively, each with its own strong and unique voice, Brave & Brilliant books entertain and engage readers with fresh and energetic approaches to storytelling and verse.